A Certain Flair for Death

JOHN F. CARR
AND
CAMDEN BENARES

Pequod Press

A CERTAIN FLAIR FOR DEATH

A Pequod Press Speculative Fiction Novel

Illustrations by Stephen Fabian

First Edition

Manufactured in the United States of America
First Printing 2013
V 10 9 8 7 6 5 4 3 2 1

ISBN: 978-0-937912-59-1

On the cover: Alan Gutierrez, A Certain Flair for Death
(*www.alangutierrez.com*)

Pequod Press
P.O. Box 80
Boalsburg, PA 16827
www.PequodPress.com

Speculative Fiction Novels by John F. Carr

Carnifex Mardi Gras

Rainbow Run (with Camden Benares)

The Crying Clown Celebration: A Certain Flair for Death (with Camden Benares)

THE
CRYING
CLOWN
CELEBRATION

BOOK ONE

A Certain Flair for DEATH

TABLE OF CONTENTS

CHAPTER 1

TRUTH BETWEEN FRIENDS

Truth is the most valuable thing we have.
Mark Twain

Fitzgerald Baker entered my life at an oblique angle. Angela Calderon, the only woman I had ever considered marrying, hired him as architect for her new therapy center. The two of them spent a great deal of time together but I assumed that it was business. I was concerned with my own counseling, and for the time being was willing to let Angela pursue her dream of establishing the Calderon Rebirth Center, a halfway house where the suicide-prone would be reborn into a positive life.

I don't know when she and Fitz became lovers, but I was sure that it was temporary, that I would resume my position as Angela's lover when her flirtation with Fitz was over. I thought I was handling the situation as well as could be expected, but Serge Dicori, my best male friend and professional colleague, held a different opinion. He told me about it over dinner.

We were eating at Khan's Mongolian Barbecue in the part of Los Angeles called the Fringes, formerly known as Hollywood; a gathering place for the eccentric, the unconventional, the artistic and the bizarre. Outside, a group of Mormon Moslems attempted to dissuade all from entering an establishment that served both pork and alcohol. Inside there was an assortment of customers:

a zebraman whose black and white striped skin was a memorial to the last zebra who died almost sixteen years ago in 2072; a couple dressed in black leather wearing a long silver chain that circled the man's neck and was secured at the woman's waist; an androgynous male with breasts grafted onto his back, who wore a loin covering of joined coins as a sign that he was a street prostitute; a group of four Asian tourists who looked Chinese but might have been Mongolian; a bison-headed werebeast with crisscrosses of scraggly fur running up and down his brown arms; a trio of light-skinned blacks who were speaking Spanish; and a scattering of mainstream-dressed people that included me and Serge.

I had gone through the line first after selecting thin slices of pork and lamb, small portions of sliced carrots and onions, lots of bean sprouts and then adding garlic, curry and barbecue oil. Serge, who hadn't eaten here previously, lingered over the selections, reading the directions and opening a conversation with the Asian woman next to him. I watched them as the Mongolian cook emptied my bowl on the circular grill and skillfully moved the food over the hot surface with two wooden sticks.

Serge's eyes followed the Asian woman as he walked to our table. She sat down in the booth against the far wall next to the zebraman. I looked questioningly at Serge who said, "I was wondering if Mongolians eat here, but she isn't Mongolian. She's an Eskimo tourist."

The trio of Spanish-speaking blacks—two women and a man—finished their meal and left. Serge's eyes were drawn to their exit. I turned my head to see what captured his attention and saw the group of Mormon Moslems clustered around the black Hispanics.

"What's going on between those Puerto Ricans and the picketing blacks?" he asked.

"The pickets are Mormon Moslems," I said, "descended from the blacks who fled California to Utah after the Big One. Some of the Moslems practiced the Mormon religion as protective coloration. Eventually the common thread of polygamy led to a blend of the two religions, but the believers were cast out of Utah about thirty years ago. Most of them returned to California for the religious and personal freedom here. I got their pitch against alcohol and pork the last time I was here. I imagine they're trying to convert the Puerto Ricans. Seeing a man with two women probably brings out the urge to proselytize.

Serge smiled and shook his head. "I knew I could depend on you for an answer, Phillip." He picked up a small portion of his meal with the chopsticks, chewed and then swallowed. "This is delicious. How did you discover this place?"

"Husein Medina treated me to dinner here in December," I answered.

"That sponger is determined to become a friend of yours, isn't he? Dinner. Invitations to that weird New Year's Eve party for both of us. What does he want from you or from us?"

"He wants me to refer people to him for his Sufi dancing classes; I'm willing to do that when it's appropriate because he does that well. From us he wants recommendations for a lay membership in The Golden Society. That I'm not willing to do."

"I can see why," said Serge. "Medina favors zeroes as followers, taking the walking wounded as students and attempting to turn them into high-energy losers. I think one of the main reasons he wanted us at his party was for diagnostic reasons. His people-picking ability is as flawed as his character. He needs someone to point out the problem people or he's going to find one of his toadies slitting his throat or setting the house on fire while he's in it."

"That's a possibility. To use his own occult terminology, his Akashic records are mostly notations of his unpaid Karmic debts. But he does recommend great restaurants."

We exchanged small portions of our dishes. Serge's was more highly spiced than my own and the meat in it was mostly beef. We agreed that Khan's technique of requiring the customer to select the ingredients created an amazing possibility for a variety of taste sensations.

As we finished the meal and sat over tea and almond cookies, I looked at our reflections in the window, seeing two men of the same size and shape, just barely under average height and weight. We were both somewhat vain, having declined second helpings to maintain trim waistlines. I was the elder by a decade but that was indicated only by the slight thinning and graying of my hair and beard. Serge's hair was still all black and thick enough to look solid. My nose was long and straight, his aquiline. His Mediterranean skin contrasted with my Nordic pallor. As he opened his lips to speak, I noticed that they were wide like mine but slightly fuller.

"Phillip, I'm glad you suggested dinner together. I haven't seen you since New Year's. In the three weeks since then, I've come to the conclusion there are some personal matters that need to be discussed. I've elected myself because we're close friends and you know I have no interest in attacking you for sport."

"Is it my personal or my professional behavior that concerns you?" I asked, as I tried to keep the uncertainty I felt from showing on my face.

"Both, Phillip."

"Sounds serious. Tell me about it."

"Your personal life is on a narrower spectrum than it has ever been, to the extent of affecting our friendship…and you know how much I value that. I don't intend to stand back while you shrink your life. I see the look on your face—please don't interrupt! I'll give you an example: to the best of my knowledge you haven't spent an evening with a woman since I maneuvered you into accompanying Nadina Towers to my birthday party in November. You haven't seen her since, have you?"

"No," I answered. *Had it been that long? Maybe I was becoming too involved in my work.*

"Here's a more personal example," continued Serge, "Our friendship is deteriorating along the fault lines of professional deformation. Formerly, when we were together, maybe twenty-five percent of our total conversation was concerned with my patients, your clients and new developments in the therapeutic field. Now, professional talk comprises almost all of your conversation whenever you pick a subject to talk about."

"I don't know about that, Serge," I said, my face beginning to flush.

"Confirmation comes from your own mouth, right now. Your level of general awareness of your own behavior is down, my friend—way down. And it's affecting your professional life as well. You're treating fewer clients and you aren't aware of your bias in selecting them."

Serge had never mirrored my own life to me before. I knew that he was sincere, that he was doing what he felt had to be done, but the whole conversation had taken on a dreamlike, surrealistic quality. I seized on his last sentence as if clutching at a railing for support. "I have a bias in selecting clients? What kind of biases are you talking about?"

"Remember your client of about two years ago, Steven Morgan?"

I nodded that I did. Steven Morgan had been seething with suppressed hostility that almost drove him to suicide. Angela had saved him.

"When you recognized that your treatment for the suicide-prone didn't produce results fast enough, you immediately brought in Angela Calderon. You did exactly what a lifestyle crisis counselor is supposed to do: get the client into therapy or a series of therapies that will restore function and recreate belief in the possibilities of life."

Serge paused. Annoyed that he wasn't getting to his point, I interjected, "What's that got to do with the client selection bias that you're accusing me of?"

Serge frowned, causing the space between his eyebrows to reshape as two symmetrical puckers. "Instead of selecting clients that you can easily help, you select clients that are difficult—this gives you the illusion of being deeply involved in life, but it's the client's life, not yours. Or you select clients that are on the borderline of suicide, clients that should be referred to someone who specializes in suicidal crises rather than lifestyle crises. I know that you've worked that corner of the mental health field before, but it isn't your specialty anymore or you wouldn't be coming to me for advice all the time on how to handle your patients."

When Serge paused for breath, I said, "I see the example coming. Karl Kashubian, right?"

I tried to keep my hand from shaking as I poured more tea.

Serge said, "Yes. You asked my advice. I suggested Oscar Kemple's

Anger Termination Therapy and you rejected it."

"Of course, I did! I see Kemple as a last resort because his procedures are not only incredibly expensive, but they are painful for the client."

"Kemple has a high success ratio."

"I know," I said, trying to keep my voice down, "but only for people who are angry at specific people. Kashubian is angry at the system that allows holly web programmers, who in many cases have no qualifications for their jobs other than the fact they convinced someone to hire them, to judge the appeal of independently produced holographic productions. Kashubian believes he is an unappreciated genius and that creativity comes from a combination of suffering and intelligence. As long as Kashubian believes that, Kemple's AT Therapy might be able to stop the suffering. But I'm convinced he would stop Kashubian's creative flow, as well."

"So how are you handling the case?"

"I've got him working on another holly show of his own and I'm helping him to get involved in minor creative pursuits where he faces no chance of rejection. When he finishes his new holly production I'm going to convince him that he has suffered enough, that he has paid his dues and brought his creativity to fruition, and that his time of suffering is over because he has finally matured as an artist."

"That sounds very good, Phillip," said Serge. "I hope, for the sake of everyone involved, that it works. Because I know what you wanted me to recommend when you asked about Kashubian and I didn't do it. My own judgment may have been clouded because I wanted you to see what it is you're doing."

"Serge, this is getting too abstract. What did you think I wanted you to recommend?"

"That I suggest you refer Kashubian to Angela as a client."

I could feel the fortune cookie slip out of my fingers. "Why would I need you to suggest that I do that?"

"Because you haven't yet accepted that Fitzgerald Baker has replaced you as Angela's lover. You want to keep the feeling that you and Angela are still closely connected and to do it you are destroying your professional and personal life with illusion maintenance."

My mouth was parched. Memories and impressions flickered like flames in my mind's eye: Angela's dramatic entrances, the click of her heels as she danced to flamenco music, her long unpolished nails gently stroking my arm as she talked to me, the scent of her Cinnabar perfume on my sheets like a signature, the cinnamon colored velvet robe that still hangs in my guest closet.

"Phillip, where are you?"

I reached out with effort and brought the teacup to my dry lips; the cup trembled slightly. I swallowed the tepid tea and then said, "Here: I'm here. And I hear what you're saying."

"Remember my season of mourning when Laura died and how I came out the other side, with your help, ready to continue living. Phillip, you still have half your life yet to live, but you are living half a life because you haven't accepted that your romantic relationship with Angela has ended—"

"It's not over!" I didn't realize I was shouting until I saw everyone in the restaurant staring at me. I picked up the check and said, "Let's take a walk."

Serge nodded. I paid the check and we left. I didn't even notice the picket line until one of the Mormon Moslems touched my sleeve. "I feel your pain," said a tall picketer, "may I offer my help?"

"Leave me alone!" I shouted. To stop me from lashing out with more than my tongue, Serge put his arm around my shoulders and guided me through the picket line. I felt anger at both the picketer and myself for overreacting. *What is wrong with me? Why this approach avoidance conflict with Angela? I hadn't seen her in several weeks yet she is always on my mind.*

We walked in silence past an antique shop full of unwanted high-tech furnishings from the last century. I said, "Things have changed, but my relationship with Angela isn't over."

Serge said gently, "I know you once hoped to enter a joint practice with her. Have you altered that plan?"

"Yes. Now that her therapy center is close to being realized there is no chance of us working together. I tried and tried to get her to update her therapy procedures, to modernize her practice, but she won't shake off Templeman's influence—that old fraud—and she persists in clinging to antiquated therapeutic methods. I've never understood how she gets such fantastic results with her old-fashioned modes of operation."

"May I tell you?"

"Certainly," I said begrudgingly.

"Therapy can be practiced as a combination of science and art. You practice with a high percentage of science. Angela practices with a high level of art. In addition, she sees suicide as a personal enemy because of her son's suicide. She attacked Steven Morgan's suicidal impulse as if it were a bull and she were the matador going in for the kill. She reminds me of those medical doctors who see death as the enemy and will do anything to extend clinical life—regardless of its quality. She will excise any part of the client's persona necessary to remove the inclination toward suicide, and then Angela infects the client with her passion for life."

At the corner kiosk we bought hot coffee from a Weeble street vendor, and then walked half a block uphill to sit on the low rock fence that bordered an unused lot. I warmed my hands, which were cool from the slight chill of a January night, and burned my mouth with the first sip of coffee.

I said, "Serge, I see that you have a different, a clearer, more clinical, perspective of Angela than I have. But I do not believe that my romantic involvement with her is over. I was her lover before Fitzgerald Baker came into her life and I will be her lover again when he's gone."

"You don't see him as a serious rival?" he asked.

"Only temporarily. Once the new therapy center is completed, he'll be involved in something else and will gradually fade out of her life."

"Would you?" Serge asked.

"Would I what?"

"Fade out of Angela's life because the professional relationship was over."

"No," I said.

"Then what makes you think he will? He's been working on another project, the Pantheon of Prophets for the Church of Prophetic Revelation. That hasn't seemed to cool his ardor. You've met him and seen him at least a dozen times. What do you know about him?"

That he's a successful architect. He seems to be well liked. He's young—too young for a lasting relationship with Angela. He's handsome, has some charm, enough attractive qualities to keep Angela interested in the flirtation."

"Phillip, what those two have is not a flirtation. It is an intense affair that's been going on for more than six months. Fitz is a formidable rival, and you haven't bothered to find out who he is as a person."

I shifted my crossed legs to a more comfortable position and replied, "I'm ready for you to tell me who he is and what you believe he has that makes him a serious rival."

"Fitzgerald Baker is a complex person with a fascinating family background, and I suspect he's highly neurotic. It's said his great-grandfather was John Fitzgerald Kennedy and his great-grandmother was Marilyn Monroe. In passing, Angela told me he suffers from a Kennedy fixation and the Monroe obsession. There is absolutely no way that Angela could have avoided becoming entangled in the twisted threads of his life because she's enthralled with his family history and has a strong response to his charisma."

"Charisma?"

"He's got it, more than Husein Medina, more than anyone I've seen. But it's erratic. He doesn't have control over it, but I've seen it shine when Angela strokes him. She doesn't do that when you're around because she is sensitive to what you feel. Marilyn Monroe was the most famous suicide of the last century and you can be sure that Angela wants to know how that has influenced his life. I'm sure Fitz has led Angela to believe that he needs the kind of love and help that she alone can provide. The only way he could be a more serious rival would be if he were a mental health professional, too. I have heard her say that he is tired of architecture and thinking of changing careers. If he becomes a therapist, he'll bind Angela to him forever."

"Serge, I appreciate what you've told me. Angela is giving a lecture in Berkeley tonight. As soon as she returns to Los Angeles, I'm going to see her: Alone, if possible. With Fitzgerald Baker, if not. I am a determined campaigner. You've made me comprehend the filters that I've erected between me and the reality of Angela. You're the best friend I could ask for."

"I hope it isn't too late," said Serge.

"It's never too late. As the clichemiester would say, "'As long as there's life, there's hope.'"

We left for our respective bodes and I began planning my campaign to regain the love and favors of Angela. First I would buy her a Mexican Santo. I knew where I could get an eighteenth century figure of St. Elizabeth, a worthy addition to her collection of primitive art. I would give it to her as a Valentine Day's present. Second, I would throw a party. With live flamenco music, her favorite. I would use that Cuban catering service to remind her of our vacation in Havana. Perhaps I had underestimated Fitz Baker, but I was a generation older, more experienced and much more knowledgeable about Angela. I was going to give him the stiffest competition he had ever faced.

CHAPTER 2

BURIED ALIVE

Death, the undiscovered country, from those bourn no traveler returns.
William Shakespeare

The viewphone chimed and flashed. I looked up from my lapreader, which displayed an article on Womb Expulsion Therapy from *Lifestyle Crisis Counselor's Journal,* and saw the caller was using my office number. I let the answermat handle it, but flipped the remote switch in my recliner to put the picture into the holly and on the picture speakers. If the caller was just another potential client with post-achievement ennui, I could refer the call to a colleague. In a society with guaranteed subsistence, many people compete for meaningful personal achievement. If they find their victories hollow they have real problems, but not necessarily anything that I would classify as a lifestyle crisis.

The only call I wanted was from Angela; I'd left messages at both her home and office. My own voice vibrated from the speakers saying, "This recording is on the answermat of Dr. Phillip Wendell. If you wish to leave a message, you may do so now." It took me a few seconds to recognize Fitzgerald Baker's face. I was accustomed to seeing him with

Angela as her faultlessly groomed escort. Now his shingled brown hair was wildly disheveled and his face twisted with strain. He was wearing a white hospital gown.

I felt a painful spasm in my lower digestive tract. I was unsure as to whether I was more worried about Fitz's unkempt state or his message.

"Phillip...I mean, Dr. Wendell. Uh. This is Fitz Baker. I'm calling about...Angela."

He paused again and tears began to stream from his eyes. He gulped, then continued, "I'm afraid I have bad news…no, terrible news." Fitz's face appeared to collapse in upon itself, as tears streamed from his eyes.

A rush of disaster scenarios, like dark storm clouds, filled the horizon of my attention. My heart stopped beating for a moment, then resumed wildly. The lapreader dropped out of my hands onto the parquet floor. I shook my head and quickly pushed the manual override switch for the answermat, while I thrust the recliner into an upright position. "This is Phillip. What's happened to Angela?"

"How did you know?" Then Baker began shaking so badly that he stopped speaking. After several deep breaths, he regained control. "Angela's dead." His voice broke again and sobs took over his vocal apparatus.

I felt as if my reason for living had just died. I rose out of the chair, my curled fingers straining for the screen. Baker shrank back from my image. If only I hadn't stopped seeing Angela. I wanted to reach right through the screen and shake Baker until his eyes popped out of his head. What kind of fate was it that had snatched Angela away from me almost at the same moment I had come to realize how much I wanted her? Without even allowing me the opportunity to tell her of my desire and love for her.

"Phillip, what's wrong?"

His voice brought me back to the here-and-now. I fell back into my chair, drained. "I'm all right," I answered. I realized I had subconsciously blamed Baker for Angela's death without evenknowing how she had died. But she has been with *him.* I gripped my armrests until my fingers were bleached of color. Somehow I had to steer my way through the miasma that was clouding my perception.

"Where are you, Fitz," I asked, shifting to my professional questioning mode.

"Santa Rosa General Hospital. Ahh…we were at her property in Windsor, checking on the pre-building excavation—" As Baker turned from the screen, I could see him brush away the tears. "The, the earthmover pushed the entire bluff over both of us... Oh, God Almighty, how could you let this happen!"

Almost a minute passed before Baker began to speak again in a strained voice. "My Call-All alarm guided the rescue crew to me, but when they found Angela, she wasn't breathing. Nothing they did revived her. She was prone on the ground with mud in her eyes. She never moved or made a sound…nothing!"

I felt my heart lurch. *Anglea dead!* I couldn't believe it. I shook my head and attempted to assume my professional face. "Is there anything I can do?"

"No. Yes. Sorry….I mean there's nothing you can do here. But I'm being released from the hospital and then I'm coming straight back to Los Angeles. To see you."

Why did Baker want to see me? He was the last person I wanted to see—at least, right now. He had never been a friend or client. Had there been a final message from Angela to me? I felt my heart leap. But no—she never regained consciousness. What did he want with me?

"Is there something you haven't told me?"

"Yes, it wasn't an accident." His eyes appeared to light up. "I'm certain it was done on purpose. I have your home address; I'll be there in about three or four hours and explain everything."

I closed my eyes and tried to make sense out of his words, my feelings, Angela's meaningless death. I didn't want to see him. And yet, I didn't want to be alone with my grief. My lovely Angela was dead....

I took a deep breath. "I'll be here. Have you told the police that it wasn't an accident?"

"Yes, but I don't think they believed me," he said, pushing his hair out of his eyes which were both bloodshot.

"Before you leave, file an information access form with the hospital, the Call-All rescue crew and the police listing me as your professional confidant. Will you do that?"

"Yes, Phillip."

"I'll be here when you arrive."

We severed the connection. I slumped back in my recliner. The orange and rust decor of my den seemed overlaid with the grayness of Angela's death. My herbal tea tasted brackish. I felt sick at heart. The sunshine shirt I was wearing seemed too bright for this somber sequence of events; I walked into the sleeproom closet and exchanged the shirt for a mottled gray and black pullover. I studied my reflection in the mirrored wall. The mixed black and gray colors of the pullover matched my mood as well as they matched my thinning hair.

I wanted to cry or beat my fists against the wall, but instead all I could do was stand in impotent anguish, clenching and unclenching my hands.

After a while, I looked out the all-weather window next to the interior passageway that led from my residence to my office in the Century City Constellation. The perfectly landscaped grounds and the bright February sunshine outside did not soothe or cheer me. Today the grounds seemed like a primitive cemetery in the flatties, those still popular two-dimensional films of the previous century that documented the past as art.

The sunshine reminded me of the brightness that Angela Calderon had brought into my life—not that we had always been in personal or professional agreement: I had thought her a too possessive mother, not only of her son's life but of his death, also. I was also convinced that her admiration of Templeman's Treatise was misplaced; Templeman's approach to counseling had too much neo-Freudianism in it for me—roots are only a part of the reality of crises as I see them.

But she was the grail and I was her knight.

No more late-night passionate arguments. No more bouts of frenzied lovemaking...Angela was dead. I felt the sting of salt in my eyes.

My throat tightened. I slowly slid down the wall to my knees, letting my head rest against the windowsill.

For twenty years Angela had been the most important part of my life. Now, only a few years older than myself, she was dead in the early part of the second half of her life. How hard it was to believe that I would never see her face, so full of mature beauty, except in the timeless rooms of memory, rooms that can be visited often, but never lived in again. How was I to live without her?

The room was dim when the last sob stopped in my chest. By the time I rose to my feet, the automatic sensors filled the room with a cheery glow. I wiped the last tears from my eyes. Enough. Time and time alone would heal my grief and I could be of no assistance to the dead. Baker was evidently in need of my assistance. I was surprised to learn that he was carrying a Call-All alarm. What was it that a holly wag had said about them when they were first advertised? "Designed for paranoids by paranoids. The complete alarm system for the completely alarmed."

My laugh came out as a harsh chortle, and I was instantly sobered.

I walked over to my computer console and sat down in the wooden swivel chair. I longed for facts because I didn't want what I was feeling. I blinked twice at my computer wallscreen and the Viennese accent of Ludwig von Drake asked, "Vat is it, Phillip?" The cartoon countenance of Ludwig, Donald Duck's uncle and Disney's mid-Twentieth Century poke of the elbow into the side of Sigmund Freud, failed to bring the usual smile that my computer antimate typically brought forth. I turned off the antimate, leaned over the keyboard and punched in my request for the Call-All rescue team on Fitzgerald Baker. When my access code was verified, I received a readout:

CALL-ALL RESCUE CREWS REPORT 45-CA954-W12-1018

SUBSCRIBER: FITZGERALD FELIX BAKER, ICID 0-915904-24-1

DATE: FEBRUARY 3, 2088

TIME OF ALARM: 1138

TIME OF RESCUE CREW ARRIVAL: 1147

NEAREST INTERSECTION: Fisher Road and Alysson Lane, Windsor.

SITUATION: Earth cave-in at construction site.

ACTION TAKEN: Rescue team dug out subscriber Baker and his companion, Angela Calderon. Also discovered body of Henry John Vulker under overturned earthmover.

SUBSCRIBER'S CONDITION: Stable and recovering at Santa Rosa General Hospital.

REMARKS: Calderon and Vulker certified dead.

CREW MEMBERS PRESENT: R.G. Hewlitt and E.M. Arsenal

END OF REPORT

I pressed the key to retain the readout and put it in a temporary file. Then pressed the print lever to obtain a hardcopy for reference. My request for the hospital report produced an immediate readout that informed me that Baker had been treated for shock and minor abrasions before being released. I requested the police report be sent to me when available and received a confirmation that it would.

Then I sat back and waited for Baker to arrive, looking at the orange walls while memories of Angela drifted along the corridors of my mind. I tried not to focus on the desolation I felt inside, tried to distance myself from a reality that had substituted disappointment for optimism, sadness for joy.

SF

CHAPTER 3

GRIEF AND GUILT

There is a lot of guilt in this situation, but what makes you think it is yours?
Sam-tio Chung

The memory of a tanned Angela in a white bathing suit on the sand of La Playa, the beach near Havana, during the winter of '75 faded when my control panel emitted a low chime and showed the flashing light indicating a visitor had entered my foyer. I pressed the holly key and got Baker's image. He was no longer wearing the hospital gown but a sheen suit of metallic blue and gold that fit smoothly over his well-muscled frame. The small rip on the shoulder indicated to me that he hadn't stopped to change clothes. Probably he had had the suit cleaned at the hospital before teleporting to the Century City vault station.

As he came closer to the camera I looked for signs of strain on his face, which was framed by shingle-cut, shoulder-length, chestnut brown hair now neatly combed. Red fatigue lines showed around the blue irises of his eyes. Beneath the straight nose there was a full mustache that partially obscured the set line of his mouth. The rigid precision with which he moved showed that he was putting an effort into controlling the stress he was under. I had just recognized him as a serious rival and now he was my companion in grief.

I pressed the control that opened the first set of doors. Fitz went through them, waited for them to close and then stepped through the second door when I punched the release. His first words were "Phillip, sorry I'm late, but the police wanted me to answer some more questions." Then his face grew taut and he added, "I need to explain this to someone who can understand. It's my fault that Angela is dead."

I took a deep breath of air and slowly expelled it. If this was a confession, it might be a good idea if I recorded it. "Fitz, do you mind if I tape this?"

"Go ahead. Nothing matters much without Angela."

I pressed the recording switch and said, "Tell me about it from the beginning."

We both sat down in my den; I back in my chair and Baker in the captain's chair next to my desk. He took a deep breath, crossed his arms over his stomach, clutched his elbows, audibly exhaled and then breathed again before speaking.

"Angela had given a speech on suicide prevention in Berkeley last night. We spent the night there and rented a car this morning to drive to Windsor. Did you know that she was planning to open The Calderon Rebirth Center, a halfway house for people recovering from suicide attempts?"

"Yes," I said, trying to keep the bitterness I felt out of my voice. If it hadn't been for her obsession with the rebirth center, we might now be together and she would still be— No, this was not the time to indulge my grief. I had to learn what he meant when he said that Angela had been murdered.

I cleared my throat and began to speak again. "Angela was aware of my early work with potential suicides. She told me about the project."

"Then you know I designed the building, a modified geodesic structure mostly below ground level."

I shook my head yes.

His voice caught and he paused to rub his red eyes. "The excavation was supposed to be finished this week. We went to check on the progress… Then the construction crew broke for lunch, we were looking at the bluff undercut when—"

Baker slumped down in his chair, burying his face in his hands. I could hear the sobs from behind his tightly pressed hands.

"I'm sorry," he said, after regaining his composure. "It's like a nightmare. I still keep hoping I'll wake up and find that none of this happened. That Angela is still alive… She was more alive than anyone I've ever known. I'd always thought I'd be the one to die first."

"I know," I said softly. I'd thought I had all the time in the world and now I had none.

In a voice pushed to exhaustion, he continued, "We were below the undercut when the entire bluff suddenly came down on top of us. I tried to block Angela from the avalanche of dirt...but I was too slow. Phillip, I don't know if I can explain the fear, the horror I felt. For Angela...myself. The dirt squeezing my eyes, filling my nose..."

He shuddered. "There wasn't supposed to be anyone operating that earthmover. I'm sure she was murdered! But I was the intended victim. Not Angela!" Baker's voice had become strident.

"Why do you believe you were the murderer's target?" I asked, wondering if this tragedy had precipitated some underlying disturbance. Regardless, I was determined to hear every word he had to say about Angela.

"Assassinations are like a blight on my family tree. I'm descended from the New England Kennedy clan and am destined to be the target of assassins. I'm aware that some people might classify me as a paranoid, but there have been several attempts on my life in the past. Look at this!"

Baker pulled open the presfast at the top of his suit, revealing dark, puckered skin low on the side of his neck. A golden chain that supported a medallion bisected the long-healed wound. "During a political rally on the University of California Berkeley campus, a woman who was never found or identified fired a laser gun at me. I was creased, but

Dennis Nash, co-student in political science and my best friend, was killed. Being in Berkeley again last week brought it all back." His voice dropping, he continued, "And now today: someone tries to get me again but kills Angela instead…"

"That's one possibility," I said, "but not the only one. Did you recognize the driver of the earthmover?"

"No. I never saw him before and he wasn't a construction worker. None of the crew knew him. He must have walked onto the site when the crew went to lunch. It was my death he wanted, not Angela's."

Baker's voice was dissonant; I wondered why he needed to feel that he was the intended victim. Did it make it easier to accept Angela's death if he took the blame? Or was the reason much deeper and murkier? Was he subconsciously seeking the assassin's bullet? He seemed adamant in asserting his responsibility for Angela's death. Would there be an attempt at atonement?

I shook my head several times as though I could throw off the questions that streaked through my mind. It wasn't my problem; he was not my client, but I was beginning to relate to him as if he were, perhaps from habit, perhaps to delay my mourning.

"Fitz, I've requested the police report. When I get it, we'll know a few more facts and be able to take a closer, more realistic, look at this tragedy. I don't think you can claim responsibility for it. Vulker's the man who was driving the earthmover and his actions have resulted in two deaths. We don't even know why he was on the site.

Baker shook his head violently. "I feel guilty, responsible. I knew what the price of involvement with me might be. I tried to tell her. But she wouldn't believe me. I should have left long ago. Why am I so damn thickheaded?!"

He slammed his open hand against the side of his leg, filling the den with a resounding slap.

I knew I should ask him to leave before I became more involved than I wanted to; after all, he had been the one who had taken Angela away from me. No, that wasn't true. I knew better. If anyone was responsible, it was Angela's dead son or Angela herself—or even me. It wasn't right to put the blame on Baker for problems that had gone unresolved long before he even met Angela.

Fitz seemed to be disguising his grief by assuming unwarranted guilt: Was I going to let him continue in that unproductive vein? Before I could answer that question to my own satisfaction, I found myself mentally reviewing Chung's principles of guilt transference therapy. If I could stop Baker from assuming the needless burden of guilt, he would be in a better reality for working through his grief.

"You're thinking that I got Angela killed, aren't you?" he asked, warily.

"No," I said. "I was trying to estimate your heart rate by the pulse in your neck. I believe it's a little high. Then I was distracted by the medallion you're wearing; it looks like a well-worn golden scarab."

"It's a family keepsake." Baker pulled the chain and amulet over his head and handed them to me.

What I had mistaken for a golden beetle was the worn casting of a boat. Sunken letters on the back spelled out Kennedy.

"My mother told me that it's a replica of the boat that John Kennedy, my great-grandfather, commanded during Hitler's war. He gave it to my great-grandmother and it has been in our branch of the family ever since."

"Marilyn Monroe?"

"Yes," said Baker. "My grandfather was born in secret, out-of-wedlock. People were very prejudiced about children without marriage in those times. My grandfather was given the family name of Marilyn Monroe, which was Baker. She changed her real name for her career in the flatties."

I handed the medallion and chain back to him. He slipped it over his head without mussing his hair and closed the presfast of his suit. Trying to bridge from Baker's past to a possible future, I asked, "Do you intend to pass on the family keepsake to your descendants?" Perhaps I was trying to avoid thinking of Angela.

"I don't know if I'll have any. I had a valve put in so my sperm goes into my bladder. The only woman I contemplated having a child with was Angela...and it wasn't the right time in her life for that. It's my fault. If I hadn't gone to Berkeley again, it might never have happened."

"Fitz, you don't really know that. Isn't it possible that you are transferring some feeling of guilt about your previous troubles in Berkeley to Angela's death in Windsor? The similarity of losing two different persons, both of whom were very close to you, could trigger that kind of transfer.

"The incidents aren't that similar. When I was a political science major at Berkeley, I was a political activist. I was interested in a government that served the people as opposed to being one of the people who served the government. I thought that Dennis Nash was my best friend; we shared the same classes and I thought we shared the same philosophy of politics. The investigation into the assassination revealed that Dennis had been recruited by Group N, the government agency in charge of neutralizing political dissent. He had been assigned to *me*. It was his job to befriend me—and it got him killed."

"How did his death change your life?"

"I gave up my political science major and transferred to the school of architecture on the Los Angeles campus.

"Then Group N got what they wanted, didn't they?"

"Yes," he said thoughtfully, "I guess they did."

"Their agent was killed as a result of employment he accepted. The fact that the job involved you doesn't mean that you created the job or asked someone to accept it. Nash was killed as a consequence of his own actions which he never revealed to you for what they really were. For all you know Group N may have had him assassinated to achieve their objective of neutralizing you."

"I hadn't thought of that…I don't know. I guess it's possible . . ."

"Have you become politically active lately?"

"No. Three years ago, after my thirty-fifth birthday, I was approached by a lawyer—" A look of distress distorted his face. "Oh…I forgot to call Angela's lawyer and tell her that Angela is…dead."

"Is Juanita Delgado still her lawyer?"

"Yes. Angela told me several times that if I had legal problems I should call Juanita and if I had personal problems I should consult you."

Damn her! How could she do that to me? Didn't she know how much I still loved her? What did she think I was made of? Or did she know me better than I knew myself? "I'll call Juanita in a little while. Don't worry about it. You were saying that you were approached by a lawyer about something political?"

"Yes, he claimed to represent a group that wanted to start a new political party and run *me* for President! I strongly discouraged him and heard nothing more about it."

"Then it doesn't seem likely that you were the target for political assassination. Do you have any business or personal enemies who might want to kill you?"

"No. I don't make enemies."

I found that statement professionally interesting, but now was not the time to explore it. I asked, "Do you know why you immediately thought Angela's death was an attempt on your life?"

"Lately I've had a feeling that my movements are being monitored. Nothing that I can identify with certainty. But it's made me edgy."

"Why don't you contact Maxi Security and let them determine if you're being monitored or not. Ask for Ronald Marlin to do the investigation. I know him and he's good." Marlin was a former client, one who had weathered a severe lifestyle crisis.

"I'll call him tomorrow. The shock of Angela's death has knocked me off my moorings. I don't know which way is up or down anymore." Fitz's voice sounded utterly void of energy or life.

"We're both suffering from grief. I suggest that after I call Juanita we both go through the release procedure at The Whole Body Center; unless you have something that you have to do before morning."

"There's nothing I have to do anymore," Baker replied. "What is this release procedure?"

"It's a therapeutic way to relieve grief, stress, tension and fatigue. It makes you feel better without making you so aware of feeling better that you feel guilty for feeling good." I tried to put enough life in my voice to make the prospect sound pleasant, but inside I felt mostly death, the death of my beloved Angela.

Baker nodded and I gave him a time to meet.

CHAPTER 4

GRIEF RELEASE THERAPY

Take the pleasant memories of the past and let the rest go.
Serge Dicori

While Fitz was in the lav, I called Juanita Delgado and told her about Angela's death. She said the appropriate words to me over the viewphone and I could see the sadness in her face, but the words sounded hollow, as condolences always do, and did nothing to fill the hollowness inside me. Next I called Serge Dicori; he was out. I left a message saying that Angela had died and that I wanted to talk with him as soon as possible. Serge would understand and would not be uncomfortable with my tears.

Fitz and I left my bode; walking along the flagstone path lined with California holly shrubs, whose bright red berries seemed to symbolize the ripeness of maturity that Angela had possessed. The shrubs gave way to trees about five hundred meters away from my complex as we approached the large earth-covered mound that housed the entrance to The Whole Body Center underground facilities. The afternoon sunlight filtered through black oaks spaced so their branches entwined overhead forming a leafy roof, creating an atmosphere reminiscent of the restored Druid shrines in England.

The sign over the open archway was wooden, a mahogany backboard with blond pine or fir carved letters which spelled out THE WHOLE BODY CENTER in a long arc. The archway frame was rough stone, giving an impression of strength, solidity and stability. Interior indirect lighting gave a subdued glow to the curved walls which were draped with fluid mosaics, smooth pastel panels of mutable constructs in patterns of shifting sand that moved when the vibration and temperature sensors responded to the presence of a person.

I had seen them the last time I had been here about a year ago; they hadn't been installed in 2077 when I had brought Angela here to help her release the grief she had felt when her son committed suicide.

As Fitz and I stepped into the anteroom, an older man of indeterminate age wearing a white tunic stepped out of a dark, curtained alcove and said, "I am your helper. May I be of service?"

"We called for reservations for the release procedure. I'm Phillip Wendell." I gestured toward Fitz and said, "My associate, Fitzgerald Baker."

Fitz said nothing. The helper said, "I have your reservations. Here are your statements of charges."

We glanced at our statements and walked over to the terminal beside the alcove to put our keycards in the slot to transfer energy credits from our accounts to The Whole Body Center.

As soon as the transactions were complete, the helper said, "Please follow me to the effigy room. There you will select an image that reminds you of Angela." He parted the curtains that partially concealed a ramp with a gradual downward slope, a ramp that curved like the arc of a huge circle. The stone-like walls, illuminated as if by a perpetual twilight, were partially covered by abstract murals. Under our feet the carpet, as thick as leaves on a forest floor in autumn, muffled any sound of footsteps. Overhead the ceiling had scattered, minuscule points of light which invited the mind to create constellations. The curved corridor placed a limit on the field of vision, a limit I knew was intended to foster curiosity as to what was ahead in the immediate future but just out of sight.

The helper guided us to the effigy room which was filled with busts of mature women—I had been asked for some details about Angela when I called for reservations; The Whole Body Center was efficient as well as thorough. Each mannequin head was costumed with domino hood and half mask, hiding the hair and part of the upper face, making many of the faces seem hauntingly familiar as if their slightly open lips were about to whisper your name.

Fitz and I strolled through the bust-lined aisles until we found a mannequin of Angela's complexion, oval face and full lips. I nodded to the helper when Baker and I had agreed that we'd found the best approximation of Angela among the effigies. I could almost imagine it was Angela with a mask over her eyes and hood over her hair: For a moment I had to struggle to force back the unbidden tears that had started to well in my eyes.

The helper pressed a button concealed beneath the back of the domino hood and said, "This way, please."

I was glad of the interruption and we followed the helper through a portal, which had not been our entrance, to emerge into another curving corridor. I expected the helper to turn right but he turned left and I recognized that I had lost my orientation to the aboveground world. He led us into a pale green room with two curved walls and two straight ones. The straight walls were lined with thumblock lockers, each faced by a chair.

No two chairs were alike except in the respect that they were all wooden with hard bottoms. There were rocking chairs, secretary chairs, throne chairs and antique school desk chairs, a greater assortment than the Neobeat cafes that pride themselves on unmatched furniture.

"Put all your clothes and possessions in a locker," said the helper.

I sat down in a captain's chair very much like the one in my den. Baker sat down near me in a chair that appeared to have been hand-fashioned from a section of church pew and began to remove his flexfiber shoes.

The helper said, "Please wait here. I'll be back soon from the effigy rooms with the others who have come to lose their grief."

I sat down and began removing my custom loafers after the helper left us.

Baker, looking surprised, asked, "Are other people going through this ceremony with us? People who didn't even know Angela?"

"Yes," I replied. "The procedures here are based on the belief that shared grief is easier to release."

"Do you believe that?"

"I believe that their system works. Whether the theory is true or complete is a secondary consideration, but it makes sense to me that getting grief out in the open before strangers can be a cathartic—"

Baker interrupted with, "You've been through this before?"

"Yes. Several times."

"Tell me what happens next."

"I think the experience will be more worthwhile for you if I don't preview it."

"Do the effects diminish with repetition?" he asked, his brow furrowed.

"Yes, for all but a few."

"What would you recommend for a client if he kept grieving after this release procedure?" asked Baker, his face taut.

"Grief rarely leaves all at once; it usually decays. The rate of decay varies with individuals and circumstances. So it depends."

"But are there things that can be done to ameliorate it?"

"There is a whole spectrum of grief abatement therapies, everything from behavioral desensitization through memory editing and restructuring, if the grief remains constant. If the grief is decreasing but at a very slow rate, there are a number of techniques to treat the mourner's symptoms until he has time to adjust to his loss."

Before I had a chance to start the next sentence, Baker asked, "What are they like?"

I replied, "The Pavlov Behavioral Institute of New Mexico has a repetitive desensitization procedure that consists of—"

"No, not that. I want to know about techniques for treating the symptoms."

"Grief assuagement through new stimuli is the most common because it is usually the most effective. The techniques can be as mundane as finding new hobbies and pastimes, or as radical as death-rebirth simulation, fantasy living with a mummer surrogate or even mindset identification alteration.

"What's a mummer surrogate?"

"A live-in actor hired to play whatever part will lessen the grief. The part of the dead person can be played as close to previous reality as possible or in the spirit of some grief-reducing fantasy. The mummer might not even play the part of the deceased person but an entirely fictional person designed to bring an end to mourning."

The helper reentered the room with three people; Baker and I glanced at them and then continued the undressing process that had slowed down during our conversation. We heard the helper give the other three mourners instructions to undress. We disrobed and waited. Although nudity is almost universally accepted, introducing people to each other while they are undressing is considered crude in most circles.

When all of the mourners were finished putting clothes and possessions into the lockers, the helper gathered us together before a door in the curved wall. Now that the rest of us were naked, the helper's white tunic seemed like a badge of office. We formed a semicircle in front of him and he performed first name introductions.

Indicating a tall, unusually thin man with almost no body hair except a few reddish blond hairs around his genitals, the helper said, "This is Wallace, who has come to mourn the death of Godfrey." Wallace looked up. I was unable to see any visible sign of grief on his face.

The helper waved his hand to encompass both the other two, a dark-skinned pair of middle-aged people who looked like siblings because the only visual differences between them were sexual. The helper said, "Roberta and Robert, who have come to mourn the death of Dale." Both members of the pair had reddened eyes and traumatized faces.

Pointing to me and then to Baker, the helper said, "Phillip and Fitzgerald, who have come to mourn the death of Angela."

Baker choked back a sob when he heard her name, while I dabbed at the tears now trickling from my eyes.

The helper led us to a doorway just beyond the lockers. Each of us was assigned a separate cubicle by the helper who said, "Inside you will find clothes that symbolize the clothes that your loved one no longer needs and dishes that represent the ones your loved one left behind. You are to break the dishes and rip the clothes. After that you are to strike the padded wall until you lose your rage or your strength. Come back to the locker room when you are finished, but take as much time as you need."

The breaking and ripping ritual had more meaning for me this time than it had the last time. I picked up a white and blue plate and smashed it against the hard wall opposite the entrance. Without analyzing what I was doing, I was soon in a frenzy, smashing dishes, ripping clothes and pounding the padded wall.

I quickly lost track of time. I stopped pounding the wall, like some punch-drunk fighter, when my arms became too heavy to lift. My body was wet with sweat and trembling exertion. I left the cubicle and entered the locker room. All the mourners were there; they were waiting for me. I started to speak to Fitz, but just as I opened my mouth, the helper said, "Please follow me."

We were led through the door in the curved wall and into a circular room; the curvature of the tiled walls was the opposite of what the mind's eye expected; the door was the point of tangency for two huge circular rooms.

The helper seated us next to each other in five of the twelve enclosure chairs which were arranged in a circle about a meter from the wall, all facing inward. The chair was like a combination of an old-fashioned barber's chair and an individual sauna shell that covered the body up to the neck. I tried to find the pattern in the arrangement of the tiles on the portion of the wall that I could see but I was unable to see through my tears.

All the others, even Wallace, were crying. The concentration of onion juice molecules in the air was just at the threshold of my olfactory perception. If I hadn't known about it, I may not have suspected that I was being unnecessarily helped to let out my tears. Using an irritant to provoke tears is an old and effective device to unlock the door of sorrow. My stream of tears seemed to be my total consciousness.

Each of us was checked by the helper to ascertain that the central nervous system stimulator, commonly called a spineline, registered as connected. He put the drinking tubes in our mouths; mine fit in the corner of my lips like a dentist's suction tool. Baker looked as concerned as if he were in a dentist's chair without a pain damper.

The dry heat inside the shell sucked the moisture out of my body. I pressed my lips on the drinking tube and received a cool squirt of water which I eagerly swallowed. Before my body had adjusted to the heat, I felt the spineline send out the sphincter release signal; my bowels contracted, almost cramped and then evacuated into the vacuum commode built into the seat of the chair. My bladder swelled and then compressed, forcing my urine out the channel and into the void of the vacuum; this was followed by a remote controlled, sexless ejaculation.

I felt empty inside, as though my internal organs had been sucked through the seat. I sagged back against the chair and rolled my head to look at Baker. His face was a pasty white and his eyes were open in an O of surprise.

Unbidden, the water tube fed me a steady stream of cool, distilled water that after the first swallow, which contained an emetic, was tasteless until it hit my stomach. I vomited into the trough below my chin. When the distilled water came back up clear, the process stopped and the drinking tube sprayed a jet stream of water that rinsed my mouth and washed my chin and beard. Even though I had known exactly what would happen, I felt weak and strangely purified as I left the chair and, along with Baker and the three others, followed the helper and entered the cleansing booth he indicated.

The cleanser was a new model. I walked in and my skin began to tingle as I felt the static electric charge in the air. I stepped forward, put my chin in the chin rest and adjusted the faceplate. Contour brushes on flexible arms emerged from the walls. They rotated against my skin as if to polish me, buffing off foreign matter, loose hair and flakes of aging skin.

I expected a vacuum hose to follow the brushes, but instead I felt compressed air being directed at me from a dozen angled nozzles. The air pressure was strong enough to make me feel that I was being buffeted by a fierce Chicago wind except that the air stream wasn't cold; it was warm enough to create an occasional drop of sweat although after the earlier sauna I had little excess moisture. When the air nozzles stopped scouring my skin, I felt as if I were a building cleaned by old-fashioned sand blasting.

From the cleansers, the helper led us into another room that looked like a chapel with heavily draped walls barely discernible in the dim light. The helper ushered us to seats in a curved pew with armrests for all occupants.

When I sat down my eyes were drawn to the altar-like throne where the holly images would appear. I was seated next to Fitzgerald Baker, who was between me and the others. He too seemed fascinated by the throne.

"This is the finishing room," the helper explained, "because this is where you are given the opportunity to complete the relationship you had with the person you mourn. Each of you, in turn, will see the blue light glow on the right arm of your seat. That will mean it is your opportunity to talk to the entity symbolized by the effigy. First you adjust the controls to make the effigy speak in the proper voice. Then you may confess past thoughts and actions, say the words that got left unsaid, wind up all the ends that were loosened by the ending of the relationship."

As he finished speaking, the hologram of an androgynous face appeared and a voice, in a hoarse whisper, said, "Robert. I'm here. Adjust the voice control so I don't have to whisper. I'll say your name five times so you can adjust the voice level. Robert, Robert..."

I listened as Robert made the voice into a contralto.

"I'm Dale, Robert. Now is the time for you to let everything out. Let this final encounter leave nothing unfinished or unsaid. Speak to me. Speak freely."

Robert was sitting on my far left; I couldn't see his face but I could hear the emotion in his voice when he spoke.

"Dale…Dale. You understood me like no one else except Roberta. You understood. I loved you... You know that. Heard it every day. There was a place, a space in my life—I didn't know was empty. Didn't know 'til you filled it…"

Robert stopped to blow his nose on a tear towel.

I had my own in my hand, occasionally wiping the tears that ran unbidden from the corners of my reddened eyes. I was feeling the empathic reaction to Robert's grief, which my mind and body were translating into expression, an expression that would help purge the grief, sorrow and absolute loss I felt due to the loss of Angela.

Robert bent forward toward the effigy and clenched his hands together in his lap. Between sobs, he said, "You were the perfect lover. You are gone. You will never be forgotten. I will love your memory forever."

Robert sat back in his chair. The voice which was cued by the helper seemed to come from the effigy's lips. It was firm and sure with the ritualized words: "I have heard you. I understand you and it is okay." The image faded when Robert said no more, and then turned to focus on Roberta.

The voice now spoke to Roberta saying, "I'm Dale, Roberta. I'll say a few words so you can adjust my voice if it needs it. I'm here, Roberta; I'm here so that you can talk to me."

Roberta said, in a soft tone that quivered with emotion, "I love you, Dale."

"I know, Roberta. Now is the time for you to let everything out. Let this final encounter leave nothing unfinished or unsaid. Speak to me. Speak freely."

I didn't know whether Roberta had adjusted the control or not, but the voice of Dale now seemed a tenor male voice instead of the contralto female voice that had spoken to Robert previously.

Roberta said, "Dale, I knew this time would come, I knew that our *ménage a trois* would not last forever. I feel such a loss. Unimaginable loss that has to be experienced to be conceivable. I weep a sea of sorrow. If tears could bring you back, you would have already floated back to our sensual chamber. My mood now is as sexless as if I had been celibate by choice for all of my life."

Her voice broke and she paused almost a minute before speaking again. "I…I…know now that that will change. I know I will have other lovers, even some that I will share with Robert. But I want you to know—I need to know that you understand—that other lovers will merely be a brief melody in my life. You were a theme…"

My mind whirled with the implications of her statements and tried to grasp the complex similarities and differences in the grief we were sharing.

The effigy's voice intoned softly but firmly, "I've heard you. I understand you and it's all right."

When the image faded it was replaced with the face of an older man, the weathered countenance of a patriarch that dominated the room with a commanding presence. The lips whispered, "Wallace, I'm here. Adjust the voice control so—"

At the sound of those words Wallace, who was evidently familiar with the controls, transformed the voice into a penetrating, almost overpowering, bass that rumbled out the rest of the beginning ritual.

I could hear the anger in Wallace's voice as he replied "Oh, no. This is no final meeting. Our final meeting will be face-to-face. People have been saying you were dead for a long time, but I know that you're not dead. You are merely dormant. I grieve. I grieve for your loss of professionalism. But most of all, I am angered that you aren't taking responsibility for your own actions. You cannot abdicate because there is no one else to oversee your projects.

"I've sought you in many places; Mount Sinai, the Wailing Wall, the Garden of Gethsemane, the Vatican. Finally, I've come here, God, to talk to you, knowing that this ritual will not escape your attention. Sooner or later, you will have to reappear or designate an empowered agent to speed the changes that must come. I've prepared myself by purification for that role to the point where I am both something more than human and also someone less than human. I've also prepared my mind by reading everything that has been written about you.

"I know that some of the writers weren't selected by you because so much of what they say is self-serving. I don't believe that you have joined into a partnership with the opposition. I believe that you've neglected things so long that you want to ignore the world and hope that it will go away. The world will not go away. You won't be left alone. You have survived disbelief. But can you survive hate? For I promise you, God, that unless you show me your face and make me understand, I will inspire believers and former nonbelievers to hate you. When there is sufficient hate, there will be no you. I do not ask for your forgiveness. I know what I'm doing. God, show me your face!"

Wallace screamed his final demand, but the effigy face remained impassive. The ritual words rumbled out: "I have heard you. I understand you and it's okay."

Wallace slumped down as if emotionally drained. I had become so involved in Wallace's drama that I'd forgotten Baker and my own grief for a few minutes.

Baker's turn came next; I saw the blue light glow on the arm of his chair. The masked oval face with the parted, sculptured lips looked even more like Angela now than it had in the effigy room. I shivered involuntarily. When Baker had the voice adjusted to the alto range, I was surprised by the intensity of the pain I felt upon hearing that familiar voice.

"I'm Angela, Fitz. Let everything out. Tell me all. Leave nothing unfinished or unsaid in this final encounter."

"Angela, you were the focal point of my existence. My life had meaning for the first time when I shared it with you. I'm going to ask Clyde to finish up the details on your rebirth center…I can't go back there. That place is…ours, I mean yours. Well, it's a good place for your Center, but it's no place for me…" He paused, to rub the tears leaking from his eyes. "No—not now. I don't know how I could ever feel reborn there. Not without you. I feel dead inside, empty, vacant. I wanted…"

Baker's sobs stopped his flow of words. I felt tears run down my cheeks and into my beard. His grief and my grief were one as I heard him continue.

"Angela, I know that you were reluctant to take me as your lover. I overcame the obstacle of being a generation younger than you are. I overcame every hindrance to explore the love of my life. But how do I overcome this loss? My mind has been strafed with missiles of despair. I feel as though the very marrow has been sucked out of my bones. I know that you made provisions for the Center to be completed from your estate. Your death has not ended your dreams, but my dream is over. I understand that it is not your fault, but it's my reality and I don't know what I will do to make it livable. If I believed in life after death, I'd join you. The only thing I have to believe in is my love for you. My love for you is my life. I can't bear to say goodbye…"

Baker exploded with shuddering wails that shook his body.

When he had quieted down, Angela's voice said, "I've heard you. I understand you and it's okay."

The blue light came on at the right arm of my chair.

The effigy said, "I'm Angela, Phillip. Tell me all. Leave nothing unfinished or unsaid in our final encounter."

"Angela," I began, "I am as grieved now as you were when your son committed suicide. I remember so many times together, beautiful times when you began to live again, to love again and to realize that life goes on."

I paused to clear my throat and wipe my eyes. "I know that although we didn't always agree on professional matters and minor questions, we had a potential for mutual happiness that we never fully explored. When you left your husband, I was ready to assume that role but the problems you had with your son's death delayed that. Blaming yourself for his death was unnecessary and it made you withdraw from the happiness you could have found. I had hoped that you would close out whatever guilt you felt about his death once The Calderon Rebirth Center was functioning. If that had happened, this incurable romantic would have proposed to you again."

I heard Baker suck in air. When I turned to face him he looked away. I rubbed my eyes with my knuckles.

I began to speak again. "Yes, there have been other women in my life, but I realize now that I never let them become as important as you. I loved you years ago. I love you still. The memories of you will be a joy to me forever."

The tears I was shedding were not tears but a christening of the new mental ship that traveled through a world no longer inhabited by Angela the late lamented love of my life.

I heard her voice say, "I've heard you. I understand you and it's okay." Some part of me knew that someday it might be all right, but most of me was feeling a cathartic release, that ideal state of letting go of the grief and retaining the memories that mattered.

The helper led us like sleepwalkers through the passageway to the physical rejuvenation room. Baker looked surprised as we were fitted with electronic exercise suits that stimulated and loosened the muscles. I let my mind drift while my body went through the most extreme postures the suit feedback system reported that I could tolerate. It was less violent than a treatment by a sadistic masseur or masseuse but much more thorough. I felt twinges in muscles I hadn't used in years.

All five of us were exhausted when we were fitted into reclining racks that realigned the heated, loosened muscles and repositioned our bones. I felt at least a centimeter taller when I left the room.

The helper directed us to five empty cubicles equipped with soundproofing to absorb the sounds of any grief we wanted to sob or scream out, and an air pressure floater that would allow us to float on air as we slept. He told us we would be awakened at dawn.

I told Fitzgerald Baker I would see him in the morning. I was too exhausted to do anything but sleep, and I hoped my dreams would be of Angela.

CHAPTER 5

A LETTER FROM BEYOND THE GRAVE

You don't know a woman until you have had a letter from her.
Ada Elverson

When I entered Juanita Delgado's well-appointed legal office around 1100, Juanita was talking to her law clerk, saying, "...and I need that before going into court. It'll reinforce our client's position that neither character redevelopment personality restructuring or surgical transformation violates the existing contract." The clerk nodded to her and then to me on his way out the door.

Juanita looked over at me and said, "I'm so sorry, Phillip. I know how close you were to Angela." There was a look of sadness in her brown eyes.

I steeled myself for the unbidden tears that appeared automatically at the mention of my beloved's name. This time it was a sprinkle instead of the usual deluge and, after dabbing at my eyes with a handkerchief, I was able to continue the conversation. "Thank you, Juanita. I know Angela was more than a client to you, she was a friend as well."

She clasped my hand. "Yes, I miss her so badly. It's been a terrible morning. I've had to contact her parents, her ex-husband and so many of her friends. I've made arrangements for the letting-go ceremony, as well. It will be held on Thursday at the Wilshire Memorial Chapel at 1500."

"I…I will be there." It wasn't where I wanted to be; I wanted to be back with Angela in some happier place at a happier time.

"Phillip! Are you all right? You look like you're about to pass out."

"I'm not doing well," I admitted, shaking my head. "Angela's gone, Juanita! I feel as if I've lost a limb, or my heart has been ripped asunder. I'm having trouble imagining a world without her." Tears began to well in my eyes.

"I know," she replied in a subdued voice. "Angela was so alive… Who could have expected her to die like this?"

I shivered, and Juanita took me in her arms. The tears began to flow again, and this time I didn't try to stop them. When I had stopped shaking, she led me over to her chair and fixed me a hot cup of coffee. I drank too much on the first sip and it scalded my tongue. My impatience to experience even a small pleasure had brought me pain.

"Juanita, did you get a copy of the police report?"

"Yes, my copy arrived just before you walked in the door. Vulker was a member of the Right to Die Society. He's on record as having made several attempts to interfere with the progress of Angela's Center. The autopsy showed that Vulker died from ingesting extract of baneberry mixed with some other drugs in a time-release capsule. Probably self-administered. Vulker is liable for a wrongful death suit if anyone wants to sue his estate, but it looks as if he had planned this for some time. The only assets in his estate are a small energy account and a few personal possessions. Everything else that he had is on short term lease with a terminal escape clause."

"So he played kamikaze."

Juanita nodded her head sadly.

"Is there anything we can do to get the *bastards* that sent him?" I was surprised at the vehemence that filled my voice.

"No. Not unless we can find a witness or a tape of the conversation ordering him to kill Angela. Personally, I don't believe he was ever given such an order. With fanatics like Vulker you don't have to be direct. It may have been entirely his own idea; I don't think we'll ever know. The police are checking to see if he's a known associate of any extremist groups; the lead detective thinks Vulker might be a member of the Berkeley Chapter of the Right to Die Society."

I toyed with the idea of infiltrating the Berkeley Right to Die Society but quickly dismissed it. How could you punish people who wanted to die? No, there was no need for vengeance: Vulker was already dead and persecuting his associates, who may or may not have been involved, would not bring Angela back.

I shook my head. "What a shameful waste… I cannot deny Vulker his right to die, but he could have martyred himself to his ideals without killing Angela."

"Her death was so senseless," Juanita said, shaking her head. She paused, then added, "Phillip, would you like some more coffee?"

"No, thanks," I croaked in reply. My throat was tight, as if a tennis ball was lodged there.

Juanita walked over to a file cabinet and removed a legal size envelope from the middle drawer. I saw my name written in Angela's distinctive cursive across the top. My breath caught; it was as though Angela's hand was clutching my heart.

After a deep breath Juanita handed it to me, saying, "Angela left this with me with instructions to give it to you when she died."

"Thank you," I muttered. My hand shook as I took the envelope.

Juanita paused a moment as if to see whether or not I was going to open the envelope and, when she saw I wasn't, she asked, "Phillip, do you know where Fitzgerald Baker is? I left messages at his home and office to notify him of the time and place of the letting-go ceremony, but he hasn't called back. I think he ought to be told what was in the police report."

"We went through the grief release procedure together at The Whole Body Center yesterday, but he was already gone when I called at dawn.

I'll try to locate him and tell him."

"*Gracias*, Phillip."

"If I don't talk to you before the service, I'll see you there Juanita."

I left her office, clutching the envelope that held a precious message from Angela. My first impulse when I left the central Los Angeles huburb was to go to the nearest privacy lodge and rent a cubicle, but I rejected the impulse. Instead, I would savor Angela's last private message to me after I finished the business of the day.

Back in my Century City office, I put the envelope from Angela into my office safe, and left messages for Baker at his home and office. Then I concentrated on discovering his whereabouts so I could tell him about the police report. I didn't know Baker well enough to know who his friends were, other than Angela and his business partner. I knew of no one else he might consider a close friend.

Baker had left The Whole Body Center before dawn, so attempting to trace his movements seemed unlikely to produce results. Where could he be? If he had found the release procedure inadequate, he might have gone someplace to grieve privately—perhaps someplace where he could be alone with his memories of Angela.

It appeared as though Angela's death had brought us closer than we had ever been while she was alive. We were brothers in grief, both sharing her as we could have never done during her life. My feelings towards Fitz Baker were all out of kilter; in one sense I resented the closeness that he had shared with Angela, the depth of which I was only now coming to realize. On the other hand, Baker was the only person who could understand the desolation and abandonment I'd been feeling since her death.

Seeing Baker made Angela, in life and death, all that much more real to me—both the pain and the joy. I hoped our time together would be short so I could go back to living my life.

Serge had implied that the well-worn path of my life had become a rut, but to me the familiar grooves matched my diminished needs and wants—especially now without my Angela.

Where would Baker go to be alone with Angela's memory? Perhaps he would want to remember her as she had been when he saw her last. I called the Los Angeles Counselors Guild on the viewphone and asked for the library.

"Library, Perkins." The screen showed the familiar face of Hyacinth Perkins.

"Hello, Hy. How are you?"

"Fine, Phillip. And you?"

"I'm managing. I need an optic thread of Angela Calderon's last lecture, the one she gave in Berkeley on Monday."

"I was sorry to hear of her untimely death. You were close to her, weren't you, Phillip?"

"Yes. I want a copy of her last lecture—maybe I should get two. One for Fitzgerald Baker, too, unless he already has one. Could you check to see if he has ordered one?"

"He had one delivered this morning. I'll send one to your office."

"Thank you, Hy. Did Fitz have his sent to his home? I'm looking for him."

"No. He had it sent to—let me check. Here it is, the Campbell Yacht Club, Key West, Florida. That help you?"

"Yes. And, thanks, Hy."

I left my office and walked to the Century City vault station. Five people emerged flashing smiles made eerie by their translucent teeth. I recognized that as a symptom of heavy indulgence in the trance drug Tranzokeen. One of them said, "There's never been anything like the Australian trance dance."

They headed for the cleansers as I went to the terminals, put my keycard in the voucher slot, punched the code for my Key West destination and went into the booth.

Inside the darkened cubicle, I felt the sensations that teleportation always induced in me: the coursing of my blood through my veins and arteries as if champagne were circulating in my body, the tingling of my skin as my brain recorded the feeling of thousands of small brushes gently stimulating the surface that connected me to the rest of the world, the lightless flash as I was transported via the energy force lines of the Earth across the continent to the southern tip of Florida.

As soon as I emerged from the Key West booth, I set the indicator on my watch to east coast time to match the local time clock on the wall. Through the all-weather windows I could see light rain in the fading twilight. I took the first tram on the enclosed tramway and got off at the Campbell Yacht Club.

Having neither membership nor guest privileges at the club, I waited until the security guard verified that Fitz was on his boat and would see me. Once I was cleared the guard opened the access door for me and said, "Turn to your right and look for berth 109."

I thanked her and went in the direction she had indicated.

My knowledge of boats is limited, mostly by lack of interest attributed to my stubborn seasickness that persists through normal doses of motion sickness preventers, but when I saw Baker's boat, the shape of it prompted me to recall the medallion he wore around his neck. Baker had two golden boats—one on his chest and one here in the water. Through the misting rain I could see the boat's name painted on the stern. It was, of course, *Angela*.

I tried to stop the unbidden question that popped into my mind: by what right did he name his boat after the woman I loved? I pushed the thought away; regret was making me more possessive after her death than I had been while she was alive. But I hadn't known they were so close then…

Baker was waiting for me on deck. "Come aboard," he said with a scowl, "I'd like to know how you found me." There was a hint of paranoia in his voice.

I walked up the sloping gangway and onto the hardwood deck. "I learned that you had ordered a copy of Angela's last lecture delivered here. I came because I wanted to tell you what was in the police report. You are in no way responsible for Angela's death."

He looked puzzled, and as I drew closer I could see his eyes were red-rimmed from lack of sleep and crying. After a slight hesitation, he said, "Come into the cabin. I'd like to hear about it."

I sat down at the small table where Baker, judging by the half-full bottle of rum, had been sitting.

"Want to join me in a drink?" he asked. There was a slight slur in his voice that indicated it wasn't his first. "Genuine Puerto Rican rum. Angela and I got it in Castano the last time we had her out."

"Sure," I said, trying to keep the anger out of my voice. "I'll have one. With coke, if you have it." I hadn't been ready to hear him say we—meaning Angela and him—in such a possessive manner. I wondered if he felt the same way towards me; it would explain his tenseness every time we were together.

He poured me four fingers of rum, put two splashes of Coca-Cola in it and asked, "What did the police find out?"

"Vulker was a member of the Right to Die Society. He had tried to stop the establishment of the Center before. There is no doubt he had planned to kill and Angela was his target. He'd taken poison before he started the earthmover."

Baker's face lost all expression, as if he too were dead.

"I know this information doesn't lessen the loss. I believe, once you realize that the entire situation was not of your making, you will be on your way to dealing with the new reality."

His face hardened. "I only wish it were that easy."

We sat in silence for a long two minutes. I sipped my drink. Both of us needed consolation; I didn't think we could get it from each other. Baker didn't move; his eyes weren't focused and his blink rate had slowed almost to a stop. I wondered if this was his first bottle.

Breaking the silence, I told him, "The letting-go ceremony will be at the Wilshire Memorial Chapel at 1500 on Thursday. There is a message on your answermat from Juanita. She made the notification per Angela's instructions." I tried to mask the hurt I felt when I said her name.

When I said Angela, Baker focused his eyes on me. "You mean her death was really not my fault."

"No, Fitz. It's not your fault in any way."

"Oh... What else did you say?"

I repeated Juanita's message.

"Thank you, Phillip. Is there anything I can do for you? I appreciate what you've done."

Baker's words were sincere, but behind them I could detect mixed emotions of some sort. I suspected he wanted to be alone. Maybe because he wanted to absorb the news I'd given him. Maybe he resented my former relationship with Angela, just as I resented his status as her last lover. Maybe he wanted to treasure his memories of her without having to acknowledge that I had such memories, too.

"You're welcome, Fitz. I'm going to leave. I have to get back to Los Angeles.

"I'll see you Thursday." He sat unmoving as I walked out of the cabin toward my rendezvous with one of the final links in my chain of memories of Angela.

Back in my den with a glass of Angela's favorite Bordeaux at my elbow, I pulled the envelope tab and began to read the first sheet of her last message:

Dear Phillip,

If you are reading this letter, it means that I have died. I know that you miss me and that things haven't worked out the way either one of us had planned. It must be strange—the whole thing is probably much more difficult for you than it was for me.

You have been an important person in my life for longer than most of the people I know. That is a truth that transcends death, just as the love we shared transcended the circumstances which prevented that love from blossoming into the most important thing in both of our lives. I know that you wanted it to be that way. There were many times when I shared your dreams.

Now I'm presuming on a relationship that has ended. I've done a very nonprofessional thing. I've taken Fitz Baker as a lover when

I intended merely to prevent his becoming seriously disturbed. He can't see his own problems clearly enough to seek help and I felt he would be offended if I suggested extensive therapy. He's an exceptional architect but he is not happy as one. He is preoccupied with the mysteries and tragedies of his family tree. One of my fears has been that he is becoming suicide-prone like his great-grandmother. (I've enclosed a genealogy chart so you can see what that involves.)

I've told no one but there have been threats made against me and the Center—I haven't told anyone because I don't really take them seriously and I couldn't stand the fuss, especially from you and Fitz. My freedom is very important to me; maybe as much as my life. This may help you understand why I was never able to give you the commitment you so dearly wanted.

I am afraid that should anything happen to me, Fitz will take my death badly. I've become very important to him. Maybe too important. He has never been comfortable about discussing death. From clues too numerous to mention, I have concluded that he suffers from a fear of assassination as well as from the fear that he might be inclined toward suicide.

If Fitz hadn't reminded me in his bright, cheerful moments of Jason, I probably would never have let him become so close. He has a charm and an aura of masculine warmth that has surfaced often enough to overwhelm me. I know that Jason never came to terms with his incestuous desires toward me. Please don't think that I'm trying to alter the past in this relationship with Fitz just because I'm old enough to be his mother. I don't think incestuous desire is one of his problems. His mother is a practicing erotic terrorist, and offered him her assistance in establishing his sex life.

That last paragraph seems to have gotten out of hand; maybe because I'm writing about the past in a future that I'll not know. Maybe I'm exaggerating Fitz's problems, an occupational hazard, but I did tell him that if he had personal problems he should see you. I will take it as a favor if you do, although I have no right to ask this of you. I wanted you to know what to expect.

I don't know what else to tell you, Phillip. My world was a better place for having known you. I loved you.

Angela

Eugene Fitzgerald Baker (Family Genealogy)

John Fitzgerald Kennedy
1917 – 1963

Eugene (Gene) Fitzgerald Baker
1961? – 2002 (See note 1.)

Marilyn Monroe (nee Norma Jean Baker) 1926 – 1962

Zelda Harrington? (See note 2.)

Zachary Fitzgerald Baker
2003 – 2056 (See note 3.)

Mary Gulik
2033 – ? (See note 4.)

Fitzgerald Felix Baker
2050 –

NOTES

1. Gene Fitzgerald Baker was probably born between 1958 and 1961. He was certain his natural parents were John F. Kennedy and Marilyn Monroe. Gene Baker was murdered in 2002.

2. Zelda Harrington was evidently an alias; her original name is unknown. She reared her son Zachary Baker in the Erisian Community; both left in 2018 according to verbal reports. The Erisian Community does not keep data on ex-residents.

3. Zachary (Zach) Baker died in 2056 in a fire suspected to be arson.

4. Mary Gulik (not a birth name) was left at a Daughters of Demeter lodge as an infant. She has no accurate information on parents, date of birth or place of birth and is inclined to present various fictions as fact.

A flood of mixed emotions crashed against the gate of my consciousness, spilling over and flowing into my awareness: First, anger that Angela has used her final letter to tell me about her last lover. Jealousy—a self-defeating urge to grasp that which cannot be held. Jealousy because Fitz Baker had been so much in her concerns. Bitterness that my romantic dreams of a future with Angela were jetsam on a desolate, ashy beach. Love for Angela that had triumphed over minor differences in life and had survived her death. Plus regret my own romantic investment in Angela was now a closed account.

I looked at the three pages again, two pages of words for me which were mostly about Fitz and Fitz's one-page genealogy chart—as if I gave a damn whether or not he was descended from Marilyn Monroe and John Kennedy. Carefully, I reread the words that Angela had written:

"There were many times when I shared your dreams." Those words reminded me of our vacation in Havana so many years ago, back when

Angela had separated from Leon, her husband. They had agreed that their young teenage son, Jason, was to spend six months with each of his parents during the year—not because that was what they thought best for a boy trying to cope with puberty, but because it was the only compromise they could agree to accept. Angela and I were going to vault to Havana from Miami after the custody transfer there at Angela's parents' bode.

Everything was very civilized on the surface. Angela's parents, Herbert and Biancha Alfaro, were equally civil to Leon and to me. Leon knew that I was Angela's lover and I knew that he was a major contributor to the problems Angela faced. We were quite polite but very distant with each other. Jason was the center of attention and exploited it fully as everyone made certain that he was ready to vault to his father's Argentine residence.

Once Angela and I stepped out of the vault station on El Prado in Havana, everything was better than I had imagined it could be. I had been infatuated before, but never in love like this. We played as if we were carefree tourists on a honeymoon—having portrait holos taken of us in the dungeon of Morro Castle, both wearing bright yellow tropical jumpsuits, visiting the ruins of the Castro Memorial, buying dark rum and clear banana liqueur on an intoxicating distillery tour, playing in the sun and sand at La Playa where I added a horde of freckles to my back, having a gin and tonic in New Harry's Bar, smoking a small reddish brown cannabis cigar rolled with the Cuban leaf weave method, making love like we were teenagers who had just mutually discovered sexual pleasure.

Havana faded from my mental screen of memories and was replaced with a series of scenes in chronological order:

Jason returning from Argentina, alternately strutting his emerging manhood and exercising boyish charm to command Angela's attention; me taking Angela and Jason to Lucasland and the Off-world Exhibition, attempting to be the kind of substitute father that I had always wanted to have; Angela, Jason and I visiting her brother and his family in their rural mid-western retreat, exploring underground caverns and eating ripe wild persimmons so delicately sweet when freshly fallen from the tree; vacationing in Madrid, just Angela and me, delighting in the Madrid Prado Museum display of the paintings of El Greco, Pablo Picasso, Salvador Dali, Ramona Diaz, Juan Notrevo and Maguerita Chemez.

The memories became hard to bear as they gave me quick flashes of what happened after Jason's final return from Argentina: My argumentative discussions with Angela about my not wanting to be second to Jason in her life; Angela telling me about discovering Jason's body in her bedroom, hanging from a ceiling beam, clothed only in her lingerie; my own guilty feeling of release after his death versus Angela's morbid mourning; going through the grief release procedure with Angela; searching the Sonoma County Russian River area to find a site for the Calderon Rebirth Center, the project which Angela quickly devoted more time and attention to than she had to her son, the project that I had let squeeze me into the background of her life and, according to the letter which I held in my hand, the background of her death.

Why hadn't she told me about the death threat?

Counsel yourself, Counselor. What do you want from Angela now? Her love. Her presence. But, now, in death there was nothing left she could give me. I hadn't believed in an afterlife since childhood; not even then, really. I was the youngest child of a loveless marriage. My sister was busy replicating my Mother's life in Missouri, attending church and acting out the other Midwestern rituals, remnants from the past. I had left home as soon as I could escape the frigid climate and equally cold relations.

What did Angela want from me? From her words, she wanted me to be willing to act professionally for Fitzgerald Baker—if he requested it.

Can I do that? Yes. Will I do that? Yes, I thought, any reason for not helping Baker if he asks for my help would be based on resentment of a reality that no longer existed.

In addition to this, few potential clients offer the kind of challenge that Baker might, the kind of challenge I need to keep my thoughts and feelings off her. Damn! If only she'd taken Vulker's threats seriously…

Or did she? She closed the letter in the past tense—I loved you. Did she have a premonition of her death...or was it another of her romantic gestures.

Stop it. The relationship with Angela is over. I can see now that if I had unleashed all my latent aggression, I could have persuaded Angela to marry me. Had I really wanted to marry Angela? Or had I just wanted a romantic ideal kept intact in my mind, untouched by the enclosed reality of marriage? After all, I had survived the loveless marriage of my parents. I wasn't in the best position to analyze my own actions and feelings but I knew one thing for certain: Angela's letting-go ceremony was on Thursday and I was determined to let go. Had to let go.…

CHAPTER 6

THE LETTING-GO CEREMONY

Yes, you can have the last word! Make a holly of yourself reading your will.
Twenty-first Century Advertisement

The reception prior to Angela's letting-go ceremony was held in the enclosed flower garden at the Wilshire Memorial Chapel. The well-tended flowers perfumed the air, giving the atmosphere of the spring that was yet to come, an atmosphere intended to be lighter than those transfer ceremonies of the past that had been filled with cut and dying flowers and with wailing, weeping mourners. Today's ceremony was intended to mark an end of mourning and a beginning of the acceptance that Angela Calderon had let go of life and that the lives of others must go on without her.

I had come alone, alone with my sorrow—although not alone in my sorrow. Serge had offered to come with me, but I had told him I would see him here. I had spent the previous evening with him, stupidly drowning my sorrow in much red wine. Serge, my true friend, drank with me but not much, showing unlimited patience with my grief and my tears. The shank of the evening had been fuzzy; this morning had been worse. I had taken a quarter-grain of codeine to banish the hangover; it worked to soften the harsh edges of the reality I longed to deny.

I was no stranger to the place or the procedure. I entered, walked along the inlaid rock path past purple irises and pale gardenias to the nearest self-service beverage bar and picked pear juice from the selection of fruit juices, coffees and teas.

With my pear juice in my left hand and my right hand free for the hand-clasping rituals of greeting, I moved down the path among the white, pink and red roses to where the family had gathered in the largest alcove, some sitting on the built-in benches, others standing in small groups. I made my way among them, speaking positive or sympathetic words, and touching hands with Herbert and Biancha Alfaro, Angela's parents; Rich, Sharon, Rita and Alicia Alfaro, Angela's brother, sister-in-law and nieces; and an assortment of cousins whom I hadn't met before and did not expect to see again.

Leon Calderon was standing by himself a short distance away from family members but not far enough away to be around the next bend of the circuitous flagstone path. He and I had settled our differences amiably after Jason's death. Then as now he looked every inch the Argentine aristocrat; his beige tailored suit and tan accessories were expensive, tasteful and appropriate. Above the low fitting collar, I could see evidence of the blend in Leon Calderon of Argentina's five major ethnic groups: His neck looked German, thick and well-muscled, the nose was Roman, the cheekbones beneath his Spanish eyes were prominent, high and quite Indian looking, the tight curl in his black hair was African.

He had his head cocked, engrossed in the classical Spanish guitar music playing throughout the garden. When I was within speaking distance, he turned slightly and said, "Hello, Phillip." He spoke to me in English, an unusual courtesy from him since we both spoke Spanish and I knew he preferred his native tongue.

"How are you, Leon?" I asked.

"I am well. And you?"

I tried to keep the flatness I felt out of my voice when I answered. "I'm okay. I hope your life is going well." I realized that the previous hostility I had felt toward Angela's ex-husband had dissolved in the solution of time. Of course, in keeping with the intended decorum of the coming ceremony, we avoided speaking of Angela's passing.

"I have remarried and have a family—both a son and a daughter. And yourself? You have married?"

"No, I haven't married."

Leon nodded. "If you seek someone to replace Angela in your life, I wish you the best of fortune in your quest."

"Thank you, Leon."

With my peripheral vision, I saw someone who might be Fitzgerald Baker in a gray and black formal formsuit, someone who had turned just before I could see his face. I excused myself from Leon's company and went in the direction that Baker had taken. After a few steps I wondered why I was following him: Maybe I merely wanted to see him again, to see him in the light of what Angela had written about him.

Before I could catch up with him, I heard someone call me by name. I turned to see my former teacher, Dr. John Benway, talking to Dr. Harold Templeman and an older woman who was seated on a bench surrounded by yellow buttercups.

"Phillip, I'm pleased to see you. You know Harold Templeman of course. This lady is his mother, Sarah Templeman."

I greeted Dr. Templeman and his mother, then asked my old mentor, "Is the current crop of students giving you a stimulating challenge?"

"Always, Phillip," Benway said, "they always do. But that's what keeps me functioning—a rebirth with every new class. How's the practice?"

"Satisfactory. I'm spending about half my time in researching some of the therapeutic techniques that haven't been granted accreditation yet. The only clients I accept now are ones who interest me, who offer me an opportunity for professional growth."

Templeman asked, "Is that what the new professionals are doing?"

I rated Templeman's manner somewhere between annoying and offensive. "Professionalism consists of doing one's best for every client; one of the best ways to maintain it, I have found, is to refer to other practitioners those clients whose situations don't create enough response in me to challenge my abilities as a counselor."

"I always thought that prejudging clients was outside the scope of lifestyle crisis counseling?"

I kept my voice at an even pitch as I replied, "Accepting a client without considering whether or not the practitioner can bring his full professional competence to bear on the situation represents to me the lack of concern for individuals that is characteristic of the inept, the careless and the nonprofessional."

Before Templeman could sputter out a response, his mother said, "Harold, please get me another cup of that delicious mint tea."

"Of course, Mother," he said, and started off toward the beverage bar. I exchanged a few more words of little significance with my former teacher about academic matters, thanked Sarah Templeman for her offered recommendation of the mint tea, told Benway that I would call him, made my excuses and left them before Templeman returned.

As soon as I turned the next curve of the flower garden path, I saw Juanita Delgado talking with Dr. Linda Duran. Both were wearing dark blue that contrasted sharply with the background of orange poppies. Seeing them together prompted me to surmise that Linda was taking over Angela's practice.

I reached them just as Clyde Burbank, Baker's partner, and his wife Eileen joined them. After greeting everyone, Clyde asked, "Has anyone seen Fitz?"

"I think I saw him earlier," I said, "but I didn't get a chance to see his face and make certain it was him."

Juanita asked Clyde, "How has Fitz been? I've screened him several times but he's never answered."

Clyde replied, "He was distraught the one time he came to the office. Didn't stay long. Said he didn't know when he'd be back."

Eileen added, "We invited Fitz to stay with us for a few days until he felt better. He just mumbled something about not being good company and left."

I mentioned that I had visited him in Key West, and told Juanita that I had given him the information on the police report and informed him about today's ceremony. A few minutes later the conversational group began to disperse. The sounds of heels striking the flagstones blended with the sounds of the Spanish guitar—Angela's favorite instrument—as if the pedestrians were performing a slowly-paced flamenco dance.

I continued my walk through the flower garden, wondering how many of the people whom I didn't know were Angela's former clients.

I was surprised at the pleasure I experienced when I saw Charmaine Dwoskin, a friend of mine and Angela's whom I hadn't seen for some time. Her brown hair shone in the sun. She had lost about five kilos since I had seen her last.

"Charmaine, how delightful to see you. You look marvelous."

"Phillip, how nice. Have you been taking care of yourself?"

"I thought I'd been until I saw you. Now I know I need to do something to make me feel as good as you look."

Her full lips curved in a smile that showed well-formed teeth. "Thank you. My body feels light and very female. I've become immersed in the delights of my underwater ballet classes. The water washed away the old Charmaine and my new figure emerged from the depths."

She stepped back and performed a graceful pirouette. The soft material of her dress flowed over her slim thighs. "In celebration of the new me I went on a shopping spree with my cousin in New Zealand. Blue is not usually my color, but this dress demanded to be mine. Wearing it makes me feel like dancing."

"I'm glad you returned," I said, grateful for this pleasant diversion from one of the most unpleasant days of my life. "Will you be in this part of the world long enough for us to go dancing sometime soon?"

"Ah, of course, but when is the question." Her face took on a serious look. "Angela so captured me with her talk of contributing to the world that I actually volunteered to be a trustee for her Center. Then I found myself doing responsible things so well that I became entangled in projects that only I can complete. And with Angela gone, there are so many things that have to be done. May we postpone for just a little while?"

"Yes. Promise that you'll let me know when your schedule slows from hectic to merely busy?"

"Certainly," she said. Somehow it seemed right that we stayed together looking at the flowers, marigolds, morning glories and tall red hollyhocks that perfumed the air.

We were both listening to *Malaguena* when Charmaine asked, "Is the music recorded?"

"Usually live. The musician's alcove is over there to our right, beyond the rose bushes. Let's go see."

As we started toward the roses, a small woman, barely a meter and a half tall and with bulging eyes, met us on the path. She glanced toward us and said, "Hello," as briskly as she was walking.

Charmaine and I both responded to her greeting. When the woman was out of hearing range, I asked, "Do you know that woman well enough to recommend that she consult someone in internal medicine? Unusually prominent eyes and a compulsively fast pace are classical symptoms of hyperthyroidism."

"Not really, Phillip, but I know who she is. That's Margaret Healy, the psychic that Angela consulted. She's still into the old psychic versus scientific mode and believes her afflictions are needed for her psychic persona."

"Angela consulted a psychic?"

"You seem shocked. Are you averse to psychic information?"

"I know psychic abilities exist in some people at some times with varying degrees of reliability. Anyone who examines the statistical evidence and the research papers without a closed mind knows that something is there. But experimental results are not always repeatable and some practitioners are out-and-out charlatans. I guess I'm just surprised to learn that Angela was seeing a psychic. She never said anything to me about it."

"Angela felt she had unfinished business with Jason and made some attempts to contact him. I'm sure she thought that you wouldn't approve; she once told me that she might be creating self-delusional conversations with him just to satisfy her own desires. Margaret Healy has a reputation for communicating with the recently dead so Angela brought her in for a second opinion."

First the letter, and now Margaret Healy the psychic. I was beginning to wonder just how well had I had known Angela?

"Jason died a long time ago," I said. "What's she doing here now?"

"Don't know. Perhaps it's her concern with the dead."

Our conversation stopped when we reached the musicians alcove where a single guitarist was bent over his instrument, giving us a view of his thick black hair while he played *Habanera* from Bizet's "Carmen."

I saw Fitzgerald Baker among the listeners on the far side of the alcove. He was wearing a black and gray patterned suit that incorporated inappropriate old-fashioned mourning bands as an integral part of both sleeves. He saw Charmaine and then me. I nudged Charmaine and nodded a greeting. He returned the gesture. His face looked ravaged, lined and drawn with lips pressed flat against his teeth as if suppressing a pained grin. There was something strange about his face but before I could identify the change, the bells tolled to inform us that Angela's letting-go ceremony would begin as soon as everyone came inside.

I felt a hand on my shoulder. I turned to find Serge, who spoke to both of us, softly so as not to interfere with the music. He seemed pleased to see Charmaine, pleased that she and I were together. He excused himself to speak to someone else and said that he would talk to me later.

The guitarist completed his selection and looked up. His name was Jover Wing—I recognized him from the holly—he was Angela's favorite guitarist. Ironically, I had intended to hire him to play at the party I had planned to give as an excuse to get Angela into my bode again. As I looked at Jover Wing's oriental appearing face with the noticeably heavy eyebrows, I remembered seeing Angela remove hairs from her eyebrows which she kept thin and shaped because she felt their fullness marred her perfect face.

At that moment a sudden realization hit me and I knew what was different about Fitzgerald Baker. I looked back at him and saw that he had shaved off his eyebrows in the ancient mourning tradition. Although he turned to join the others filing inside, it was obvious that he was not the least bit ready to let go of Angela.

As Charmaine and I walked the path that led from the garden to the ceremonial room, she whispered, "Fitz's in terrible condition, isn't he?"

"Yes," I answered. "He can't seem to let go of Angela."

"When I first saw Fitz," Charmaine said, "I felt that he was one of the most alive and vibrant men I'd met. But then I realized his words didn't match his emanations. It took me a while to realize that when he was glowing it was from some pleasurable stroke that Angela had given him. When she walked out of the room, he faded into gray. He barely functioned unless she was nearby."

We entered the ceremonial room where the plush carpeting and drapes muffled most of the noise of the crowd as they found seats. Each row of contour chairs was spaced far enough away from the row in front to provide an access aisle from side to side. Gaps in each row at irregular intervals allowed the attendees to move up the sloping floor toward the back of the room if they wished. Charmaine and I sat in the fifth row; Serge nodded to us from nearby. I had lost track of Baker as he moved toward the rear wall of the theater-like room.

The bell continued tolling as people entered and sat in the seats covered with pastel, sculptured brocade in patterns that matched the drapes on both side walls. I glanced around and saw that the room was almost full, which meant the ceremony would start soon because the rear wall was movable and had been positioned to accommodate the number of people who had gathered in the flower garden. It was a subtle touch but one that helped everyone believe the ceremony was well attended.

The house lights dimmed. A pattern of moving lights that looked like candle flames appeared on the draperies, winking off and on in a pattern that led the eye to the small stage which was the focal point of the room.

All lights went out. A hologram of Angela appeared, lifelike enough to make me catch my breath. I could have sworn there was a hint of her Cinnabar perfume in the air. She was wearing the only jewelry I remembered her wearing—a large ruby ring in an antique gold setting and tiny ruby balls in her pierced ears. My heart felt pierced; the ruby earrings resembled drops of my heart's blood.

Angela was dressed in a two-piece tailored suit of red and gray velvet with matching gray boots and gloves. The only part of her skin that showed was her flawlessly made-up face. She turned in a quarter circle as if surveying the room, returned to center position on the stage and spoke. "Hello, everyone. Thank you for coming. I'd like to speak to each of you individually but that really isn't practical. The fact that you're here shows that we were important to one another. I'm glad you cared enough to come.

The staging was so professional my analytical self pondered on how much time, money and energy Angela had spent on this funeral presentation. The imaging was state-of-the art and the camera work was worthy of a Hollywood studio. Did she update it every year? Or was this an image in amber, so-to-speak? I had known her well, or thought I had, and I'd never heard any mention of a death drama, as they were commonly called.

"First I would like to express my appreciation to my parents who always did their best for me, beginning with my early childhood in Barcelona and Miami and continuing through my education and professional career. One of my greatest comforts was knowing I always had your love and support..."

"As Angela continued her words to other relatives, most of whom I didn't know, I found myself remembering bits and pieces of the past—Angela lifting her red and black silk skirt in a Spanish dance. Angela squirting red wine into my mouth from a *bota*. Angela lying beside me in peaceful post-coital sleep. Her mention of Leon jerked me back from that past and into the present.

"...I want to thank my ex-husband, Leon Calderon, for the pleasant memories of our early days together when the world was ours alone. I was so happy then, blossoming first into womanhood, and then into motherhood."

Leon Calderon smiled, as though reviewing pleasant memories.

Then Angela's aspect seemed to grow as she reared back and her voice became louder. "One of the great events of my life was giving birth to our son, Jason. He was such an attractive child, physically and mentally. Maybe most parents feel their young are the hope of the future. I know we did. Maybe it was our own expectations of Jason as well as our own expectations of ourselves that made life so difficult for the child who became an adolescent but never an adult…"

She paused as tears glistened in her eyes. "We both loved Jason, so much that when we no longer loved each other we resented each other's claim on Jason's love."

"It has taken me a long time to accept the premature death of my son." She paused for a moment and then continued in a strident voice. "I have created The Calderon Rebirth Center not only to serve those who suffer in the same manner that he did but also to serve as a memorial to Jason. Now that the Center is a certainty, I believe my son's death was not in vain—at least, not totally."

She dipped her head, lifted it and rose up on her toes. "And I want my ex-husband to know that I forgive him for whatever he may have contributed to the death of our son."

I knew that Angela hadn't made a permanent adjustment to Jason's death, but this hostility was a facet of Angela I had never seen or heard before. Charmaine's hand touched mine in reassurance; I must have reacted strongly to take her attention away from the stage.

I looked at Leon Calderon: His entire body was rigid; his blanched face looked ten years older, ten hard years older.

"I want to thank Dr. Harold Templeman for his professional guidance," Angela continued, "Dr. Linda Duran for her willingness take over my practice, Dr. Serge Dicori for his professional assistance, Dr. Phillip Wendell for his loving friendship and understanding…"

I savored those words, the last ones I would get from her, and put them among my pleasant memories of Angela.

When my attention returned to what she was saying, I heard, "...Fitzgerald Baker, the architect who designed the building for The Calderon Rebirth Center for his many efforts on my behalf and for the pleasure of his company. Fitz understood the importance of the Center to my life and contributed freely of his time and resources not only to the project but also to me personally. He was a source of comfort, of solace, of reassurance. He accepted my reality and enhanced it."

I fought the irrational jealousy that left an angry knot in my throat. Fitz would have never become so close to her had I not foolishly taken Angela for granted. It was my own ego and hubris that was to blame. To me Angela had been an element of nature—like the wind, or the rain, or the sun—and I had expected her to be there whenever it was convenient for me, or I needed her. Fitzgerald had only filled the shoes I had left vacant. And now she was gone and her words were for him…

I squeezed my eyelids together so tightly I could see a flash of white light.

"Fitz never knew my son but I feel that they had much in common, a charisma, a love of life that left the world better for their passing. Fitz, I sincerely hope the advice and information I have given you will help you in the future as your efforts for me helped me in the recent past. You are an unusual and valuable person. May you find fulfillment in your future."

There was a strangled sob—an unseemly display of sadness—from somewhere behind and to my left. I was sure that it was from Fitzgerald

Baker, but my sense of decorum kept me from looking.

Charmaine's hand squeezed mine as Angela said, "I wish to thank the trustees—Vivian Arnold, Enrique Rodriquez, Fay DeRouen, Charmaine Dwoskin and William Pinewood—for agreeing to carry on the work that will culminate in The Calderon Rebirth Center. You are friends in the truest sense of the word.

"Now I am going to say goodbye to all of you—relatives, lovers, friends, associates, clients and acquaintances. It wasn't a long life but it was a full one and you helped make it so. I have said my last words to you and made all my last requests of you except for this one final request: Let go of your memories of me unless they bring you pleasure. There is a time in every relationship for hanging on and for releasing. My time for hanging on is over; I ask you to join me in letting go."

Her image disappeared.

I don't know how long I sat there without moving, maybe a minute or two, before Charmaine said, "I have a meeting in twenty minutes with the other trustees. It was good to see you and I'll call when I have some room for dancing in my schedule."

"Thank you, Charmaine," I said, my voice sounding flat and mechanical to my ears.

Charmaine left. I glanced around for another minute, reminded myself that there was not time for hanging on, no person to hang onto and it was past letting go time. I tried to force myself to let go of the idea of Angela as if it could be done by an act of will. Serge asked if I wanted company but I told him I'd rather be alone.

Outside the chapel, there was a crowd around Margaret Healy—a devastated-looking Fitz among them. Dr. Templeman was standing there with a look of boyish impatience on his face as his mother spoke with Margaret.

When I got near them, I heard Margaret Healy say, "But she hasn't released her essence yet. She spoke of wanting to move her hands. To push the dirt away."

A cold chill moved up my spine.

Fitz asked, "Where is she now? Does she still think she's buried alive?"

I could scarcely believe I was hearing him correctly. Angela was dead. In lieu of a messiah who could restore life to the dead—and there hadn't been a claimant for that role since the assassination of Jesus Ortega—Angela was no longer a physical part of this reality. Her essence had left her corporal remains. Why couldn't Baker accept that?

Margaret, her bulging eyes and twittering movements, giving her the aspect of a predatory bird, answered, "She feels trapped in a lonely place. It is cold and tight. Voices come to her, begging her to come. She tries to move her body but cannot. She's frightened. She hasn't realized yet she's free of the body."

"What can I do?" Fitz asked, in a voice bordering on terror.

"Stop calling her back! Your desire for her to be alive is strong. It is interfering with her process. I have talked to her. I will keep telling her it is time for her to go on. Time for her to be transformed. She hasn't accepted that yet, because you won't release her.

Fitz looked like a disaster victim. A middle-aged, over-dressed lady took Fitz into her arms and he broke out into cries that reminded me of a woman in childbirth.

I forced myself to walk past them. I didn't know whether it was true or not. Anyone could have found out the circumstances of Angela's death and, of course, her body was in the University of California Medical Center morgue waiting for organ harvesting or whatever medical use they would put it to. That was public knowledge.

I didn't know whether Margaret Healy was giving genuine psychic information out or not. I didn't know whether Angela had accepted her own death or not; I wasn't sure I wanted to know. But I was accepting it: I was letting go. At least I was telling myself I was letting go, as I blinked away the tears in my eyes.

CHAPTER 7

PARATIME

Nostalgia isn't what it used to be
Simone Signoret

During the next month the grief and desolation that had draped over my life like a veil after Angela's death began to lift. Even my clients appeared to be responding to my improved attitude: Karl Kashubian was beginning the final edit of his new holographic production and Anita Watson had left therapy to return to school at the Western Anthropological Institute. Serge and I had dinner together twice and our talks were improving my perspective of Angela and our former relationship. There had been no word from Fitzgerald Baker and I was privately relieved to find that he had been able to cope with his sorrow without my help.

In early March, Charmaine Dwoskin screened me at my office. I was delighted to see her smiling face.

"Hello, Phillip. Aren't you the handsome man who promised to dance with me and hinted at other assorted delights? I've completed the tasks of my office. The burdens now lie in other, more capable, hands. I am now entitled to party, party, and more party. How's your schedule?"

"Wednesday and Saturday are free. No appointments or meetings either day."

"Would you like to dance?"

I said yes. "Wednesday is a good day for me."

"Do you have any ideas on where to go dancing?" she asked.

I thought for a moment. "How about dancing our way through the past at Paratime?"

"What a perfectly wonderful idea! Shall I meet you there? I'm still staying in Windsor."

"Let's meet at Paratime. Wednesday around 1700 in the 1980s' sound garden."

On Wednesday I teleported to the vault station in the Mojave desert; the station served only Paratime, an entertainment complex that occupied five square kilos of climate-controlled desert and offered the best of the past in ten-year segments back to 1900. The diversions of the nineteenth and eighteenth centuries were divided into larger sections that captured the spirit of those times: The Gay Nineties; The American Civil War, Gold Rush, Frontier Days, The Westward Expansion, The American Independence Movement, The Colonial Period, The Early Immigrants, American Indian Cultures.

At the entrance, I placed my keycard in the voucher slot and was admitted to the changing room. I opened a thumblock cabinet and put all my clothes and possessions, except my watch and keycard into it. I slipped my keycard into my watchband and went to the clothes rack.

Moving around the other patrons who were selecting garments, I slipped into a pair of foam sandals and a plain white flimsy toga of the one-size-fits-all type. Flimsies were made of paper and the ultimate in throwaway clothes. Outside the changing room I caught the tram that traveled back in time stopping at each of the long malls that presented a concentrated simulation of the past.

When the tram stopped at the 1980s, I got off, put my keycard in the voucher slot, exchanged my sandals for a pair of dark green simulated suede shoes, traded my toga for a flimsy replica of a century-old, green-patterned shirtjac-trouser combo and left the changing room to step onto a sidewalk mall made of old grayish beige concrete. Most of the buildings had huge windows to reveal the merchandise, activities, entertainments or services available inside.

I merged with the scattering of pedestrians and strolled past an organic fast food restaurant, a high tech furniture store and a Starbucks coffeehouse that featured live entertainment. I paused for a moment in front of a Primal Scream therapy center and thought how much more sophisticated the therapy field has become in a hundred years. Imagining how a client from the 1980s would respond to cultural cross-fertilization therapy, the procedures necessary to avoid culture shock and reentry trauma following extensive teleporting, was mindboggling. The past can be a pleasant place to visit but a modern person couldn't live there without extensive adjustment; some of my colleagues have treated long-term Paratime employees for temporal disorientation and past shock.

Continuing down the 1980s' mall, I reached the sound garden, entered, selected two xylophone mallets from the available assortment and began walking along the curving paths bordered by dwarf trees. Each tree had a variety of metallic objects hanging from its branches like mechanical fruit, obsolete objects from the automotive and aerospace industries of that era, obscure artifacts whose curved lines and complex fittings gave little hint as to function. Each item was utilized for its sound potential. I struck out spontaneously with my mallets, tapping tapering pipes, conto red panels, hemispheric containers and sculptured steel parts, occasionally repeating several blows to create a simple tune segment that blended into the cacophony created by other sound garden players.

When I reached the center of the garden where all the paths converged, I sat down on a wooden bench, closed my eyes and listened to the composite sound, which soon lulled me into an alpha state. A short time later, I felt a hand on my arm and heard Charmaine say, "There you are."

I looked up and saw Charmaine in an aqua and gold sheath flimsy with gold pumps. I rose to my feet. "Hello, Charmaine." We embraced briefly and then sat down; her flimsy was slit past her knees on both sides, revealing shapely thighs as she crossed her firm dancer's legs.

"How nice to find you waiting here. Not too long, I hope."

"No, but it wouldn't matter if it had. You're worth waiting for."

She smiled. "You make me feel appreciated."

"Good. I intend to continue doing so. As a French friend once said to me: 'A man should always let a woman know how much he appreciates her. For if he does not appreciate her, he should not be with her."

"Your French accent is charming perhaps we should have dinner in a French restaurant later."

"Great idea. Are you ready to go dancing?"

"Yes. I've been languishing behind a desk lately so I'd like to start with something energetic but more modern than the Charleston, shimmy and varsity drag."

"We can start with 1940s' big band music at Avalon Ballroom in 1940s. After dancing with the nosties there, we can dance forward in time."

We left the sound garden, past the space shuttle exhibit into the Grand Mall and took the tram to the 1940s' mall. We passed Hitler's War battlefield and made our way past the dinner quarter to the Avalon Ballroom.

The interior of the Avalon was supposed to represent a ballroom of the forties; I was no expert but it looked authentic to me: Dim, colored lights that rotated light and shadow across the waxed floor, carpeted stairs that led to a balcony with small tables for intimate conversation or dancer watching, tables with long tablecloths that lined both sides of the dance floor. The bandstand looked like a stage set for a musical flattie out of the forties. The holo of the band, which was in sync with the recordings being played, could be taken for real musicians in the subdued lighting.

Like swing era dancers, we jitterbugged to Charley Barnett's "Skyliner" and Artie Shaw's "Frenesi." Then we sat down over a couple of 1940's cocktails and made casual conversation as we listened to Duke Ellington's "Satin Doll," an intricate, sophisticated work, which was followed by

Tommy Dorsey's simplistic "Boogie Woogie." After we finished our drinks, I asked, "Where next?"

Charmaine replied, "How about something more exciting?"

"The 2020s flash?"

"Let's do it."

We left the 1940s' nosties in their ballroom. Charmaine snuggled next to me and we walked to the end of the 1940s mall, past the souvenir shops, before making a right turn to the Grand Mall. A left turn would have taken us back into the 1930s and the Great Depression or further down the Roaring Twenties. At the 2020's entrance we docked our keycards and entered the changing room where we got new flimsies. We selected similar caftans with red and white irregular horizontal stripes with touch-tight closures. Red vinyl dancing shoes completed our costumes. The mirrored inside surface of the caftan felt cool against my skin as we joined the strollers along the 2020s mall, some of whom were going into a HoloDome to see the first holographic films.

We entered the dancehall called The Flash Cube and received our makeup kits when we paid the entrance fee. In the unisex makeup room, we put on the heavy stylized makeup that was traditional for dancing the flash. The emphasis was on exaggerating the eyes. I carefully closed my right eye and with black makeup I darkened the lids and entire orbit of the eye. Then I traced the bone structure around the eye in white, filling in the corners so the eye socket seemed mostly eyeball. With black makeup I made a large outline around the eye which hid my eyebrows and drew radiating lines to simulate eyelashes. I did the other eye similarly and drew in fake eyebrows on my forehead. With the crimson tube, I reddened my lips.

In the mirror I could see that Charmaine's eyebrows were slanted up; she added colored sequins for a harlequin look. Charmaine and I both looked like caricatures of excited voyeurs—exactly the right look for dancing the flash. The makeup was as effective as a mask; I might not have recognized Charmaine if I hadn't seen her put on the makeup.

She laughed and said, "You look like a sad raccoon. Here, let me."

She used a small brush to paint turned up corners on my lips. Then she added black smile lines around my eyes. "Now you look like a gay raccoon."

We both laughed, although carefully so as not to mess our makeup.

Out on the dance floor, the movements of the flash, which I hadn't danced for a while became familiar again. Charmaine was an exceptional dancer, sensuous yet free, following my lead as we moved to the bass beat of the drums under the multicolored lights that flashed on and off in synchronization with the music.

Charmaine whirled out of my arms when the saxophone began to scream out the melody. When Charmaine faced me again, we touched palms—as in a child's pattycake ritual—to the rhythm of the bass and drums. The saxophone climbed up and down the melody line growing harsher; the bright colored lights dimmed, leaving just enough light reflecting from the mirrored walls for me to see Charmaine. We met the sound with thrusts of our bodies, turning and gyrating to the hypnotic beat.

The saxophone began to honk, leading up to the big flash. We loosened the touch-tight fasteners on our caftans with synchronized movements as the sax grew louder. When the bright lights flashed on and all the dancers shouted "Flash", we opened our caftans wide and flashed our bare torsos without missing a beat.

I noticed that Charmaine had crimsoned her nipples and scattered sequins in her pubic hair.

Later when we left The Flash Cube, I asked her, "Shall we visit 2030 and dance the frenzy?"

"Why don't we skip a decade and try some Brownian motion."

We turned right into the time tunnel, bypassed the 2030 exit, and entered the 2040 decade. There we shed our caftans and removed our makeup. Charmaine picked a black and tan tunic dress flimsy and I picked a brown shirtsuit. We entered the mall next to a small religious shop that sold mementos of the miracles of Jesus Ortega. Neither of us was tempted by the window display; Charmaine is Jewish and I'm a Buddhist. The Second Coming of Jesus was a minor factor in our lives.

At the next doorway a shill—or a shifter pretending to be a shill—said, "You're just in time for the big show. Right this way to see a re-creation of the events that took place when the Ortegans launched their first generation ship.

We walked on, ignoring the barker. He stopped his spiel and said to our backs, "As you Will."

Soon we reached the Roundhouse, a modified dome, where we could enjoy the Brownian motion created by A.U. Brown—commonly known as Goldie Brown to the many whom had enjoyed the Brownian motion domes. Inside we donned the brown unisex capes that housed the charged hoop that repelled all other hoops that came within a one meter range.

Some purists might insist that Brownian motion isn't dancing since many of the motions are for balance or direction maintenance and most partners are separated soon after they start, only finding each other when the music ends. Skilled partners practice staying within two meters of each other and synchronizing their arm movements to the beat. For most dancers, the dance steps are whatever is needed to maintain balance as sections of the dished floor around the trampoline center rise and fall in time with the recorded sounds of Goldie and the Brownouts or some other motion group.

Charmaine and I started off fine but were soon scrambling to stay upright as the smooth, padded floor rippled beneath us and then dipped. Then we both lost our balance, grabbed for each other and were repelled by the hoops in our costumes. Soon I was bouncing around like a bumper car in one of the 1950's amusement parks.

The path of least resistance brought me to the trampoline center and I bounced high on purpose, looking for Charmaine among the other dancers. On the third bounce I saw her. I began to move in her direction as well as I could but lost sight of her until we both found ourselves on the trampoline at the same time. We made a synchronized jump together—if you can call being two meters apart together—and managed to remain partners until the music ended with an amplified discord.

Charmaine said, "I'm browned out."

I laughed and answered, "That's true for two."

"Let's have dinner. Stuffed mushrooms. Wine. A suave Frenchman beside me."

"How about *Chez Andre* in the 2050s, *Cherie*?"

"*Oui*."

We made our exit and caught the time tram to 2050; there we changed into the colorful dinner clothes of that era. Charmaine found a midnight blue gown that emphasized her sexual attributes with crimson decoration that outlined her breasts, crotch and hips. As she changed, I saw that she hadn't removed the crimson from her nipples or the sequins from her pubic hair. Somehow, knowing her body was decorated beneath her dress was tantalizing.

I wore a black and white tuxform with the transparent vertical panels that revealed both nipples and the hair on my chest and thighs; the stuffed codpiece I wore was white, as was the tie, which was pre-tied in a love knot.

Over chateaubriand, salad, stuffed mushrooms and Burgundy, Charmaine said, "Phillip, I saw one of those printed T shirts in the 1980's mall today. It said: 'IT'S YOUR BODY. USE IT OR LOSE IT!'

May I impose on you to recommend an exercise therapy that would also be amusing?"

"Last week I read about a new therapy that utilizes dance movements. I know it provides good exercise, and it sounded more amusing than therapeutic."

"Tell me more."

"It's called symbology therapy by the originator, Anton Wykowski. Have you heard of him?"

"Wasn't he one of the great ballet dancers of the forties and fifties?" she asked.

"Yes, and later a ballet instructor," I replied. "Now he has a studio in Mendocino for conducting symbology therapy. Wykowski has developed sets of standardized positions and movements of dance that have strictly defined meanings, based on traditional ballet, dance history, mime, body language and the sign language used by the deaf. Once a client has learned the Wykowski Movements, each dancer develops, with Wykowski's assistance—a dance sequence depicting any conflicts he or she is experiencing. The dance is performed to music selected by the client against a backdrop on which computer graphics and Jungian archetypical scenery, symbolic of the dancer's inner disturbances, are projected. They are preselected by the client to complete the nonverbal presentation. Wykowski claims the performance acts as a cathartic for deep rooted emotional traumas and blocks. Does that procedure appeal to you?"

"Hmm. Sounds like enough skill could recreate an experience, or an experience train, but with the greater possibility of concentrating on my emotions. So often I tend to be involved in finding the right words at the expense of the experience. Then later the feelings come out, when the opportunity to vent them is gone. Being a trustee has given me some different experiences."

Charmaine's hands frequently moved as she spoke, graceful gestures and gentle caresses were a part of her. Now she moved some of the table things, seeking an outer order that reflected her next words: "But that only expresses the feelings. Will it bring—"

"There is a feedback session after the client dances. Experienced symbology dancers give their reactions and suggestions in dance under Wykowski's direction. This enables the client to change and subsequently alter the dance to match new developments. I think it holds potential for nonverbal people or for people who use over-verbalization as a way of avoiding communication. For you, it would be mostly physical exercise unless your trusteeship is creating some conflicts that you can't resolve."

She shook her head. "My feelings have to do with responsibility. My brother lectured me on accomplishment, as if I would disappear in a puff of smoke unless I was useful in this world. You carry responsibility as if it were your skin." She reached over and touched my hand. "But I have no sense of unresolved conflict with any of the people involved in the Center. Except perhaps a certain annoyance. Pinewood—one of the other trustees, if you remember—broke his leg at an inconvenient time. However," she said with a smile, "I don't suspect his intentions.

"Then Juanita Delgado became entangled with a case involving implied retention of personality in a performance contract when I needed her legal expertise. And, of course, Fitz Baker. Either he wouldn't show for meetings at all or he would bring that eerie grief thief with him. And—"

"Fitz hired a mummer!" I exclaimed.

"You bet. I got goose bumps all up and down my back the first time I saw her. For a moment, I really thought she was Angela! Until I focused on the way she was dressed. Angela had a class act, sensual but aloof. This one practically had both breasts hanging out and a skirt tighter than skin. Then I realized Fitz had her made-up to match his sexual fantasy image. So obvious that it was painful to watch. And distracting—the way he looked at her."

Charmaine shook her head sadly. "Her presence was bad enough, but when she started to act the part it became intolerable. Then the trustees, myself included, voted to exclude her from Center business. Rather than attend without her, Fitz turned over the architectural duties to his partner."

So Fitz hadn't released his grief. Hiring a mummer to play the role of Angela, that was a total rejection of adjustment. I wondered why he was willing to let go of Angela's major work when he couldn't accept her death.

"Are you still here? You look far away."

"I was just thinking about Fitz."

"Not Angela?"

"No. Except peripherally. I had hoped Fitz would have adjusted to Angela's death by now."

"He doesn't even glow like he used to," Charmaine added. "There's little trace of the charisma that made his father's career."

"Fitz's father? You knew him?"

I tried to recall the name on the genealogy chart; I couldn't. What's his name?" I asked.

"Zach Baker was his professional name."

Zach Baker. Zach Baker? Performance. The name was vaguely familiar. Maybe some form of show business. Maybe athletics.

I said, "Tell me about him."

"He was an auggie star."

Now I remembered. The auggies—Augment Sensory Stimulation, mostly used for sensory stimulation sex opera films. They became popular around 2045 after the New Puritanism died of terminal dullness. I'd seen my share of them as a young man, but I couldn't remember Zach Baker. At the time I hadn't been interested in the actors, at least not the male ones.

"After dessert, would you like to check the 2050's cinema to see if they have any of Zach Baker's auggies?"

"Now, hold on a bit," Charmaine said, her eyes brightening. "I can see the therapist with a professional gleam of curiosity in his eye, but how do I rate in all of this?"

"You're my top priority, Charmaine. Beneath this cool exterior there is smoldering lust, ready to emerge at the slightest provocation."

"I do believe I'll skip dessert."

We rented a privacy cubicle in the Private Eye, an auggie cinema, and got a readout of the available auggies. There were several starring Zach Baker. We requested a plot summary and a preview of the first one listed. The list began:

Oh, Sister *stars Zach Baker as Cord and Tawny Page as Laura. Cord and his half-brother Wayne (Jim Rixon) live in a quadmingle marriage with Laura and Janice (Michelle Fox). When Laura's stepsister Dolores (Maria Arnoldi), a former nun who had just left her unfrocked priest husband, becomes a temporary house guest, the quadmingle develops emotional fault lines and sexual stress pockets as Dolores tries to make the household into a pentaflexive.*

Charmaine said, "*Oh, Sister* has the right flavor for me; a nun with sexual desires still has the spice of forbidden decadence. If it appeals to you there's no need to check out the rest."

"It seems right to me."

Charmaine and I made ourselves comfortable on the double lounge. I punched in the request for *Oh, Sister*. Within seconds the opening credits flashed on the wrap-around screen. We both put on headbands to get the benefits of augmented sensory stimulation. The track selector switch had four positions: forward was off; left was for female gender identification, right for male and back for neuter. I selected the male track and watched Charmaine pick the female track.

Zach Baker was obviously the star of the show. When I first saw him, I could sense his star quality, his charisma. I looked for any resemblance to John F. Kennedy. There was some but I was surprised to realize that Fitz looked more like John F. Kennedy than his father did.

Once the opening scenes had established who was who, the sexual encounters began and it became obvious that the actors had been selected for theatrical ability as well as for visual appeal. Tanned, blonde Tawny Page looked like a legendary Amazonian who was geared for copulation instead of combat. Michelle Fox was small, well-formed, dark and sultry.

Zach Baker and Jim Rixon were both well-built but neither sported the giant genitals popular in sex films predating the auggies. The auggies had appealed to an aware audience who wouldn't mistake quantity for quality.

When Maria came to visit, I felt Zach's instant lust, which was obviously reciprocated. Charmaine and I pressed closer together as the action progressed with sexy movements and double entendres like "I don't know why so many ex-priests are getting divorced; maybe they just aren't ordained for marriage."

The sexually climatic scene was the final sexual encounter between Zach and Maria just prior to Maria's departure to join a religious retreat with elaborate sexual rituals. By the time Zach and Maria had their clothes off, so did we. Fondling each other as we watched, we felt the hot wire excitement of two accomplished actors who were also sexual athletes bringing us to an intense level of sexual excitement. By the time Maria was putting her clothes back on, we were too aroused to wait. We coupled on the couch.

When I looked around next, the screen was dark. Charmaine and I left for the Paratime Hotel where we used the auggie stimulation as a point of departure for a more elaborate sexual encounter. I never thought of Angela once.

Oh, Sister
SF

CHAPTER 8

RITES OF THE CRYING CLOWN

Send in the clowns.
Stephen Sondheim

Less than a week after my visit to Paratime with Charmaine, I was listening to my answermat, making notes of requests for appointments and cancellations, when I recognized Fitz's voice. I looked up at the screen: He was saying, "Phillip, this is Fitz Baker. I, ahh…I need to see you professionally. I saw the head thread, *The Crying Clown Rites...* and something snapped—"

His voice stopped and he cradled his head; I was surprised at how gaunt his face appeared when he looked up again. "I did something I would have never done in my right mind. I want, no...I need to see you. But I want you to see *The Crying Clown Rites* first. I'll pay your usual rates for the time and expense. *Please* call me after you've watched it."

The challenge of accepting Fitz as a client, after first recognizing him as a rival and then accepting him as a companion in grief, was enormous. A challenge I was not sure I was up to. I knew that helping Fitz was Angela's last request of me. I also knew it was an unfair one, at least from my point of view. I was uncertain as to what to do so I decided to postpone my decision until after my next client, who was due any moment, had left.

While I was waiting, I decided to investigate the head thread Fitz Baker had requested me to see. I punched in a request for information on my datapad for *The Crying Clown Rites* and the readout displayed:

HEAD THREAD IS THE DESIGNATION FOR A THREAD-LIKE RECORDING MADE FROM AN ADAPTATION OF THE HOLOGRAPHIC DREAM RECORDER. THIS ADAPTATION ALLOWS THE DIRECTOR TO TRANSFER MENTAL VISUALIZATIONS, ENHANCED BY COMPUT ER GRAPHICS, TO A DIGITAL RECEIVER FROM WHICH HOLOGRAPHIC IMAGES CAN BE PROJECTED USING ANY STANDARD HOLOGRAPHIC DEVICE.

I downloaded a copy before Ruth Ashland arrived. Ruth had recently taken four weeks of a six-week course at the Ibanez Character Transformation Center. She dumped the course when she realized her new emerging character was in conflict with her core personality. We were exploring whether she should go back to her old character or change her personality. I found her old character colorless and had decided that any change in her personality would be a plus. It was clients like Ruth—I had taken her on as a favor to a former client—who had brought me to mid-career ennui.

Ruth, a tall, nervous woman, entered the office and sat down.

"Hello, Ruth. How are you today?"

"I'm feeling ready to attack the problem of getting a combination of a resilient character and a relaxed personality."

During the next hour I readied Ruth for the Kemmler Foundation of Personality Redevelopment. Before she left she was looking forward to meeting Kemmler's crew, while I was exhausted by my final exploration of her self-imposed limitations. I resolved to treat no more bland clients; the satisfaction of helping was less rewarding than the pain of boredom.

I rescheduled my remaining appointment of the day and left my office, missing the daydreams of Angela that had been a part of my daily existence for too long. Emerging from the inside corridor into my home, I bent down to pet my cat before turning on the holly. It took less than a few seconds to access the head thread from my office terminal.

I transferred the film to the holly and the legend: THE CRYING CLOWN RITES, A ROALD VALLEN PRODUCTION appeared on the stage. The opening credits were few: Vallen had evidently done most of the technical tasks as well as the creative work.

The opening holographic scene appeared as detailed as if it had been photographed from the real world instead of being formed in its creator's mind: The sun is shining on a truncated, honeycombed pyramid over two hundred meters high. A tall, male adolescent rides the pedramp over the top. As he crouches down and then stands again when certain of his balance, the background noise pulsates like surf.

In a close-up shot the pedramp rider's strong features are highlighted. His full lips are curved in an almost smile; his gray eyes have numerous red squiggles as if he had been without sleep or had consumed excessive alcohol or drugs. A violet Logan crystal is implanted in his forehead like a third eye. A blue and gold Indian headdress tops his oval face. His chest is covered by a crudely altered metal breastplate, his legs by chaps of reptile skins. A codpiece shaped like an elephant's trunk dangles from his crotch.

He exits from the pedramp when it reaches the bottom of the pyramid onto a yellow brick road.

US

Although I have never been there, I recognized the locale as Teener Town, a former commercial disney that had been seized by the target customers. The squatters had taken hostages and fought all challengers. When the owners capitulated, the occupiers denied entrance to anyone over eighteen, added new and dangerous rides and created their version of an adolescent paradise. Most adult outsiders saw it as a perilous slum. The residents and would-be residents saw it as an under-eighteen utopia.

I continued to watch, looking and listening for anything that might pertain to Fitz.

The tall teener stares up and down the empty road then checks the charge of the stun stick attached to his belt. He turns at the scraping sound of a door opening and sees three pre-teens emerging from one of the small blue houses. Two shuffle like drunks, but the third had the speedy, jerky walk of a user of one of the berserker drugs. All three wave their electronic tinglers at him in obvious hostility.

They exchange a few words that are mostly esoteric gang slang before the violence starts. The berserker charges the teener, stumbles and continues toward him, staggering and out of control. The teener flattens the stunned berserker with a single, powerful blow. The other two prepubes, obviously unskilled in team combat, don't coordinate their attack and soon join their companion stretched out on the yellow brick roadbed.

Soon the background noise rises to the level where it can be identified as the sound of crowd panic. When the first group of desperate runners comes by, the teener grabs an adolescent girl and pulls her into an empty house. He slaps her until she stops her hysterical sobbing. "What's going on?"

"Someone let the press packs in," she says between gasps. "They've killed some of the leos and the zippers can't stop them."

He releases her and begins his own frantic efforts to escape the hunters who prey on isolated settlements for the human merchandise that is sold to slavers, organ bankers, homicidal game runners, human experimenters and assorted sadists. His efforts continue until he is dusted with mickey gas from a zepcraft and is taken prisoner.

I made a note to ask Fitz if he was ever taken hostage or taken prisoner.

The next few scenes documented the brutal separation and imprisonment of the captured teeners.

After most of the other prisoners have been shipped out of their temporary jail, one of the guards—who seems more humane than the rest—tells the tall teener, who has been identified as Robbie: "Don't take it so bad. You're the lucky one. Most of 'em are going to end up in off-world mines or in the organ banks. You turds are the pretty ones and we've got special plans for you."

None of the prisoners seem reassured by his words.

At the end of a long ride in a blue hoverbus with opaque windows, the teener is taken to a holding place in what appears to be a wilderness preserve. As part of his indoctrination, he is questioned by an older man, with an almost hairless, baby face, who responds to the youngster's insulting reply with a quick fist. The man then tells Robbie to show proper respect or he will be sold for pet food.

After a period of weeks in which the teener, who now has a small scar where his Logan crystal used to be, is fed well and forced into body building exercises. Next he becomes the property of a hardened man in his late middle years named Spenser. Spenser begins the relationship by punching the teener in the stomach with a strong blow. Satisfied by the youngster's physical condition and resistance to pain, he buys the teener and tells him that he is changing his name from Robbie Borden to Robinson Spenser and taking him home with him as his new son.

Robinson is driven in an escape-proof turbo rover to the Jackson Hole Enclave where he meets Mrs. Spenser, a woman still somewhat unbalanced due to the recent murder and sexual mutilation of the two Spenser children.

In the ensuing weeks, Robinson learns what he can about the community in which he is a prisoner. It seems to be an amalgamation of influences: Neo-Puritanism, prairie homesteader, private game preserve with carefully selected modern conveniences, and some folkways, mores and secrets that are fully understood only by the initiated.

Robinson manages to establish a working relationship with the stern, unsmiling Spenser who seems unchanging, while the emotional bond with his putative mother grows as she shows new signs of animation. She helps nurse him back to health after he is badly beaten by the father of a teenage girl whom he seduced. When he learns that Spenser protected him from a more severe beating than what he received, he is surprised.

While Robinson is still bedridden, Spenser says, "They took the Murray girl in with you to see Doc Nichols. The semen test was negative; otherwise there would have been a marriage after the Rites."

Robinson's face seems to indicate that he hears the capital R of rites in Spenser's voice, but that he has no idea of what they might be or who participates.

I wondered if Fitz had a teenage affair that turned out poorly as I watched the scenes of increasingly cold weather and Robinson doing his chores.

Spenser leaves with several of his guns on one of his periodic hunting trips. Mrs. Spenser and Robinson spend their evenings in mostly silent communication gazing at the flames in the fireplace. The night before Spenser returns, a male neighbor comes by late and asks Mrs. Spenser to tell her husband that there will be another hunt.

"One broke through the barrier about an hour ago."

Robinson looks as if he has questions, but doesn't speak. When Spenser returns and hears of the hunt, he orders Robinson to load the rover for both of them. The energy Robinson puts into the task demonstrates his enthusiasm for being included.

During the drive Spenser tells his foster son about the founding of their community when he says: "Forty-eight years ago a group of wealthy men banded together to break away from the sickness and weakness on the outside. Even then the government of the United States had surrendered most of its powers to the universal welfare state, the World Committee. We pooled our resources and bought up the town of Jackson Hole and most of the surrounding country. At the turn of the century, Jackson Hole was an enclave for the rich until the Welfare Riots of the twenties tore up the place pretty good, and left a lot of dead behind.

"Some of the others already owned sizable holdings hereabouts so it wasn't too difficult. A group of like-minded men decided to create a world based on the firm truths of the nineteenth century, with enough modern conveniences to eliminate the drudgery of that era."

Spenser's conversation continues with an enigmatic reference to deep waters in the stillest lake. Then, in reply to the uncomprehending expression on Robinson's face, he adds, "I don't want you to be surprised by anything you see during the next few days. We live a different life from most of those on the outside. And have different needs to satisfy."

The rest of the trip passes in silence as if to let the information settle in the mind of Robinson. When they arrive at their destination, the Anderson ranch, the young man attempts to get more information about the hunt. The only ones who seem willing to talk about it are those who are prospective members; none of whom know any more than he does—or, at least, so they claim.

After all the expected hunters arrive, about sixty of them, they divide themselves into squads of three. Spenser, Robinson and a man named Manners, all equipped with rifles and backpacks, begin their trek through a deep, rocky ravine which is near the last sighting of their game. Robinson clutches the obviously unfamiliar rifle close to his chest.

Several hours later, they find the first sign of their quarry, broken branches in a dead tree. Robinson looks carefully at the broken limbs. A close-up shot shows no claw marks but it does show the whiteness of Robinson's fingers as they grip his weapon.

They are still seeking more signs of their moving target when they hear a loud rifle shot. All three men run toward the sound. There is a quick flash of movement in a stand of trees. Robinson's youth allows him to reach the spot where the quarry was running before the others. His face shows shock and surprise when he sees the track of their prey in a patch of damp ground. It is the boot print of a human being.

Spenser and Manners catch up with Robinson and express their approval of his finding the track. They motion for him to lead on.

Robinson, with the other two a short distance behind him, hurries up a small knoll through clusters of snow-covered trees and bushes. A man in a brown parka is zigzagging down the other side. Spenser raises his rifle. The loud sound of the shot is quickly followed by a close-up of the intruder's brown parka blossoming with blood as he jerks and falls to the ground.

As if halted by an invisible wall, Robinson stops when he reaches the victim whose fluttering eyelids indicate he is still alive.

Spenser, now beside the rigid boy, says, "Your shot. Whoever reaches the skeet first gets the kill.

Robinson moves his rifle slightly, as much toward Spenser and Manners as the man on the ground. The sound of other hunters rapidly approaching the scene is drowned out by Spenser's voice when he starts to direct Robinson's rifle toward the wounded man and says, in a commanding tone, "Kill him, boy!"

With an uncomprehending look on his face, Robinson pulls the trigger and a third, bloody eye is drilled in the forehead of the barrier jumper. Other hunters yell their congratulations and pound Robinson on the back. Robinson's eyes look as if there is no one at home in his skull.

After the hunt, Robinson's relationship with his foster parents begins to change. Mrs. Spenser seems to avoid him as much as possible while Mr. Spenser, like the rest of the enclavers, pays him more attention.

As I watched these scenes, I wondered if they paralleled the circumstances of Fitz's early life.

When Robinson confronts his foster mother with the fact that she is avoiding him, she confesses that she is becoming as afraid of him as she is of her husband. Later, at a supervised meeting in the youth hall, Robinson notices that many of the youngsters seem subdued. He asks about the low spirits and is told that it is the last meeting before the Rites, and the last time they will all be together. When Robinson presses for more information, his informant checks to make sure he's not being overheard and says, "Only those who have survived them know what the Crying Clown Rites are and are not. It is forbidden to talk of them. My older brother Stephen went to the Rites three years ago and never returned."

Now I knew we were into the universal experience, wondering what the rites of passage into adulthood would be and knowing that they would not be fair. Nor would they be explained. And all the time spent waiting would add importance to the question: Am I destined to die young?

Robinson was sick during his waiting period—a long bout with fever that caused him to lose weight and strength, a period followed by an emotional numbness, then a relapse triggered by Mrs. Spenser's plea for Robbie's help in her efforts to avoid Mr. Spenser's sexual advances.

Robinson's belated response brings him to the bedroom door too late, and he overhears her and Spenser in the throes of passion.

The relapse doesn't end until Mrs. Spenser comes to the sick bed and begs him to get well. "Robbie, you must eat. There are only nine days before the Rites. If you are not strong, I will lose you too. Do it for Mother, please."

Several days later Robinson is out of bed and back to his chores. He appears comforted by the established routine of mindless chores. A routine which is interrupted by Spenser, who summons him to his den. "It is forbidden for a father, or anyone else, to discuss the Rites or the Crying Clown Celebration that follows. But there are a few things I am permitted to say: The Rites will begin at dusk tomorrow and will end at sunrise the following morning. No matter how great the pain and discomfort, it will all come to an end in less than twelve hours. Try to survive one hour at a time."

"Where will they take place?" asks Robinson.

"On a hilltop outside of town. Later, during the Rites, remember this was not something we wanted to do."

Robbie looks puzzled.

"The Rites grew without warning and from seemingly nowhere. Now they are a part of everything that is Jackson Hole." Robinson looks pale and ill; he says nothing more, but appears numb beyond physical or mental expression.

The hill where the Rites are to be conducted is crowned with a circle of old, majestic pine trees, which tower over a fire pit blackened by long use. Those who are to be initiated examine the area, some perplexed by the metal rings embedded in the trees, some talking to themselves about how they could escape were it not for the barrier around the enclave, all of them apprehensive about the ordeal to come.

After a pile of wood has been brought to the fire pit and a truckload of chains has been unloaded, an older man with a stern face addresses the assembled initiates. In a military voice so stern as to negate the possibility of meaningful feedback, he says, "You will be asked to do many things you do not understand. Do them and do not ask any questions. I want all of you to disrobe."

Almost all of the initiates begin to strip and expose their skin to the chilling wind. One initiate, an older man from the outside, cries out, "I'm not takin' off my fuckin' clothes! You're gonna have to come and take them off yourself, old man."

Before his words are lost in the wind, an enclaver knocks down the defiant initiate with a single blow of an ax handle. As soon as he hits the ground, two other enclavers are standing over him. One draws a knife and quickly removes the man's clothes as if he were skinning an animal of its hide.

A nearby initiate begins an unstable laugh that seems to border on hysteria; he is silenced by a hard blow to the small of the back delivered by the skinner's companion.

Robinson clenches his hands together trying to control his shaking which, judging from the expression on his face, is as much from fear as from cold.

I made a mental note to ask Fitz what his fears are.

The enclavers drag the unconscious man to a tall, thick pine. There, with chains and stakes, and by use of the embedded ring, the initiate is bonded to the tree. Soon all the other initiates are similarly chained, without further resistance, which they seemed to realize would only encourage their captors in their cruelty.

Around the fire pit, which is now leaping with flames as darkness falls, the enclavers pass around animal-skin bags filled with wine and liquor. Some of the men stagger while buckdancing. One enclaver, wearing clown makeup and carrying a wineskin large enough to hold five liters, begins making the rounds of the chained victims, reciting some incantation and squirting red wine into open mouths.

The clown stops before Robinson: Blue makeup is the base that shows on his forehead beneath the white hair that is combed forward; blue ears show their lobes below the hair that half covers them. The nose is a red bulb; the mouth a white downturned arc that looks like drained skin around a deep, open wound. Red, bloodlike tears are painted on blue cheeks. They well from white-lined eyes, each covered with a black cross.

For a moment I became lost in the symbolism. Was it the simple pun of the cross-eyed clown? Or was it the symbol of archaic Christianity that glorified the suffering the cross represented?

Then the clown-priest delivers his bad joke or damning prayer in the sing-song voice of ritual that remains sacred long after it has lost its value: "Here, take this wine, "The blood of our heart. Let it transform, or set you apart." The clown squirts the wine into Robinson's mouth, completing the ritual of symbolic cannibalism. He swallows eagerly. It will make him feel warmer but at the expense of losing body heat, the body heat that if retained might help him survive the coldness of the night and the sadism of his captors.

SF

On Robinson's left, the chained youth speaks through gritted teeth as soon as the clown passes out of hearing. Why don't they let us go? I don't have to go through this anymore. I can hold my breath and die." He squeezes his eyes tightly shut, compresses his lips and moves the muscles of his face as if to close his nose. He bows out against the tree, his body muscles straining. Then he slumps forward, his head falling to his chest.

The sound of renewed breathing is as harsh as self-betrayal.

Robinson's head drops too. His eyes are closed. Exhaustion has brought him the temporary release of sleep.

The view shifts back and forth between the enclavers around the fire and the initiates chained to the trees. Each return of focus to the fireside shows the flames at a lower level. Occasionally one of the initiates groans or cries out, but most are asleep or silent, their faces blue or ashen and eyelids lined with frost.

When the focus returns to Robinson, he is still chained to the tree, slumped in sleep, unconsciousness or dead. The slight movement of his chest reveals that he is still breathing. On the horizon is the first blush of dawn. The blue-faced clown, who has exchanged his wineskin for a bloody hunting knife, approaches Robinson and speaks into his ear, "Wake up, Son. There are only a few more hours left to go."

I recognized the clown as Spenser just as the surprise of his identity hits Robinson's face.

"Quiet. You're not supposed to know who I am," Spenser says, as he guides his blade to the left side of his foster son's chest and inscribes a circle around the left nipple. As the blood wells out, he makes a similar incision circumscribing the right nipple. The blood runs down Robinson's chest and drips off his floating ribs to add to the stains on the darkened ground.

A white-faced clown carrying a wire basket with several containers in it joins the duo. Spenser sheathes his knife and then dips his hands into a bowl as if to cleanse them. When he removes them they look shiny as if coated with oil.

Spenser squats in front of Robinson. With his left hand he holds his foster son's genitals, while his right hand probes for the anus. He finds it and forces a finger inside. He begins the motions that roughly stimulate the prostate gland, quickly bringing Robinson to orgasm without any variation in his mechanical technique. Robinson jerks and writhes as if he were experiencing as much pain as pleasure. Tears fill his eyes.

Using another vessel from the wire basket, Spenser makes a mixture of Robinson's tears, blood and ejaculate. He dips his finger into the compound and draws a large X on Robinson's forehead, followed by a pentacle on the left cheek and a pyramid with an eye at the top on the right. The remaining mixture is used to make a circle with radiating lines around the initiate's navel.

The scene dissolves in the darkness of the predawn hours. The next image is of the beginning sunrise.

Two clowns are making the rounds of the trees, inspecting the hanging initiates for signs of life. As they reach the tree to which Robinson is chained, one calls out.

"Bring a blanket and a stretcher. This one's alive and breathing." Two attendants wrap him tightly, like a mother's embrace, in the blanket and load him on the stretcher: a series of close-ups show frostbite on Robinson's hands, toes, ears and nose. He appears to be barely conscious.

As the stretcher nears the ambulance, an obviously female clown with red polka dots covering her face approaches the stretcher and peers into Robinson's face. The clown says something in a high, choked voice garbled by emotion.

"Mom?" asks Robinson in a croaking voice.

"Are you all right, Son?"

Through chattering teeth, he answers, "I...I don't know."

The woman asks one of the attendants how Robinson is doing.

"Not so good," whispers the man. "Like the others, he's suffering from acute hypothermia. If we can get him to the hospital in time, we might be able to save his life."

Robinson's eyes close as if he is surrendering consciousness. One of the stretcher bearers says to the clown, "Out of the way, lady. He's going into shock. Got to get him into the ambulance where it's warmer."

The clown steps back; but when Robinson is inside the ambulance, she keeps one of the doors open so she can watch him. The attendants, in answer to another summons, leave to pick up another survivor. The ambulance driver yells back, "Get in or get out. If he loses much more body heat, he'll be a corpsicle. Close that damned door!"

The polka-dotted clown gets in, pulls the door shut and covers Robinson's body with her own as if to smother him with the warmth of her flesh.

As if the slam of the back door had been a starter's signal, the ambulance driver revs up his turbine and races the vehicle over the rough trail through the trees. On a downhill curve he hits a patch of melting ice and barely avoids crashing into a tree that looks almost half as wide as the ambulance. The rear end swings around wildly as the driver struggles to regain control.

In the back, the polka-dotted clown is thrown off Robinson's body and onto the floor near the rear door. When the vehicle is back under control, the clown gets up, revealing a suit thoroughly dampened by the melted snow and slush that puddles the rear deck. The clown peels off the wet costume revealing her marshmallow flesh for a few seconds before she crawls under the blankets with the semi-conscious survivor of the initiation.

The driver is intent on the hazardous road and is unaware of the motions behind him. The mutual shivering of boy and woman become mutual warmth, then sensual heat, and then the fire of sexual desire in consummation.

As the spasms of orgasm lose their intensity, Robinson opens his eyes in wonder as he sees the polka-dotted clown face above him. He looks puzzled for a moment, then, with frostbitten fingers that barely bend, he wipes off the red and white makeup and sees the face of his foster mother.

"Mother," he cries, in a tortured voice.

Sobbing, she says, "I'm sorry...they told me heat was the only thing that might...that might save you. Oh God! What have I done?"

With a look of horror upon his face, Robinson pushes her away and off the cot they share. She looks at his distorted face and begins screaming. He covers his ears with his hands to shut out the sound. When that fails, he lashes out at her screaming mouth.

Mrs. Spenser bangs her head against the side of the ambulance, still screaming. As if they had a will all their own, Robinson's hands try to cover her mouth and, when that fails, try to squeeze her throat closed. Underneath the remainder of the smeared makeup, her face turns from pinkish red to purple.

Slowly becoming aware that the screaming has stopped, Robinson stops choking his mother. Her bulging, lifeless eyes are silent testimony that she will never scream or breathe again.

The ambulance stops. The back door is jerked open. The driver asks in a harsh yell, "What the hell did you do to her?"

Robinson drives his foot with all his strength straight into his accuser's face, then scrambles out of the ambulance into the hospital parking lot.

Several clowns yell at him as he starts to run through the lot. He staggers against a truck and picks up an ax from the truck bed. His pursuers slow down as he menaces them with his newly found weapon.

The blue clown steps forward. His voice is choked and loud when he says, "Son, don't you know who you are? Or what you've done? You killed her...Your mother."

Robinson turns and sees a clown trying to sneak up behind him. "You've tricked me for the last time," he screams, swinging the ax with all his strength and burying the head in Spenser's skull.

The tableau is frozen with shock except for Robinson who drops the ax handle and sprints away nude into the trees at the edge of the lot. There is a loud crack of rifle fire followed by the solid sound of impact as the bullet hits a pine tree just missing Robinson. He continues to run, rests for a moment, and runs again until he has rounded a hill and is out of the line of fire. The thrum of a zepcraft in the distance catches his attention. He turns back but sees no pursuers. He looks at the ground and inspects it carefully; there are no signs or tracks to indicate which way he has traveled.

He moves carefully now, avoiding the many snowy patches that will show prints of his bare feet. He seems oblivious to the rocky surface and the brisk wind that makes the trees groan. Near a small clearing, he carefully buries himself in a snow bank, brushing the snow over himself like a blanket. The sounds of his hunters fade into the distance. His eyes are staring at a blue flower on the edge of the clearing, illuminated by the dawn and making a long shadow that reaches toward him.

When the focus returns to Robinson, the sun is shining directly into his staring, unseeing eyes. The final shot shows unblinking eyes and a blue flower that casts no shadow.

CHAPTER 9

FREUD REVISTED

I see Freudian psychology as Freud's problem.
Sam-tio Chung

Long after the black letter THE END, superimposed on the white snow, had faded from view I was still sitting in my recliner, ruminating about what I had seen. Vallen's *The Crying Clown Rites* was very different from his work in documentaries. His holoprod of *Selfishness Out Of Control* had been a brilliant exposé of the Control organization and their inhumane practices of personality reduction and ego erosion. His latest work, regardless of whether it was fiction or fact, was a packaged nightmare with a deeper and wider reality than the common horror hollies.

Of course, I was somewhat distrustful of the blatant Freudianism in Vallen's head thread. It could have been titled *Oedipal Robinson Out West.* And Vallen's brief appearance as the hunt victim would leave any psychoanalyst worth his couch tugging at his beard.

While Freud did do some innovative work in the field of emotional health, he never realized his own limitations, especially in the area of understanding his own problems. There is some evidence to indicate that psychoanalysis has helped some people at some times; however, there is just as much evidence that it increases dysfunctional behavior in others. One school of thought is that Freud was unable or unwilling to believe that his personal worldview didn't encompass all of reality; another school believes that Freud overindulged himself in the use of cocaine.

Actually, both schools are correct, just incomplete in their understanding: I believe Freud's belief in the universality of the Oedipal complex was a defense of his personality structure and that some of his theories were delusions brought about by the elation of cocaine usage and the disorientation created by cocaine withdrawal.

Freud or Vallen certainly would have been challenging clients… But enough woolgathering. My focus should be on Fitz: What did the head thread mean to him? Did he see himself as Robinson, traumatized by his mother's (Angela's) betrayal, and afraid that he might follow a similar spiral of self-destruction? Or had the mummer taken advantage of Fitz's uncentered ego to place him in a form of psychological bondage that reminded him of Robinson's internment in the Jackson Hole Enclave? For the first time since Angela's death, I felt vitally involved in my work again.

I decided to call Fitz and set a time for an appointment.

I was just about to hang up when Fitz's face filled the screen. He looked like an unkempt zombie as he mumbled "Hello" in an emotionally flat voice.

"Hello, Fitz. I've seen *The Crying Clown Rites* and I called to give you an appointment for counseling. I have all of tomorrow afternoon free. Is that a good time for you?"

"I don't have any good times. Tomorrow afternoon will be no worse than any other time."

"I'll expect you at my office at 1400 if that suits you," I said, trying to keep the worry I was feeling out of my voice.

"I'll be there."

"I'd like some information first, that is, if it won't disturb you unduly?"

"I won't be disturbed; I've got my medpack." Fitz held up his right arm and showed me the biofeedback medpack strapped to his wrist. It was a compact unit containing light-emitting diodes to indicate operation, depletion or malfunction; drugs; a hypospray to inject them and the monitoring equipment necessary to regulate the dosage according to metabolic conditions.

"What drugs are you currently taking?"

"Just Noanx to keep my anxiety level down. Angela told me it was all right for short term use."

"How long have you been using Noanx?" I wondered how long Angela had been doing therapeutic patchwork on him.

"Just a day so far."

"I'd like for you to set it at minimum maintenance sometime before you come see me tomorrow. Can you do that?"

"Yes. What else?"

"Fitz, it will save us a lot of time if you will tape some information for me and transfer it into my computer. I'd like as much background information as you can give me, a brief detailed oral autobiography, plus a summary of recent events that you believe have contributed to your present problems. Are you up to that?"

"I've got nothing else to do."

I gave Fitz the access code for the record mode of my computer. Just as I was getting ready to end the conversation, he asked, "You said you've seen *The Crying Clown Rites?*"

I nodded. "I just finished viewing it. There will be a copy in my office tomorrow that we can see on the holly if that would be helpful in understanding your reactions to it."

Fitz cringed. "NO! …I mean, no. I wouldn't want to see it again. That's why I wanted you to view it before I came in for counseling. I'm not going to look at that damned thing ever again." He wiped his forehead with his palm and I could see the blinking diode that indicated Noanx was being injected into his wrist.

By the time I was able to close the conversation, Fitz was back to his

Noanx pallor and I had to reassure him that I was not going to desensitize him to the head thread. I had never considered doing that. Whatever his problems were, they were merely symbolized by *The Crying Clown Rites*. To desensitize him to its content without exploring the meaning of that content for Fitz would be a cosmetic approach to the problem—the kind of practitioners who do that would treat leprosy with makeup.

Wait one minute! I thought, laughing to myself. I was beginning to get that protective urge about Fitz that I always felt with my serious patients. Did that mean I wanted to treat Fitz? He had already accepted me as his therapist—albeit at Angela's urging. And it had been Angela's last request… But could I really help him?

Maybe it was time I examined my deeper feelings about Fitz: There was some anger, jealousy too; a little guilt, pity and compassion. Also curiosity. I wasn't sure how much I owed Angela—if anything at all. It was clear from her last message that we had not been on the same page, or even chapter. So if I was going to do this, it wasn't going to be for her alone. The question was: What did I want to do?

My client load was low, the lowest it had been since my first year of practice. And I'll admit it; I was bored. Now that Angela was out of my life my picture of the future was opaque. I needed something to engage myself in the here and now.

Charmaine? No, wasn't that what Fitz was doing with his mummer surrogate of Angela? I liked Charmaine; she was fun, she was sexy. But I didn't need her as a crutch.

I needed time to put Angela's passing in perspective before I considered another relationship. Besides, I didn't know enough about Charmaine, her past and present, or how she saw her future.

Fitz was the safer choice of the two. And he needed my help… And, just maybe, I needed him.

Since I had the rest of the afternoon free, I decided to review *The Crying Clown Rites*, starting at the end and working backwards, to see if I could learn why it had precipitated Fitz's collapse. Robinson had died after killing both his foster parents shortly after his sexual encounter with his foster mother. If Fitz suffered from Freud's problem, Mrs. Spenser could be a stand-in for Fitz's mother. Which might mean Angela was the previous stand-in. Fitz had thought he was the cause of Angela's death and that paralleled Robinson being the cause of Mrs. Spenser's death.

I needed to know more about his relationships with women. Charmaine had mentioned Fitz's charisma more than once. When I saw her next week, I would have to obtain her perspective on him. She was also the one who had told me Fitz had hired an actress as a grief thief.

I made a quick note on my datapad: Try to set up interview with Fitz's mummer surrogate.

The apparent meaningless violence of the clown initiation rites might possibly have more significance to Fitz than they held for me. Mystery schools and secret societies tend to use terror, symbolic violence, drugs, theatrics, promised rewards and other techniques in combinations to give the initiate a different way of viewing reality. Some of them, like the Skoptsi's Baptism of Fire or the Illuminati's Rite of Light, were every bit as violent as the Clown Rites; the major difference was the emphasis the Jackson Hole clowns placed on surviving under hostile and lethal conditions. I would need to hear Fitz's bio tape and have a talk with him before I really understood what the head thread meant to him.

I decided to go down to the basement pool and swim my thrice-weekly kilometer to wash away Fitz's problems.

After my swim I went home, changed into my dark green caftan and vaulted to San Francisco for the monthly gourmet dinner of the Synchronicity Society. I joined Serge in the bar for an aperitif. We hugged each other warmly and he said, "Phillip, you're looking much better."

"Thanks, Serge. I'm feeling good."

He smiled. "Is there a new lady in your life?"

"I recently went to Paratime with Charmaine Dwoskin, and we had a great time."

"I'm pleased, Phillip. She's attractive, charming and intelligent."

"She's the first woman I've been interested in since Angela died."

I was able to say Angela's name without a catch in my voice. Serge evidently noticed.

"You seem to have ended your mourning period. I was worried about you."

"Angela exists only in my memories; I am no longer haunted by her ghost. Once I finish her last request, I'm sure I will have complete acceptance of everything that has happened."

"Her last request? What's that?"

"In a letter she left with Juanita, Angela asked me to counsel Fitz if he asked for my help."

Serge sighed. "And he has asked for it and you are going to give it?"

"Yes," I said, trying not to sound as defensive as I was beginning to feel. Fitz, with his obsession with assassination, his fixation on Angela, and the Kennedy albatross fastened around his throat, was one of the most interesting clients I'd been involved with in years. It wasn't as though I were Angela's puppet.

"Phillip. Phillip. You never could say no to Angela. Are you sure this will end it?"

I could feel my face redden; Serge was being more paternal than fraternal. "Yes," I said, "this will end it."

Sensing my anger, he changed the subject. "As you know, on Tuesdays I go out to the Fringes for free counseling at the Mind Shaft. Well, I have this new patient, a dwarf, who claims he's the real Allen Heart—the guest pest. I'll admit—except for the scars from where a tattoo was removed from his face—he does look like Heart.

"His story is that he insulted the King of the Dwarfs, while interviewing him on The Allen Heart Hour, and the dwarf king repaid his insult by kidnapping him and taking him to a chop shop where they turned him into a dwarf. Don't laugh ...this is serious. Then the dwarfs took him to Moria—a dwarf underworld beneath the cliffs of La Jolla."

I stared to laugh, but stopped when I saw Serge's face redden.

"I checked and there really is such a place. Anyway, after they took him prisoner they tried to ransom him off to the IBC network, but the network had already made a switch with a Heart clone and they weren't buying..."

After Serge's story and an aperitif I was in much better spirits. When I glimpsed the time, I realized I had better check the seating chart. Serge was scheduled to sit next to Dr. Linda Duran, who had taken over Angela's practice. I was to sit at another table between Dr. Julian Greenberg and Dr. Stephanie Biwerse. I parted with Serge and made my way to my table.

Stephanie spoke first, saying, "Phillip, I'm delighted to see you. It seems so appropriate that we're sitting together. I dreamed of you last night."

Julian added, "Stephanie told me about the dream. You can be assured that it has no Freudian implications."

"Good. That's refreshing. What kind of implications does it have?"

"I'm not sure," said Stephanie. "I was in a pastry shop to buy some fresh napoleons and the clerk said they had some just coming out of the oven. At that moment, you came out of the kitchen dressed in a white shirt and pants, wearing a baker's hat and carrying a tray of thirteen napoleons. I hope it means more to you than it does to me."

"Thirteen used to be called a baker's dozen," Julian said. "Is that significant?"

I could feel my forehead furrow. "The name Baker is significant. I have a new client whose last name is Baker."

Further discussion was postponed as the waiters began to serve the first course. The Synchronicity Society never announces the menu in advance, a custom dating back to its beginning. The food was superb: water chestnut soup, tossed green salad, asparagus au gratin, buttered julienne carrots, lyonnaise potatoes, stuffed mushrooms, green beans with almonds, roast suckling pig and, for dessert—napoleons.

Stephanie asked, "Are you going to eat thirteen napoleons, Phillip?

Just to make my dream come true?"

"But I was bringing them to you."

"Ahh...yes. But I only wanted an even dozen."

"Then I'll eat only one. It can symbolize an extra napoleon in the baker's dozen."

We joked about the synchronicity of dreams and reality over the after-dinner cognac. Julian talked about the success of his new book intended for professionals titled *Therapeutic Implications of Quantum Taoism*. He said that he had declined his latest holly offer, which was to be a guest on the Allen Heart Hour. Stephanie asked him why he refused.

Julian said, "I view what Allen Heart passes off as interviewing as a type of attack therapy, which I see as a childish rendition of 'Anything You Can Do, I Can Do Better.' Heart specializes in setting-up his guests so he can make their most cherished beliefs, desires and aspirations appear trivial, absurd or downright crazy. A few of them might find the publicity worth the embarrassment or pain—I don't. My problem is not energy credits, it's finding enough time."

Stephanie nodded our agreement. Julian's talk of Allen Heart reminded me of Serge's story about Heart's dwarf double. I related his tale and we ended up swapping stories on our most unusual clients for the next hour. That train of talk brought Fitz Baker to mind. I began to wonder if he had completed his autobiography yet. When the conversation slowed down, I excused myself, stopped for a moment to bid good night to Serge and the people at his table, then vaulted back to Los Angeles.

Once I was home I checked the computer and discovered Fitz had fed his autobiographical tape into it. I listened immediately: *My name is Fitzgerald Felix Baker. I was born thirty-eight years ago in 2050. My mother is named Mary Gulik. My father, who died when I was six years old, was the auggie star Zachary Fitzgerald Baker—known professionally as Zach Baker. He was the grandson of Marilyn Monroe and John Fitzgerald Kennedy."* He laughed uneasily as if this statement often brought laughter or incredulity.

"Neither of my parents was ever married. Although my mother visited my father frequently when I was young, she seldom took me with her. He never lived with us. I can remember Mary asking him, while I was supposed to be taking a nap during the last time we visited, if the three of us couldn't live together. He said it would never work because he had never wanted a family, because he was thirty years older than she was and because she had gotten pregnant on purpose without his knowledge. He went on to say that he had doubted whether I was his child or not, even though I resembled childhood pictures of his father and grandfather. He told Mary that she came into his life as an auggie bawd and that was all right but she was always acting as if the relationship was more than that and it wasn't, hadn't been and wasn't going to be. Mary picked me up and left. The next I heard of my father was that he had died in a fire.

Mary left me with Isobel Grant shortly after my father died. She told me she needed a long vacation by herself to recover from the shock of my father's death. I learned later that her recovery vacation was spent as a member of the shock troupe of the erotic terrorists.

Aunt Isobel—aunt was a courtesy title; my mother was an abandoned child with no known relatives—reared me in the Sacramento huburb. She enrolled me in the huburb youth union that provided basic education and communal childcare.

At puberty, I began to have troubles in the union. My union mates had learned that my father had been a sexual celebrity, and somehow that was supposed to make me an expert on sex. In trying to fulfill that role, I imitated my father and that caused some problems with the parents of the female students. Aunt Isobel handled the complaints by agreeing to put me on restriction, which caused me to act out against her.

With the help of my faculty adviser and friend, Julia Tracton, I was able to transfer to the Free Thought Communal School in Berkeley, a school with a neo-Marcusian outlook on society and the educational process. When I finished there I entered the University of California at Berkeley as a political science major. I had decided to emulate my great-grandfather and change the world through politics. My Aunt Isobel encouraged and nurtured my interest in politics and governmental change.

At Berkeley I was befriended by Dennis Nash, who became my political mentor as well as the sort of older brother I had never had and always wanted. In those days I felt I had a genuine calling to serve the people and I asked not why I should do it but only how I could do it. I believed that with Dennis as my advisor and confidant I could restore responsible and responsive government.

That dream died when an assassin attacked Dennis and me. I've thought and thought about that and am still unable to decide whether Dennis was attempting to save my life or not when he was killed. When the investigation revealed that Dennis was a government agent assigned to befriend and influence me in my political aspirations, I was dumbfounded—it brought my life to a halt.

I never went back to the campus to officially withdraw from classes, but I withdrew from everyone and spent six months in a secluded cabin near the Russian River that I rented under an assumed name. I stayed in the cabin most of the time, sleeping a lot and eating very little, hoping some magic answer would come to me.

When no answer came and I became sated with the companionship of trees, I left the forest cabin and drifted south to Los Angeles. I went to the University of California at Los Angeles and was accepted in their school of architecture, a secondary interest of mine, but one that seemed safe to explore.

After I graduated and gathered some practical experience, I joined Clyde Burbank in a partnership that has been very successful. We accumulated so much energy credit that several years ago Clyde experienced a success crisis. A friend suggested that he consult Angela for professional help. He did so and was gratified by the results. At his party to celebrate the successful conclusion of his therapy, I met Angela and she changed my life.

Before meeting Angela, my sex life was very erratic—long periods of promiscuous activity, alternating with short spans of celibacy. After Angela and I met, it took four or five months for me to convince her to see me on a personal level and even longer for us to become lovers, but once we became lovers I quit going to sex clubs and began to have emotional stability in my life for the first time.

I was growing dissatisfied with the field of architecture when I met Angela. She reawakened my interest because she was so enthusiastic about her Rebirth Center. Then I received the commission from the Church of Prophetic Revelation. Suddenly I had two exciting buildings to design and both clients were willing to let me devote as much time as necessary to produce the best results.

Then I learned that the Church project, a structure to be called the Pantheon of Prophets, was given to me, not because they believed I was the best architect for the project, but because some of their financial backers believed I would become as important a figure in next century's politics as my great-grandfather was in the last century. The Church's stated goal is total consciousness, yet they wanted me on their side for political gain. I was sorely disappointed to learn that people of such lofty goals were willing to use such tawdry means. I identify with John Kennedy to a certain degree and I'm no more tolerant of people making political use of me than he was.

Angela and I shared everything and when I told her about my disappointment with the Pantheon building she wrapped me in the cocoon of her love. I admit to being dependent on her, but it was the mutual dependency of two people whose total was more than a sum of their parts. She needed me too; many times late at night she would awaken screaming Jason's name and crying for hours. I believe I was of some consolation to her.

Angela's death hit me harder than any other trauma or combination of traumas in my life. She was everything to me. Angela died on the site of her Center that I designed for her. Architecture no longer provides consolation for me. Buildings seem hollow shells, just as I have become a hollow shell of a person.

Angela was very interested in the suicide of my great-grandmother, Marilyn Monroe. I used this interest and the Center I was designing for her to make the relationship into more than she had intended, more than I ever got from any other woman. I was more prepared for my own death than for hers.

I knew of no way to fill the void in my existence that her death created.

I tried to resume living, but I felt like an unclaimed clone. Nothing seemed to help. In desperation, I hired Estelle Zimmer, a mummer surrogate, to help me adjust to my loss, to help me find diversions, other interests, to have someone to hold me closely when I awoke from nightmares or strange dreams…

Even drugs offer me little protection from visions of Angela dead and decaying, dreams where I have a harem of women but all are dressed in black as if mourning, dreams of dying after an eternity of torture that is both mental and physical.

As a distraction Estelle and I went to see The Crying Clown Rites *and the results were disastrous. I don't think it was just because Mrs. Spenser appeared to me to be a mature, matronly version of Marilyn Monroe. It had to be more than that, but I don't know what because Angela is not here to tell me and no one will ever take her place in my heart.*

I became irrational, desperately disturbed as we watched the head thread. Right after the scene where Robinson kills his mother, I ran out of the theater screaming, and then vomited in the mall. I remember hammering my fists against the theater wall as if I could batter the building down while tears ran out of my eyes and curses streamed from my mouth.

When Estelle tried to calm me down and drag me from the wall, I hit her with my fists and told her to go the Hell away. I don't know why I did that. It was not like me at all. I've never hit a woman before….

I came home in a fog. To escape the horrors in my mind I took an Oblivion Blue and went to bed. I strapped on the Noanx medpack when I awakened, and a few hours later called you. I know now that my outburst was a cry for help. I'm following Angela's advice in consulting you. And, because you loved Angela too. I'm not sure if I like or dislike you, but I know you can understand my pain… I saw it etched into your face when you talked to Angela at the Whole Body Center.

I really don't want to do anything, but I can't remain in the state I'm in. I'm in desperate need of help. I'm afraid that if I don't get help, I'll hurt someone again—or myself.

I was not sure if I was as disturbed by the flat and dispassionate way in which Fitz had said his words or the revelation that he had known Angela far longer than I had ever realized. It took a minute for me to sort my personal emotions from my professional ones.

There was no doubt in my mind, even though the Noanx might account for some of his flatness of affect, that Fitz needed professional help. I got chills remembering the way he described hitting Estelle Zimmer in much the same manner he might recount the demolition of a building to a client. *What if he needs more help than I could provide?*

Yet, he asked for me, and what would happen if I deserted him, too? Fitz had already been abandoned by every significant person in his life, including the ones he loved the most. If I failed him now, he might even decline professional assistance. Even worse, he could attack another innocent person or hurt himself.

I needed more data to make a decision of this magnitude. After our first session or two, I could see if a rapport was developing and just how serious his emotional state was. Then, if I believed I couldn't help him, I could make an enlightened recommendation.

CHAPTER 10

BEGINNING COUNSELING

Even the longest journey begins with a single step.
Sam-tio Chung

Fitz was ten minutes late for our 1400 counseling session. I made a mental note to check if any of the available research data indicated that there was a correlation between the use of Noanx and a decrease in punctuality.

I saw Fitz on the portal screen and pressed the keys to open the door. He was wearing a murky gray jelab that echoed the sallowness of his complexion. As he made his way into my office, he moved as if his back was stiff or painful. He lowered himself with both hands into the oak captain's chair as we exchanged greetings.

"Are you having problems with your back?" I asked.

"I haven't been doing my exercises lately so my back is a trifle stiff and somewhat weak."

I asked him what exercises he was doing and recommended that he continue with them so as not to add physical problems to his crisis state.

"Then you believe I'm experiencing a lifestyle crisis?" he asked.

"I'm working with you on that assumption," I said. "You're obviously dissatisfied with what is occurring in your life now. I'm willing to do my best to help you through this time of change."

"I know I'm unhappy. Depressed. Don't know how to change, or even what to change."

"Does the idea of changing threaten you?"

Fitz ran his fingers through his thick brown hair before answering.

"Probably. I'm not sure I'm capable of making successful changes in my life. I know I haven't been able to cope with Angela's…death."

I didn't believe that rehashing Angela's demise at this time would be productive so I changed the subject. "We can change anything in your behavior or your mind-set. What we'll do is determine what new behaviors are needed and desired by you."

"I know I have a resistance to change."

"Of course, we all do. We're creatures of habit. But you are getting signals that it's time to change. These feelings of anxiety you are experiencing carry both the signal of the need for change and the energy that will be necessary to make that possible. All we are going to do is find the ways to make effective change as easily as possible."

"I don't want to make my life any more complicated than it already is. I just want this pain to end!" His voice rose in a crescendo until he was shouting.

I made calming motions with my hands. "Fitz, you're already going through change. And pain is part of the process. I know you may see a change of routine, even going on with things, as a betrayal to Angela, but that's wrong. You need to find a way to accept these changes and go on with your life. There's nothing you, or anyone else on this plane of existence, can do for Angela now. Only acceptance will bring an end to your pain."

Fitz took a deep breath, crossed his legs, readjusted his position in the captain's chair and asked, "How does the procedure work?"

"My approach is flexible. There is no pattern that requires your conformance. Together, we are going to explore your life. When we find an area that needs attention, we'll take care of it."

"When do we start? Now? I'm not sure I'm ready."

"We've already started," I said, making more calming motions with my hands. "Your being here is a sign that you're ready."

He nodded, as if accepting the truth of my words.

"Fitz, I know *The Crying Clown Rites* affected you deeply. I also know that you have no desire to see it again. What I would like to do now is merely ask you a few questions about your reactions to it so that I can understand why it caused such a strong response when you viewed it with Estelle."

"I'm not ready to do that."

"I think you are, or you wouldn't have asked me to see it before this session. *The Crying Clown Rites* is teeming with symbolism, some obvious, some convoluted, some obscure. Together we can see what relates to you—"

"I don't want to talk about it!" he shouted, rising out of his chair.

"You do want to understand why you hurt Estelle, don't you?"

He dropped back into his seat and brought his hands up to his face. "Yes...yes. I don't want to hurt anyone else."

"I know, and I believe you. Together we can learn what drove you to violence and release it. You can be free. I want to help you win that freedom."

He let his hands fall and said, "I know, you do. It just hurts so damn much..."

"Your feelings will change with time and acceptance. But only if we do this together. Now, in *The Crying Clown Rites,* Robinson was closely watched almost all of the time after he left Teener Town. Does that relate to your suspicion that you are being monitored?" I decided to approach the subject of Mrs. Spenser's death slowly in order not to provoke his already excited emotions—or potential for violence.

"No. I don't think so. I followed your suggestion that I have Maxi Security investigate my suspicions. Ronald Marlin reported that a government agent was monitoring me because our firm is being considered for a government project. They're wasting their time and the government's money since I won't take the job. It isn't fruitful to do creative work for a political organization; no matter how the project is conceived, the end result is never creative—just political."

With his flair for digression, I was ready to believe that Fitz had given up a great political career. I bored in. "Were you concerned about political considerations in *The Crying Clown Rites?*"

"No. There were few political elements, just small-town conservatism and an attempt to evade the modern world through escape and disbelief. I've found it before in these small enclaves, like the Eisenhower Enclave and Dutch's World.

"Was the architecture significant?"

He almost smiled. "Not at all. Pseudo-frontier functional structures are as boring to me as huburbs and just as stagnant."

"Robinson was a prisoner prior to being taken to the Jackson Hole Enclave and remained a prisoner once he was there. Is that significant to you?"

"Yes... After my father died—you have listened to the tape I played into your computer? The autobiographical tape."

I nodded affirmatively. "Your father died when you were six."

"Yes and Mary—my mother insisted I call her Mary, never Mother or Mom or Mommy, just Mary. She left me with Aunt Isobel in the Sacramento huburb. I felt a prisoner there. The huburb youth union socialized me and educated me to the standards of the parents of my peer group. That structure was as narrow and tight to me as the enclave environment was to Robinson."

"What other parallels do you see?"

"In the head thread, Robinson was beaten and restricted when he attempted to have a sex life. Among his peers he was the one from outside who had the knowledge of sex. When my union peers exploded into puberty, I was awarded the position of sexual expert because my father had been a sex star and my real mother was an erotic terrorist. But I didn't know any more than anyone else because Aunt Isobel wasn't interested in sex."

"Didn't you have sexual education in the union?"

"Sure, but the course addressed itself to the problems that the authors' generation had, not the ones that were current."

"How did you deal with that problem?"

"I managed to see all of my father's auggies, with the help of an affluent fellow student. Then I began to put what I had seen into practice. My sexual success caused problems with the parents of girls who were more ready for puberty than their parents were. Aunt Isobel agreed to put me on restriction, a psychological prison with invisible bars that blocked most spontaneous or pleasurable activities."

"What did you do about that?" I asked.

"My friend on the faculty, Julia Tracton, helped me transfer to the Free Thought Communal School in Berkeley."

"What did your Aunt Isobel think or do when she found out?"

"I told her about it after it was all arranged and I was packed ready to go. She just accepted it in her cold, stoic manner."

"What did your mother think about it?"

"She didn't know. I hadn't seen her in almost a year, but the next time I saw her—she came to Berkeley after I'd been there a few months—she was very accepting of the situation. In her own way she attempted to demonstrate that she wanted the best for me even if she wasn't willing to spend much time with me."

"Was there anything in the Berkeley commune that corresponded to the Jackson Hole Enclave environment?"

"No," said Fitz, "I don't think so."

"After Robinson was punished for seducing the girl, the next intensely dramatic scene was his participation in the hunt for the barrier jumper. What was your reaction?"

SF

"I identified myself with Robinson in his confusion. But in the actual thrill kill scene I found myself identifying with the victim. I saw the hunters as all the assassins lurking around my family tree, the ones who killed my great-grandfather John Kennedy, his younger brother Robert, and all the others, including my grandfather Gene Baker and my father."

"And how did you feel?" I asked, pleased that Fitz was being so responsive and open.

"As if I was a prisoner of my own past." There was a haunted look in Fitz's eyes as he continued. "Like I was predestined to experience the blight of murder, suicide and disappearances that kills the fruit of my family tree. And then, when they chained Robinson to the ancient pine tree during the initiation rites, I felt I was chained to my own family tree and it would cause my death before I made my rite of passage, before I could discover how to live I would look death in the face. It seemed even more terrible that the face of death would be the face of a clown, crying instead of laughing—the final betrayal of the child in me who trusted the world."

I waited until his breathing returned to normal before asking him any more questions. "Was there anything else that made the head thread seem like it was indexed to your life in that scene?"

"Spenser said the enclave was founded thirty-eight years ago. This is my thirty-eighth year. It seemed like more than a coincidence."

"It's what Jung called synchronicity, meaningful coincidence without apparent cause. What else seemed to parallel your life?" I asked.

"I felt that Robinson feared the initiation rites and that his fear was increased because he knew nothing about them, no details to focus upon. I have suffered all my life from unknown fears. It's been a terrible curse."

"We will deal with your fears. The belief that they are unknown is mostly illusion, and reluctance on your part to give them identity which might make them more real or more frightening. As we explore them and give those fears their proper names, you will discover that naming them gives you power over them."

"That doesn't make sense." Fitz said, shaking his head. "In some societies there is a belief that to know a person's true name gives the knower a power over that person, an edge in dealing with him."

"Not really. Some organizations allow their members to remain anonymous."

"Yes, but isn't that limited to tribal-oriented groups?" he asked.

"Not always. The purpose is to let people who feel powerless and fearful retain the illusion of being unknown as a psychological protective device."

"Does it work?" he asked.

"Like any other tool. It's useful for some and detrimental to others. For those who are starting from a very uncertain place, it can help them on their path to maturation. If they can't let go of the tool when it is no longer needed, then the tool is a handicap. It's analogous to the medpack you are using now. For the present time it works and that's fine, but the treatment plan is to get you to the point where it is excess baggage."

Fitz tensed up. "I'm not ready to give it up."

"That's reasonable, Fitz. Just as Robinson didn't want to give up his Teener Town costume when he was captured. He would have stopped wearing it eventually when it no longer matched his lifestyle, but he was forced to give it up before he was ready. We don't have to hurry. Your time schedule is your own. You are not Robinson who was forced into a lifestyle with no other alternative except death, which is—"

"Like when the initiate who had been friendly to Robinson suddenly arched his chest so the knife entered his heart, he made that choice."

"What did that remind you of?"

"The death of Dennis and the depression I felt afterwards."

"Was there anything else in the actual initiation that seemed pertinent to what you are experiencing now?"

"The senseless violence reminded me of being buried alive with Angela."

"Yes, and you blamed yourself for her death until you learned what really happened. You mentioned on the tape that Mrs. Spenser reminded you of Marilyn Monroe, but did you identify her death with the death of Angela?"

"No. Robinson's reaction to the horror he experienced caused him to kill Mrs. Spenser. I know that I was not responsible for Angela's death."

I was pleased to learn that he no longer took responsibility for Angela's death, for if he still had it would have been a major obstacle to any real therapeutic progress. I asked, "Do you see parallels between the Robinson-Mrs. Spenser relationship and your relationship with Angela?"

"Is that your way of asking if I feel there was a strong element of the Oedipus complex in my love for Angela?"

"Yes."

"Well—there wasn't. Between the neo-Marcusian school in Berkeley and Angela's interest in Freud as interpreted by Templeman, I have a thorough knowledge of the Oedipus complex and I have not been victimized by it. My mother was an erotic terrorist, not one of those shy persons who couldn't mention sex. When I left Sacramento and moved to Berkeley, she came to visit me. She told me that if I was ever interested she was quite ready to have sex with me anytime I wanted."

"I see. That's quite unusual." I tried not to be judgmental, and wondered if maybe Fitz had misinterpreted his mother's words. I needed to interview her in person. "Do you mind if I talk to her about it?"

"No. Feel free to talk to anyone who you think can help you to understand me."

"Do you think your mother would be willing?" I asked.

"Willing is a good word to describe my mother's sexual orientation. I'm sure she would be willing to talk, too."

I couldn't help but notice the hostility in his voice.

"Where does she live?"

"I'm not sure," Fitz answered, "but Aunt Isobel would know. She's listed in the Sacramento huburb directory as Isobel Grant."

"Thank you, Fitz. I have one more question about *The Crying Clown Rites*. You mentioned on the tape that you got violent with Estelle

Zimmer when she tried to comfort you outside the theater. Can you tell me why her attempt to help you increased your agitation?"

"Because…she, she wasn't Angela."

I could sense Fitz's growing anxiety. In an effort to calm him before the level of distress triggered his medpack, I asked, "Have you any experience with breathing meditation?"

"No."

"I'd like to teach the technique to you. It brings relaxation without medication. You're dressed properly for it. No tight fitting clothes. Since you're having problems with your back, I think a firm couch would be the best place for you to relax and try it."

Fitz moved from the captain's chair to the chocolate couch against the pastel yellow wall. I rolled my swivel chair over closer to the couch.

As soon as he was settled, I asked, "Are you feeling comfortable?"

"Yes," he replied.

"Let your muscles relax. If you feel any tension anywhere, increase the tension and then let it go. The muscles will automatically relax when you let the tension go. Breathe through your nose without making an effort to draw the air in. Expand your diaphragm and the air will flow into your diaphragm and lungs. Now let the air flow outward to complete the breath. Keep your focus on your breathing. If a thought or a feeling enters your mind, you don't have to examine it—just recognize it and let it go."

I watched to see that Fitz was breathing correctly, then I set the chimer for twenty minutes and the alpha brain wave state.

I remained seated until the chimer sounded; Fitz stirred and I shut it off. "Don't get up abruptly. How do you feel?"

"Relaxed, very relaxed."

"I'd like for you to do that breathing meditation four times a day, twenty minutes each time, for the next two weeks. You'll find it more relaxing when it becomes a habit. Will you do that?"

"Yes. I've come here for help and I'm not going to reject it."

"Good. I have a mood chart I want you to take home and keep

up-to-date. Once a week you can plug it into your datapad and it will feed the data into my computer. I also have a fear management notebook that will help you name your fears and start the process of conquering them."

"How am I going to keep track of all this…?"

"I'll set up a tickler file with your datapad. It will remind you what to do and when to do it."

"Here is a list of exercises to help your back. These exercises are not intended to replace your back exercises but to supplement them. Your outlook and mood are heavily influenced by what your body tells you. If you keep active and keep your muscles toned you will feel better. That may sound ridiculously simple, but usually the techniques that work best are the most basic."

Fitz nodded to signify he understood.

"We'll set up an appointment schedule now if you want."

"Please."

"And I'll give you the emergency number so you can either call me or another qualified crisis professional should anything happen that needs immediate attention." It took only a few moments to enter the necessary data from my office computer into Fitz's datapad. It pleased me to see him walk out the door with more energy than he had used to enter it.

CHAPTER 11

THE GRIEF THIEF

Imitation is the sincerest form of flattery.
C.C. Colton

As I replayed the tape of our first session on the holly, I noted that Fitz, despite his medication, had displayed more emotion than I had expected. As a lifestyle crisis counselor, my professional duty was to chart a route from where my client was to a place where he could comfortably live and grow. To do this I didn't have to be an expert in conducting whatever therapeutic experiences Fitz would go through, but I did have to know the therapeutic possibilities well enough to select appropriate experiences and to be the movable bridge that would span the emotional chasms in his life. I was not trained to treat character disorders or psychosis; their treatment required a regimen of biological, pharmaceutical, and therapeutic treatments that I wasn't prepared to orchestrate.

Not that Fitz didn't have problems; he was certainly emotionally repressed, suffering from a depression he refused to recognize, slightly paranoid and suicidal—as well as fixated on Angela's death. I noted with ironic detachment that an outside observer might have said I shared some of Fitz's symptoms. I hoped this would not lead to over-identification; I didn't think so. Usually, I was best able to help those patients whom I identified with most. And, most importantly, Fitz needed me; another rejection at this point in his life might be disastrous.

The overall plan would be a loosely structured reciprocal therapy, an interactive exchange of emotional outlooks between client and therapist. The challenge of entering a disturbed person's life on the emotional level was avoided by many professionals because of its burnout potential, but I believed that Fitz's situation demanded it.

Looking back at the release procedure at The Whole Body Center, I could see that the process had begun then, the process by which both Fitz and I would jointly reshape our lives without a primary love interest in the late Angela Calderon.

The name of a therapy, a new one that I'd read about recently was eluding my memory. What was it? Had I read about it in *Therapy Trends*? Language translation therapy? No. That wasn't it. No matter what languages Fitz's problems were expressed in or translated into and back from, they would be no more liable to lend themselves to intellectual symbolic solution.

Could it have been conversion analysis? Since I only have partial recall—I'm convinced total recall would be a curse; I'm certain I've forgotten a lot that I don't need or want to remember—I requested a readout on conversion analysis theory and practice on my datapad. It read like a combination of shock therapy, to destroy an existing mindset, and a series of intimidation strategies disguised as revealing experiences, which would convert the client into a true believer of intangible gobbledygook.

Implosion therapy? No. That was best for phobias. Prolonged and intimate contact with a phobic object or situation seemed a torturous route to any new reality.

Then I remembered the article on womb expulsion therapy I had read in *Lifestyle Crisis Counselor's Journal.* Just what I was looking for. I would take Fitz back to the birth experience, give him rebirth, a new chance for basic trust, acceptance and, most important of all, a sense of continuing growth that was a never-ending process.

I called Dr. Wanda Spellman, the originator of womb expulsion therapy, and made an appointment to discuss the possibility of applying her therapy to my client. My next call was to Isobel Grant in the Sacramento huburb, but my effort to locate Mary Gulik through her was thwarted by her answermat which asked me to leave my name and number plus a brief statement about why I called and if I wanted to be called back.

Until then I hadn't realized how much I had been looking forward to feminine companionship—even if only for talk. Charmaine Dwoskin, when I screened, told me she was busy working on her new dance routine, but would love for me to see her perform in her dance therapy class. On impulse I called Michelle Chamonix only to discover that an erratic electrical storm was blocking all circuits to Martinique. The Weather Control Corporation must be having a feud with Carib Communications.

I even screened Nadina Towers but hung up when all I got was her answermat.

Was I missing Angela so much that I was searching for a substitute? Or was my need for a woman's company merely an expression of my appreciation for the differences between the sexes? I wasn't sure so I combined work and my desire for female companionship by locating Estelle Zimmer, through the mummer surrogate affiliation service, and making an appointment to discuss her now terminated relationship with Fitz.

The tube ride to the address Estelle Zimmer had given me was as short as our phone conversation had been. She kept her screen dimmed out, claiming that she didn't have her makeup on. I wondered if her face would show, beneath the makeup, the effects of Fitz's fist.

Her house was old, elegant California Spanish with white stucco walls and red tile roof nestled in among the newer structures in Baldwin Hills. I rang the bell. When the ident panel glowed, I pressed my keycard against it and faced the portal camera.

Estelle opened the door herself and said, "Come in. I'm glad you're here."

Her voice sounded even more like Angela's alto in person than it had over the screen, but it was the shock of seeing her that made my knees buckle. She looked like Angela's twin! The bright brown eyes. The black hair worn like a Spanish Madonna. The dark red blouse, the black full skirt, both handwoven, and the black and red shawl all looking as if they had been designed in Madrid. She even smelled of Cinnabar—Angela's signature perfume.

She moved aside. I staggered past her and almost collapsed onto a Mediterranean couch. Over the couch was a surrealistic painting in the style of Magritte that depicted a matador's cape and sword upon an operating table in a room that appeared to be a chapel. I recognized it as Angela's work, a painting she had probably given to Fitz, who had placed it here.

"Coffee?" she asked, "with a taste of Spanish brandy?" I nodded and she left the room; her walk registered as being different from Angela's walk. I felt relieved.

She brought out the coffee, brandy and cups on a Toledo tray and sat them down on the coffee table. She poured and handed me one.

As I took a sip of the strong brew, she said, "I'm sorry that my resemblance to Angela was such a shock to you. Fitz told me that you and Angela had known each other for a long time. I hadn't realized it might be traumatic for you to see me portraying her. I was thinking of me, trying to get feedback on my professional abilities. Are you all right?"

She reached out to touch me as Angela would have; I drew back.

"Yes. Now that I've seen you walk and can look at you closely, I can see you're not Angela."

"How is my walk different?" she asked, her brow furrowed in concentration.

"You take longer strides."

"Of course. I'm taller. I'll have to remember that when I walk. I know the facial lines are different but the makeup minimizes the differences between my appearance and hers, doesn't it?"

"Yes. I...ah...what shall I call you?"

"Call me Estelle—unless you wish to call me Angela."

"Thank you, Estelle. Please call me Phillip." I paused for a moment trying to remember what I had intended to say before I had the unexpected reaction to her incredible resemblance to Angela. She looked like Angela with a deep tan, Angela as she had been with me in Havana.

She asked, "Is my skin different from hers? You seem to be staring at my bare arms."

"They're the same color as Angela's was when she had a good tan. Are you of Spanish extraction?"

"Mexican and German."

"Your furnishings and decorations all look Spanish."

"They are. Fitz rented this bode and had it furnished like this for me as a stage on which I appear as Angela. He hung her painting there—I don't have her artistic ability—but he accepted that. When you called, I thought it might be Fitz calling to apologize for losing control, interested in resuming the relationship."

"I don't think you'll be seeing Fitz again. As I told you on the phone, he's seeing me because he is in a lifestyle crisis."

"Don't you think that my performance as Angela will help him see their relationship in a better perspective?"

I closed my eyes for a moment to block this false image of Angela that was as real as my fondest memories; I could feel myself losing my own perspective. "No, I don't. Your professional presentation of Angela is superb. You can tell that by my reactions to your Angela persona.

"However, having you as a substitute for Angela is not going to help Fitz move past her death. Fitz and Angela's relationship was limited by factors in their individual identities that they were unwilling to change. Angela's death ended the relationship, but Fitz is still clinging to the idea of Angela. I believe that he has recognized that pretending Angela is alive is of no further use to him."

"Phillip, how much of that belief is rooted in your love for Angela?"

I paused for a second, as though slapped. I forced myself to calmly take a sip of my coffee, then I said, "I loved Angela. I had my own fantasies about her which were no more realistic than Fitz's fantasies. I'm in the process of adjusting to life without Angela because there is no alternative that is acceptable to me.

"Fitz, on the other hand, is in the midst of a major lifestyle crisis; Angela's death and his viewing of *The Crying Clown Rites* are two major factors in that crisis. I want Fitz to be able to reach more of his potential, whatever that might be. My love for Angela is a factor only to the extent that she wanted me to help Fitz to the best of my ability—only if he asked me for it."

"Is there any way I can help?" Estelle asked. "Either in the role of Angela, or as myself?" She sounded both as sincere and as manipulative as Angela might have sounded when she wanted her way.

"You care for Fitz, don't you?" I asked.

"Yes. I wouldn't have accepted the role of Angela if I hadn't felt there was a real possibility of an emotional link between us. Although Fitz canceled my contract verbally, I'm staying here until the rent contract expires at the end of next month in case he changes his mind. He needs help."

"You can help me help him."

"How?" she asked.

"By telling me about your relationship with Fitz and by answering a few questions."

"I'll do that if you'll promise to notify me or have Fitz contact me if there is anything else I can do to help him in the next six weeks. After that I start rehearsing for a secondary role in a musical comedy based on the life of the Green Jinni—musical comedy is what I trained for in the More Fun Community. I tried mummer surrogate work just to get a wide range of emotional content into my experience.

"And what happened to me? I fell into the oldest acting trap of all;

I became emotionally involved in exactly the way the script specified I was to act."

"I understand, Estelle. I don't know if there is any way you can help Fitz as Angela or as Estelle, but if I learn that there is, I'll tell you."

"Good. We've got a contract. What do you want to know?"

"I'd like for you to give me a summary of your relationship with Fitz and let me ask questions about anything that piques my professional interest. Does that suit you?"

"You realize that you're giving an actress an open invitation to talk about her work?"

"Yes," I said, with a smile. "I've known actresses and actors before, both socially and professionally. I perceive that you are secure enough within yourself and in your profession that you don't need to boost your ego by convincing me that you are good at the things you do. I'm already convinced of that."

"Phillip, you're an expert at the limited compliment."

I felt myself blush.

Estelle smiled. "Well, when the agency notified me that Fitz wanted to interview me as a possible surrogate for the late Angela Calderon, I did a quick study of her. I knew Fitz was the son of the late auggie star Zach Baker and that was enough to encourage me to agree to the interview. Usually I don't take surrogate roles which involve a sexual commitment. Not that I suffer from a neo-Puritan hangover, just that I prefer to select my lovers without reference to my professional life. I once portrayed a man's deceased sister for him on his last night on Earth, unaware of the possibility of incest. You see he—"

I interrupted this potentially interesting anecdote to get the conversation back to Fitz and Angela by asking, "what materials did you use for your quick study of Angela?"

"Fitz supplied the agency with her recorded public appearances, a detailed biography, a copy of her letting-go hologram—"

"Fitz had a bootleg copy of Angela's letting-go ceremony."

"Yes, plays it twice a day."

"It's no wonder he had to reject you. Every day he was comparing your performance not only to his memories, which would change with time, but to her final hologram, the one where she appeared as she wanted her final appearance to be."

"It was a tough role to play. I wasn't just a fascinating lover and companion; the role also required that I be his advisor and resolver of doubts. Although he supplied me with all of Angela's papers and a duplicate of her library I don't have the kind of experience and knowledge to make up for the confidence that he sometimes lacked. I hope, now that he has you for a counselor, that I might resume the role of lover and companion."

"You've become very fond of Fitz."

"Yes...while right now Fitz is confused and immature, underneath there's a potentially strong character and an engaging personality. His presentation of himself isn't polished, but he has the capability of being a great actor. If Fitz solves his life problems, his star quality will emerge. You're going to help him aren't you? Help him become the person he was destined to be?"

"To the best of my ability." It was obvious her commitment to Fitz had gone over any professional boundaries.

Estelle continued to tell me of her time in the role of Angela with a few side excursions into her personal and professional life to give me the background for the way she handled the role. I realized that regardless of whether it was Freudian or not, Fitz had looked to Angela for the kind of emotional support that is more commonly sought from a parent than from a lover. As Estelle explained how Fitz described Angela's responses in the daily feedback sessions with Estelle, I saw more evidence that Angela had been using Fitz as a replacement for her dead son Jason.

I knew that at least a portion of that identification was attributable to the influence of Dr. Templeman's neo-Freudianism on Angela. I'd have to talk to Dr. Spellman about that to see if womb expulsion therapy had any remedial effect on parent-child dependence. What I didn't want was Fitz to build a new dependency on me. I was too late to help Angela, but I wasn't too late for Fitz.

After getting a good idea of Estelle's life as Fitz's grief thief, I asked her, "what did you think of *The Crying Clown Rites*?"

"I found it a superbly done bit of theater. A bit bizarre. Full of the brutality that heterosexual males get trapped into when they can't or don't relate to women. Although I'm a little too old, I would have loved to have done Sylvia's role—the young girl Robinson seduces. But there weren't any actors in that production were there?"

Estelle looked worried, as though contemplating a future without acting and actors. She shook her head, as though to clear it, before continuing. "I was completely into the experience of viewing it and didn't realize Fitz was upset until he dashed out of the theater."

"You followed him?"

"Yes. I found him in the alley, beating his fists against the wall."

"What was he saying?"

"Not a thing. Fitz was gulping deep breaths and holding them while smashing the wall. When he couldn't hold his breath anymore, he would stop, gasp, fill his lungs with air and begin again. He didn't say anything intelligible until I touched him and then he turned to me and shouted: "Get away. Get out of my life!"

"Phillip, do you think he'll ever want me back in it?" She touched her face as though remembering Fitz hitting it.

"I doubt it. Probably not in the role of Angela. It is possible, but not likely, that he will be able to recognize you as Estelle in the future. Right now he sees you as an incomplete Angela, whom he doesn't want. I don't think he would want the real Angela either if he weren't in such emotional trouble."

"Are you sure your personal feelings about Angela are not influencing you in saying that?"

I swallowed a mouthful of the same gritty irritation that Angela had provoked in me a few times in the past, maybe even more often than that. "I realized a long time ago that being a therapist was one of the best places to hide emotionally in our society. It's a place where self-examination can easily be avoided by focusing on the problems of others. When I recognized that, I stopped my training and began to explore who I was. I resumed my training when I was satisfied I had found out."

When Estelle gave me the same tolerant grin Angela used to display whenever she claimed I was being smug, I decided it was time to leave. I made a graceful exit but had a night of restless dreams, dreams of Estelle Zimmer and Angela Calderon.

CHAPTER 12

POLITICS AND RELIGION

What we need is not freedom of religion but freedom from religion.
Isobel Grant

When Isobel Grant returned my call, she appeared willing—although not eager—to see me and we arranged a mutually convenient time. Later that afternoon I vaulted to the Sacramento huburb, which was virtually identical to the Philadelphia huburb or any other huburb any place in the world. The huburb was in the shape of a torus with a hub and spokes, an earthbound imitation of the skyisland colonies at the Earth-Luna libration points. The huburbs managed to retain all the disadvantages of the skyislands—inbred communities and restricted architectural horizons—without the environment of space which made the skyislands functional and more daring.

As I looked around at the wheel-shaped facilities for half a million people, the lyrics from an old song danced through my mind; I sang softly to myself in my limited voice "I've seen your cities; they're all the same." Of course, Sacramento being the center of California politics makes the ambiance slightly different. The prime in-group is politically oriented, people with second-rate minds and dubious ethics, political insiders who preach the greatest good for the greatest number while practicing a sophisticated form of thievery, extortion and dishonesty. As I searched for a lift to take me to K level where Isobel Grant's abode was, I felt an almost overwhelming empathy for my client who was haunted by the specter of anarchist Guy Fawkes.

Isobel Grant opened the portal of K2359 after assuring herself of my identity. She looked just as she had on the screen: short cropped blonde hair, almost hairless eyebrows, a small nose with a slight upturn, pale blue eyes set close together, a small mouth and an undistinguished chin. Her body looked solid but her gray smock concealed the shape of her bust and hips as well as obscuring her waistline. The bode's furnishings were much like her, selected to match her plainness, almost as if becoming nondescript were an art form which she was attempting to perfect.

After a perfunctory greeting, Isobel asked, "How is Fitz, Dr. Wendell?"

"He's improving. I've had several sessions with him and I see definite signs of progress."

"What is Fitz's problem this time?"

"The woman he loved was murdered and Fitz was almost killed."

She frowned. She had a one-track mind with a single rail; I was beginning to see the driving force behind some of Fitz's emotional problems. "He always did play around. I knew he was oversexed. Inherited it probably."

"From his mother or his father?" I asked. Trying to explain that sex had nothing to do with Fitz's murder struck me as non-productive; Isobel wasn't interested in any information that didn't reinforce her already set-in-concrete mindset.

"From Mary. Sex was always one of her hobbies. Thought it highly overrated myself. Zach Baker was oversexed too. But who knows if he was Fitz's father or not?"

"Wouldn't Mary Gulik know?"

"Maybe, but that doesn't mean she'd tell."

"Is she a secretive woman?"

"No. Just lies a lot. She once said, 'Revealing the mundane truth is a failure of the imagination.'"

"She sounds like a most unusual woman." I said.

"She is. We aren't alike at all. We're complementary friends, compatible but different. She's a mystic who reads data into random numbers; I'm a militant agnostic with a firm foundation in general semantics. Her causes are sexual, mine political."

"I see. When I talked to you on the screen, you told me that you would be willing to see me but that you didn't want to discuss anything over the phone. Why is that?"

"In Sacramento, the pols tap screens like students tap beer kegs. I've formed the habit of protecting myself and Mary."

"Protecting yourselves from whom?"

Her eyes brightened. "The betrayers of the public trust who buy and scheme their way into political office. Mary wants people to have their full sexual rights and I want people to have their full religious rights. Organized religions should be taxed like any other franchise business."

I started to argue with her—since the political breakup of the thirties, the only groups or institutions that were regularly taxed were those who enjoyed it as a form of masochism or were too large to fit into a teleportation vault, but realized it would be a waste of time and against my own best interest. Instead I said, "I have no quarrel with the way you see things."

"Of course not. You're intelligent and not looking for someone to victimize. Are you politically active?"

"Only to the extent of keeping informed of the issues and the candidates, then casting either a yes vote for the best candidate or a no vote for the most offensive office seeker."

"I have some pamphlets that I want to give you before you go. Tell me one thing; do you think Fitz might go into politics after you counsel him? He ought to be tired of that architecture nonsense by now."

"I'm confident that I can help Fitz through his crisis, but I'm not sure whether he will continue as an architect or not. He hasn't given any indication that he intends to resume his former interest in politics. You encouraged him in his political pursuits, didn't you?"

"Of course. He could have gone into politics and really separated the state from the churches, stopped the religious subsidies and official recognition of religious organizations."

"Does Fitz share your religious views?"

"He did when he lived here. I taught him that when the first Constitution of this country was written, the authors included a requirement for freedom of religion. That wasn't good enough. What we need is freedom from religion. Religious salespersons should have the same status as those in any other kind of sales. Now they use their privileged status to harass citizens, punish those who disagree with them about anything and use public funds for private goals of no scientifically established value."

When she paused for breath, I endeavored to bring the conversation back to my areas of interest by saying, "Did Mary Gulik approve of your politics and how they might influence Fitz?"

"Mary was only interested in politics as it related to sex. If Fitz had gone into politics, she'd have tried to get a government grant for sexual research or a series of art museums devoted to the history of the sexual experience. She wasn't much interested in Fitz after Zach died."

"I'd like to talk to her about Fitz after I talk to you. Can you put me in touch with her?"

"I know where you can find her during the spring college recess, but I don't know where she'll be until then."

"Where?" I asked.

"She'll be staying at the Burdette Hotel on Fifth St. in Atlanta, Georgia. I don't remember the address but it's near the Georgia Tech campus. She'll be registered as Hildegarde Pendragon."

After noting the address on my datapad, I asked, "Can you tell me anything about the circumstances of Fitz's birth? That's one of the main things I wanted to ask his mother about."

"Oh. You've heard about the virgin birth?"

"Virgin birth! No."

"It's a complete fabrication, a story invented by Mary to put on the world. I'll get us some apple cider and tell you about it."

Isobel got up and left the room while I pondered many ramifications of the symbology of virgin birth. She returned quickly with the cider poured into two large earth-colored ceramic mugs. We each sipped the drinks and then she began to speak. "I like children but never intended to have any of my own. I used to babysit for Victor and Varma Young. They had a precocious young son named Omar—I had political hopes for him for a while, but he took up their crusade for sexual freedom through erotic terrorism. I met Mary through the Youngs. She used to join them in their sexual forays."

"What sort of things did they do?"

"Open sexual encounters in public, erotic outrages, public demonstrations, media hypes—the usual stuff. I never cared for it but I'm willing to believe that it does no more harm than any other kind of preaching. Victor Young had grand ideas. He considered himself the spiritual descendant of Felix Pendragon, the founder of the League of Erotic Terrorists. Victor and Varma wanted Zach Baker to perform in an auggie promoting erotic terrorism and they enlisted Mary in the cause."

Isobel Grant wet her throat with a long swallow of apple cider from the plain mug. I asked, "Was the virgin birth idea part of the auggie plot?"

"I don't think so. When Zachary Baker broke a leg and ruptured a disc because a sleeping loft collapsed during the filming of an auggie, he thought someone was trying to kill him. He stayed in a secluded private hospital with guards who were supposed to keep everyone out. Mary claims to have disguised herself as a nurse, slipped into Zach's room where she gave him a blow job, spat the ejaculate into a hypodermic and impregnated herself by using the hypo to perforate her hymen."

"Do you suppose there's any truth to that story?"

"Who knows? It could have happened that way. But if she had a hymen it had been put in by surgery."

I started to laugh—surprised by this display of humor—when she shut me up with a stiff-necked glare.

"Mary," she continued, "was sexually active long before she met Zach Baker."

"Were you around when Fitz was born?"

"Mary had Fitz delivered by a midwife somewhere in New Mexico. When I saw Fitz for the first time as a baby..." She paused for a moment with her head tilted and I thought I saw a tear in one eye. Then she cleared her throat and continued, "Well, he was several months old and already registered as a Citizen."

"Do you believe that Zach Baker was Fitz's father?"

"Mary claimed that. Zach never did. Who knows?"

"Fitz wears a golden PT boat stamped Kennedy around his neck—"

"So he still wears that!" she interrupted.

"Yes," I said. "Fitz told me it was passed down through the family."

"Mary always claimed Marilyn Monroe got it from John Kennedy, and Mary told me that she stole the gold boat from Zach after he died. I should never have told Fitz that story. The first time I saw it around Fitz's neck was after Zach was killed by an arsonist. Fitz threw a temper tantrum here when he realized that Mary wasn't coming back to get him. I told him I'd take away his little golden boat if he ever did that again and we never had any more trouble until he decided that he was a rutting machine like his father. I had to put him on restriction to stop his catting around."

"I know, Fitz mentioned that to me." I did my best to keep my voice neutral.

"I could have helped him study political science here in Sacramento if that Tracton woman hadn't led him to Berkeley by the pubic hairs," Isobel said, practically spitting out the words. "She'd probably still be hanging around him acting like a bitch in heat if she hadn't killed herself."

"She committed suicide!"

"Crashed her floater into a solar-energy collection station."

"When was this?"

"Long time ago. A few months after she took Fitz away from me."

"What was the official verdict on her death?"

"Suicide by misadventure. Fitz thought she'd been murdered; he always did have an over-active imagination. It was all those John Kennedy and Marilyn Monroe stories Mary used to fill his head with. Thought he was royalty as a boy, until I knocked *that* nonsense out of his head. People are still dropping dead all around him, though. He never had much luck with friends, like that college roommate who was murdered. Sounds like things haven't changed much."

"Is there anything else you can tell me about Fitz or the circumstances of his birth?"

"No. Mary told several versions of the virgin conception story but she never said much about his birth. Fitz asked her once if childbirth was painful. She just told him yes and changed the subject like she didn't want to talk about it. Which any woman can understand."

Isobel looked at her old-fashioned wristwatch pointedly.

It was just as well, I was getting anxious to leave her sterile and confining bode. "Thank you very much for your time, Ms. Grant. I must return to Los Angeles. Is there anything that you want me to tell Fitz?"

"He didn't give you any message for me, did he?"

"No."

Her lips drew back as she spoke. "If he asks about me, tell him that I asked about him." She put some pamphlets in my hand before I got out the door and recommended that I purchase a copy of *What Great Men Think of Religion* by Ira D. Cardif at the Samuel Clemens Bookstore next to the vault station.

CHAPTER 13

WOMB EXPULSION THERAPY

I Can Help You Be Born Again.
Wanda Spellman, M.D.

Dr. Wanda Ernesta Spellman, a black-skinned, gray-haired, middle-aged woman with a matronly figure which filled her blue medical tunic, admitted Fitz and me to her suite in the Manhattan tall-wall. She said hello to me and then turned to Fitz. "Fitzgerald Baker, I'm pleased to meet you. Dr. Wendell didn't mention what a handsome man you are."

"Thank you. I'm looking forward to today's experience."

Fitz was making an effort to be charming and interesting, and he no longer wore the medpack strapped to his arm. It boded well that he was once more relating to the world in an active, positive manner. The amount of his personality exhibited in interactions had steadily increased since his first appointment with me.

"I know that Dr. Wendell has discussed womb expulsion therapy with you," Dr. Spellman said. "However, I thought that I would give you a summary now so you can ask any questions you might have. Please sit down, both of you."

Fitz and I sat down on one of a pair of semi-circular couches. Dr. Spellman sat opposite us. When we were all settled, she continued.

"Dr. Otto Rank, in 1924, published *The Trauma of Birth* which explained a psychological system built upon Sigmund Freud's statement that the infant's physiological responses at birth remain the prototype of later anxiety. The cardiac and respiratory acceleration, the overwhelming sensory stimulation becomes the basic pattern on which future anxiety is overlaid.

"Life in the womb is blissful and the shock of separation from the intrauterine environment creates a primal imprint on the consciousness of an individual. The split between mother and child at birth is a major change to which both must adapt. The child loses the only intimate contact known. What the child gains, ideally, is intimate contact with a loving family.

"If the child does not experience a nurturing environment, if the intimate contact is not reestablished or is withdrawn, the child's emotional development is often retarded and distorted."

Dr. Spellman paused for a moment, giving Fitz or me a chance to speak. I had discussed the theory and practice of womb expulsion therapy with her previously. Fitz said nothing and Dr. Spellman continued.

"Dr. Stanislav Grof, some years after Rank's death, used Rank's conceptual framework in his own theory which divided the perinatal experience into four perinatal matrices—"

Fitz asked, "What does perinatal mean, exactly?"

"It means occurring at the time of birth. The first matrix is primal union with the mother, the intrauterine experience before the onset of delivery. The second is antagonism with the mother caused first by chemical changes and then by contractions in a closed uterine system, closed because the cervix has not yet opened. Third is synergism with the mother; the cervix is open and the process of propulsion through the birth canal is accomplished by joint effort of mother and child. The final stage, the fourth matrix, is separation from the mother, the ending of the symbiotic union and the beginning of a new type of relationship.

"If that's clear to you, I'll describe the procedure of womb expulsion." She paused.

Fitz and I nodded to show our understanding.

Dr. Spellman looked at Fitz and said, "To begin with, you will relax in the womb room, gently supported in a saline solution so you will feel like you are floating. The background sounds will be a simulation of the mother's heartbeat and the gentle sounds of fluid in motion. The foreground will be a hypnotic tape that will help you regress to the first perinatal matrix."

Fitz stopped Dr. Spellman's flow of words by saying, "I've had a number of experiences I'm not at all interested in reliving. Hypnotic regression sounds dangerous. I don't want to re-experience my traumas."

"That won't happen, Mr. Baker. The tape moves you back along your time line from one mildly pleasant experience to another. The regression will be smooth and benign."

To reassure Fitz, I added, "I've listened to the tape and I'm certain that it won't cause you any anxiety."

Fitz said, "Thank you." to me and "Please continue." to Dr. Spellman.

She smiled at both of us. "Once you are regressed back to the womb, a second tape will be played. This tape will prepare you for your union with two nonphysical beings. In Jungian terms, the anima and the animus. In religious terms, the goddess and the god with you as the godling. I like to think of them as the eternal mother and the eternal father, but some people perceive them as two guardians or aspects of the individual functioning at the supraself level.

"Your guardians will be with you during the first perinatal matrix. You will be as aware of them then as you are of Dr. Wendell and me now. They will leave you during the second matrix to rejoin you in the fourth matrix for a lasting relationship that will help you come to terms with your past and be ready for the future."

Dr. Spellman paused to see if Fitz had any further reservations about the procedure.

"The guardians are a new concept to me," said Fitz. "I'm not sure that the procedure will work or be of any benefit."

"The procedure works for almost everyone with a high degree of success. The guardians are an old concept, frequently invoked during initiations into the Middle Eastern mystic groups, the Greek mystery schools, magical organizations, Silva mind control, Yacqui warrior knowledge, Australian Aborigine dreamtime, Arica, Dr. Modesto's centralism and others."

I said, "Fitz, you can look at this experience as a rite of passage toward individuation. It will be a great help in dealing with the traumatic experiences you've had."

"How?"

"After you experience your birth and reunion with the guardians, Dr. Spellman and I will guide you along your time line to the present. The guardians will help you look at the events in your life with a mature viewpoint. That will resolve some conflicts easily. Others will require that Dr. Spellman and I assist. If there are any traumas that require more attention than can be given them during this session—and that may well be the case—those traumatic experiences will be left in the care of the guardians so they can be dealt with in appropriate future therapy sessions."

The three of us tied up the conversational loose ends and entered the womb room. Dr. Spellman asked Fitz to disrobe. Then she guided him into the rubbery womb simulator, had him lie down in the saline solution with his head supported near the opening to the chute that represented the birth canal. I noticed her eyes spent more time on Fitz than they did on the controls.

On the way back to the console, she turned to me and said, "Fitzgerald does bear an uncanny likeness to former President John F. Kennedy. I thought your story was complete bunk until I laid my eyes on him. I've always had this fantasy about going back in time to the early nineteen-sixties, Camelot—as it was called. I'm from an old Boston Black family myself, or Boston Brahmans as we were called in those less enlightened times. I would have done a lot to help the Civil Rights Movement—maybe even met the President. I was a lot prettier when I was a girl. And we all know how much *he* liked girls."

Nonplussed, I had to focus on each word as I talked to keep from stammering. "Fitz does bear a likeness to his great-grandfather." It was hard to imagine Dr. Spellman having such an active fantasy life, but placid exteriors often held banked fires. Serge had remarked on more than one occasion that I depended too much on surface appearances; I'd have to take that criticism more seriously.

"Likeness! He could be his twin brother. If it wasn't for the Cloning Laws..."

When we got back to her control console, Dr. Spellman motioned for me to sit down beside her. She pressed the keys on her control panel and the womb opening began to close. From the invisible breathing opening in the top of the womb, I could hear the heartbeat sound and the fluid murmurs as the recording began with "Tense your toes. Feel the tension in the muscles. Now release the tension..."

As the recording continued, instructing Fitz in a systematic relaxation technique, Dr. Spellman turned to me and said, "Fitz can't hear us but we will hear him. The womb mike will pick up anything he says. Although he will soon perceive himself as a fetus, his responses will have the characteristics of an adult."

"Good. I have great hopes for his development through this symbolic rebirth."

The recording was now instructing Fitz in deep breathing and focusing on the warmth he felt. The neutral voice said, "Through your closed eyes you can sense a warm glow, a reddish orange glow like sunlight perceived through eyelids. A little later you will see two points of white light. Those two lights will become two beings that will guide and help you."

I had to make a mental effort to stay alert; Dr. Spellman's recording was effective.

Dr. Spellman looked at the monitor controls on her console and said, "Mr. Baker should be in a state of oceanic bliss now. I'll verify that."

She flipped a switch that amplified the sounds from inside the womb simulator and asked Fitz via her intercom, "How are you?"

Fitz's voice sounded deeper, more relaxed than I'd ever heard it when he answered, "Light and energy are enveloping me. Everything is right."

"Are the two guardians with you?" Dr. Spellman asked.

"Yes, they are here."

"Good. When they leave, you will have additional experiences and then they will rejoin you to remain with you forever."

"Must you leave?" Fitz asked.

Evidently Fitz was questioning the guardians. Dr. Spellman cut off the intercom and said to me, "I'll let him have a few more moments with the guardians and then we'll move him into perinatal matrix two."

"What happens next?"

She answered, "With this control I'll add traces of decomposed blood and iron rust to simulate the chemical changes that occur in the womb just before the contractions begin."

"What will Fitz experience when you do that?"

"We'll ask. The usual symptoms are much like a severe alcoholic hangover."

Approximately five minutes after she pulled the switch that released the blood and iron, I heard Fitz making sputtering noises."

"What's happening?" asked Dr. Spellman.

There was a gagging noise, then Fitz cried out, "I feel sick. Ah... I'm being poisoned!"

Dr. Spellman turned her head and said, "It's time to start the contractions. She turned a knob to the right and I could see the rubbery outside of the womb simulator tighten as if a partial vacuum had been created inside. Intellectually I knew that the effect was created by metal arms embedded in the latex skin, but it looked like a huge invisible hand was squeezing a syringe.

From inside the closed womb, Fitz cried, "Demons, monsters, THE CLOWN WITH THE BLUE FACE!"

The contractions increased in frequency and severity.

"No exit. NO EXIT." Fitz was shouting at the top of his voice. I looked at Dr. Spellman; she smiled back to reassure me.

"I'm in hell and there's no exit!"

In her professional voice, Dr. Spellman said, "There's always some confusion and disorientation during the birth procedure."

"HELP! HELP!" These cries were followed by a paroxysm of coughing and shuddering.

Dr. Spellman continued, "He must experience the negative aspects of the womb to be ready to leave it.

"NIGHT. DARKNESS. MY SOUL IS DYING! I'M FORSAKEN. THERE IS NO EXIT."

Taking that as her cue, Dr. Spellman pressed a button and I could see the cervix begin to open. "Phase two is over and phase three begins."

Through the cervix opening, I could see Fitz struggling, simulating the muscular movement the fetus must make to promote birth.

"What are you experiencing?" Dr. Spellman asked.

"PAIN. Too much pain… Shit. Piss. Blood. Mucus. And that cord is in my way. HELP ME!"

"That's all very typical. The experience is painful and the fact that he is aware of the umbilical cord is good. It means he is ready for birth."

Dr. Spellman turned a handle on her console and the top of Fitz's head emerged slowly from the cervix. I heard him sputter, "The pain, the goddamn pain. I'm suffocating! Can't you see?" His voice was hoarse.

"Dr. Spellman, is he short of air? His voice sounds thin and forced."

Before she could answer, Fitz—in more of a croak than a voice—asked, "Are you blind?"

Dr. Spellman turned the handle all the way to the right, Fitz—gleaming from some lubricant—was expelled from the womb onto the cushioned foam before us. His face was blue. Spellman was frozen at the console.

I jumped up, ran over and snatched the twisted chain around Fitz's neck and jerked hard. The chain broke and slipped out of my hand leaving the golden boat. Fitz gasped and then began to breathe.

I looked at Dr. Spellman; she was staring at Fitz's erection. I yelled, "Get some Thorazine!"

She ran over to a large white cabinet and returned with a hypospray. After we got the Thorazine into Fitz, he started to breathe normally. "I'm sorry. I didn't notice that he was wearing any jewelry when he went into the womb."

I was too angry to answer coherently.

By the time Fitz was feeling the effects of the Thorazine, I had my own feelings contained. I reassured myself that no experience or experiment was a failure.

"I'm sorry," she said, shaking her head. "I don't know how that could have happened. My procedures are strict and I don't deviate from them."

If you'd have paid more attention to your job than Fitz's genitals, this would not have happened, I thought. "I think you might want to re-evaluate your procedures, Dr. Spellman."

"You won't report this, will you?"

I shook my head in disgust. I didn't see any value in reporting her to the American Psychological Association, a toothless organization if there ever was one, and since there were no permanent physical injuries the New York Police Department wouldn't be interested.

We agreed that phase four couldn't be initiated now. When Fitz was ready to travel, I took him back to Los Angeles. Neither of us was sure the rebirth was what we had intended it to be, but I assured Fitz that he had undergone an experience that would help me to deal with his lifestyle crisis—I hoped my optimism would be justified by future events.

CHAPTER 14

MOTHER MARY

Sex is too important to be taken seriously.
Mary Gulik

After the aborted womb expulsion therapy, Fitz suffered a setback: his mood was withdrawn and he seemed uninterested in the flow of life. Dr. Spellman had suggested another session to unite Fitz with the guardians he had experienced during the first stage of her therapy. Since Fitz's crisis symptoms had not occurred previously among her clients, I had serious reservations about subjecting him to what would be an experimental session with no firm guidelines. And, in light of her 'personal' and unprofessional interest in Fitz, I was leery of anything else she might suggest.

When I discussed the matter with Fitz, he said, "I would be interested to know if what happened during my rebirth was a reenactment of my birth. Other than that, I have no interest in the experience. I don't remember any guardians and I don't want to remember them."

I, like Fitz, was interested in whether or not the birth simulation echoed his own perinatal experiences. My eagerness to talk with Mary

Gulik had increased proportionately; I was pleased when she called me shortly after I screened the Burdette Hotel in Atlanta, Georgia. The hotel had had a reservation for Mary under the name Isobel Grant had told me she would be using, Hildegarde Pendragon.

On the screen, I saw a woman approximately my age with reddish brown hair that was thick and full. Her hair had graceful waves that ended in a slight curl where her hair stopped at the neckline, as abruptly as if it had been cut by a guillotine. She had a prominent nose and a firm chin line. Although she was not a classically pretty woman, she was strikingly handsome. Her makeup was as bold as the canvases of the expressionists. She reminded me of a painting by Jawlensky I had seen in the Norton Simon Museum. Her first words were, "I'm Hildegarde. I presume you are Phillip."

"I am. I'd like to talk with you about Fitzgerald."

"She looked at me archly and said, "I don't recall having a client named Fitzgerald and I never discuss such things over the phone."

"Your son, Fitzgerald Baker, is my client. I'm his lifestyle crisis counselor. I'd like to discuss him with you in person. Perhaps, later today?"

"My schedule is full this evening."

"Tomorrow then. Breakfast, brunch, lunch, tiffin or dinner, whatever is convenient."

With a mixture of coyness and lasciviousness, she asked, "Are you willing to pay for my time?"

I knew she was looking for an emotional response to work off of, so I kept my face blank and said yes.

"At what rate?"

"The same rate as I charge for my time."

"Then I'll buy brunch," she said with a smile that made me feel as though I'd just passed some type of test. "Here in room 523 at 1100 and be prompt."

She cut me off before I could reply. It seemed that Mary Gulik had many of the same traits that had made Angela both engaging and exhausting at the same time—but never dull. Maybe there were more similarities than differences between Fitz and myself—I shoved that thought away and began making arrangements to reschedule my appointments for tomorrow. One client, who believed he was being persecuted by a conspiracy of holly programmers, was sure that I had been suborned by sinister forces. I spent so long reassuring him I was late for my next client; I wondered what they all would do if *I* had a lifestyle crisis.

I rose early the next morning and teleported to the northwest Atlanta vault station, arriving early enough to walk to the Burdette Hotel on Fifth. I knocked on the unscreened door at 1055.

"Come in, Phillip," Mary Gulik said. She was wearing a courtesan's peignoir of pastel green that was almost the color of her eyes. It was mostly open in front, showing the swell of her breasts and a flash of thigh when she turned to usher me in.

I said hello as I tried to decide on the best approach. I had been too long without a woman not to be interested, but she was the mother of one of my clients; not that she seemed worried about any relationship between Fitz and me. I knew from both Fitz and Isobel that she could be difficult and enjoyed improving upon the truth so I was certain that any stuffiness on my part would make me fair game for a put on or mind games. I decided to be relaxed and let her define our roles, which I was sure she'd do with or without my help.

"May I call you Mary?" I asked.

"Don't use that name today. Today I'm Hildegarde, a historic figure of sexual expression, a legend in her own time."

Entering into the spirit of her game, I said, "Hello, Hildegarde. Having brunch with you is a dramatic way for this day to start."

"I do admire a man who is not only prompt but also fast on the uptake. Do you like fast women?"

"Of course. They can be the best kind."

She walked over to the autoserv, giving me a chance to appreciate the curve of her hips, and began putting the meal on the small table. I looked around; the room was dominated by a king size bed. I was beginning to think I was going to have less to say about the direction of this meeting than I'd planned.

She recaptured my attention by saying, "It's charming that you like fast women. I've never understood the prejudice that some men have against them. If the man is interested, his chances with a fast woman are better; if he isn't interested, why should he care at all about her sexual habits? Isobel told me that you're a lifestyle crisis counselor and know all about strange behavior. Can you tell me why some men are hostile to sexually active women?"

"Could be any of several reasons or a combination of them: sexual insecurity, repression, paranoia, ignorance and envy are the most common."

As she set out the eggs benedict and champagne, she said, "I do believe that you know what you're talking about. Felix Pendragon couldn't have said it better. Will you pop my cork for me?"

As I opened the bottle of champagne, I asked, "Are Felix Pendragon and Hildegarde related?"

"Only in the hot blooded sense. Not by bloodlines. Both were celebrants of the sexual experience."

I punctuated her sentence with the pop of the cork.

"You're timing is admirable, Phillip. Will you pour?"

I poured the bubbly liquid into two champagne glasses and extended one toward her.

"Just put it on the table, darling. I don't want to touch yet. Not even fingers. It would break the sexual tension."

She picked up the glass with long, slim fingers. Her nails were bright red and starred with diamond dust. She raised the glass and said, "To Felix Pendragon, founder of the League of Erotic Terrorists and benefactor of humanity."

"Felix Pendragon is an unusual name. Was it his birth name?"

"No more than Hildegarde, who is now my spirit guide." She moved her long legs in such a way I could hear the silk whisper of her peignoir as it rubbed together, causing me to wonder if she wore anything underneath.

I hadn't realized how dry my throat was until I saw that I had drained my glass. She finished hers and said, "Fill them again. Your turn to make the toast."

I filled the glasses and said, "To increased sexual awareness."

"You are a most interesting gentleman, Phillip, and quite handsome. The touch of gray in the hair and the hint of a receding hairline give you that experienced look, a look quite different from most of the males in the life of Hildegarde."

"Tell me about Hildegarde."

"See how you are. You are charming and devious. Getting a lady to talk about herself. Intoxicating her with champagne and clever talk. I know you are interested in knowing about Fitz and I may tell you, but first I'll tell you about Hildegarde while we eat."

We sat down and began the meal; I moved slowly as my head was beginning to float. I needed some food to balance the alcohol intake on an empty stomach.

"The records on Hildegarde never gave her last name. Her first name may have been an alias. She was a legendary figure of sexual expression like Mary Magdalene, Poppaea Sabina, and Maria Theresa, Catherine the Great, Isadora Duncan, Alysson Dancer and Robin Jefferson. I used the last name of Pendragon because she was a contemporary of Felix Pendragon. He may even have known her. She toured the southern college circuit and was frequently in Atlanta when Felix helped form the first interracial sexual freedom group here when the general level of consciousness was so low that schools were segregated on the basis of color and, sometimes, gender. Some people even took pride in such ignorance. Can you imagine such a thing?"

"I can imagine it. I've seen ignorance in action before. What did Hildegarde do on the college circuit? Lecture? Demonstrate?"

"Oh, no. She was a whore. She copped with sexually starved students for a reasonable fee. Hildegarde made enough to live her life in the style she desired. She wasn't the legendary whore with a heart of gold; she was a whore who gave good service and was willing to make change."

When she paused to take another mouthful of the eggs, I asked, "What was Hildegarde's background?"

"She was of a genteel southern family, a patriot during Hitler's War, one of the dedicated Victory Girls. Are you familiar with Victory Girls?"

I paused with my filled fork on the way to my mouth and said, "No, I'm not. Who were they?"

"They were the dedicated women who contributed to the health and well-being of service men by copping with them. After the war they got a lot of bad press and Hildegarde shifted her attention to the veterans going to college on the G.I. Bill of Rights. She turned professional and worked the college circuit for the next two decades, giving sexual solace to the oppressed minority group called students."

I poured more champagne, since our flutes were empty. Mary lowered heavy lidded eyes and said, "Phillip, I do believe you are plying me with this bubbly brew."

Answering in the same pseudo sophisticated southern style, I said, "What kind of gentleman would I be if I asked a lady questions while she had a parched throat?"

"You do have marvelous manners. I've quite forgotten what I was saying."

"You were telling me of the legendary Hildegarde, but you hadn't yet told me why you are here as her."

"I am here on a prurient pilgrimage, honoring Hildegarde by a reenactment of her famous fraternity row gang bangs. Students still need sex at Georgia Tech even though the days when southern girls only copped for love or because the boy was just too cute to resist are over. Timid youths with brains are still pushed into technical disciplines. I'm here to do the same as Hildegarde. To cop like crazy with those who are ready and terrorize the rest by the example of sexual freedom in action.

"Tonight, while most of the students are off campus for spring recess, I'll knock at the door of the Phi Kappa house and ask for the member in charge of sexual recreation. Some of my partners will have the sexual experience of their lives. I'll help those introverted future engineers develop their social and sexual skills as my contribution to the tradition of service that Hildegarde knew so well."

By this time we had finished our meal and half the champagne. I asked, "Shall I pour you some more?"

"Yes, but I must lie down after brunch. We southern ladies are prone to attacks of frailty you know. Bring your chair over beside the bed."

I put the champagne and the glasses on the bedside table and then brought my chair to the right side of the bed. She lay down, propped up by pillows in a manner that exposed one breast. She pressed her empty glass over her breast and said, "I want you to lick that drop off my nipple."

"Would you answer a question while I do?"

"I just might."

"How did you meet Zach Baker?" I asked and began teasing her nipple with my tongue."

"I fell in love with him when I saw the auggie *Fucking Around on Friday*. My friend and companion in erotic terrorism, Victor Young, who wanted Zach to do a film promoting the League of Erotic Terrorists, introduced me to him."

I raised my head when she stopped talking. She exposed the other breast, picked up the champagne bottle and let a few drops spill on the dry nipple. She winked at me and asked, "Do you have another question?"

"Was Fitz's birth difficult?"

"Yes, he almost strangled on the umbilical cord. I think the midwife went into religious ecstasy when she saw his head break through the hymen. I know that Isobel told you about the immaculate conception and the virgin birth, so I don't have to tell you about that."

She stopped talking. I stopped licking. She opened her peignoir completely, revealing round breasts, a smooth stomach and a thatch of brownish pubic hair. She held the champagne in her right hand, poised above her body, and said, "You get one question."

"Was Zach Fitz's father and did he give you the golden PT boat for Fitz?"

Splashing the rest of the champagne over her stomach and thighs, she said, "That's two questions, you charming seducer, but I'll answer them while you finish the champagne.

I moved over to the bed. Mary unzipped my jumpsuit with a practiced hand.

"Zach never formally recognized Fitz as his child, but there was never any doubt in my mind as to how and when I got pregnant. Zach intended for the Kennedy boat to be interred with him in the Motion Picture Hall of Fame. I wanted Fitz to have it so he would have the security of knowing his ancestry, a security I never had. I had to cop with a security guard and a creepy mortuary attendant to get it, but if you tell Fitz that, I can prove it didn't happen that way."

She pushed me over on my back and guided my erect member into her moist vagina. I started to say something and she put her fingers in my mouth while saying, "Remember to call me Hildegarde."

We copped with a familiarity rare among first-time lovers. When the rhythm reached its supreme level of intensity, she said, "Come with me, Phillip."

I exploded and moaned "Hildegarde" at the same time, just as she had programmed me to.

Later, as I left the Burdette Hotel and headed west to Los Angeles, I wondered if she had told me the truth. Perhaps she had, perhaps not. At least her physical response had been honest; I had forgotten to give her the fee for her time and she had forgotten to ask for it.

CHAPTER 15

LUNCH WITH SERGE

An old house is best to burn, old horse to ride, old books to read, and old wine to drink, so are old friends more trusty to use.
Leonard Wright

When Fitz came into my office for his next appointment, I told him that I had met his mother and she had told me how he had almost strangled at birth, which confirmed the reality of his experience with Dr. Spellman.

"Are you sure she told the truth?" he asked. "She devotes a lot of her energy to putting on the world."

"I believe she told me the truth about that. When she was thinking about something else, I asked her if your birth was difficult, giving her no clue as to whether or not I suspected any specific difficulty. Her response was immediate. She said you'd almost strangled on the umbilical cord. She didn't elaborate, which, according to what you and Isobel Grant told me, is her pattern when she's lying."

Fitz's eyes seemed to bore into mine. "That means there was something else she was thinking about, was it sex with you?"

I hadn't thought much about my experience with Mary, maybe

because it had been inevitable from the moment we met, maybe because I hadn't wanted to think that it might have run counter to the best interests of my client. It wasn't as if I had seduced her….

"Yes, Mary and I found each other sexually attractive." I tried to keep from cringing.

"You copped with her, didn't you?"

While there was no accusation in the tone of Fitz's voice, there was an intangible sense of great emotion being held tightly in thrall. I wished that I could give him any other answer but the truth. Wearily, I said, "Yes, we made love together."

I saw no overt sign of disapproval from Fitz, but there was a shift in his posture and in the air. I felt as though I were diminished in his eyes and it left a bitter aftertaste in my mouth. I resolved not to repeat this mistake. It was not one I'd ever made before, but the meeting had been so 'staged' that it hadn't seemed real—more like something out of a farce, and I had responded in kind. Incorrectly, as it turned out.

Neither of us spoke for some time. Finally, I broke the silence, saying, "Fitz, I want to apologize for my unprofessional behavior. I didn't give you or your mother the respect both of you deserve. If you'd like a referral and the name of another counselor I'll do my best to match you up with a good one."

Fitz shook his head. "That's not what I want. That's not what Angela wanted either. My mother is a manipulative, man-hating bitch. You didn't stand a chance. She uses her sex as a weapon against me, my manhood, my friends—even my girlfriends, she would seduce them too."

"She struck me as unconventional, Fitz, but I didn't see any evidence of hatred or contempt towards me or men in general."

"Of course not. She was in her 'seductress' role, a part that she plays to perfection. She's had so much practice. She tried it on me, too—Don't look so shocked!"

"It's hard to believe. She's an attractive woman; she doesn't…"

"Of course, but not if you knew her. True, I am her son, but she's like a Cuckoo bird; she laid the egg in my aunt's nest and flew away. She only returned to perform my 'sexual initiation,' as she called it: 'to learn good sexual technique and hygiene from someone qualified.' I rejected her—and she's never forgiven me. Nor have *I* forgiven her!"

Today there were very few behaviors that were frowned on, unlike the Neo-Puritan days of the Thirties; however, incest was one behavior still almost universally condemned. I didn't want to believe Fitz, but he was very convincing....

However, I needed to get the focus of our conversation back on Fitz; not on my non-professional and idiotic behavior with his mother. "Fitz, I'd like to know what is going on in your life. Have you seen your partner Clyde Burbank lately?"

"No. Clyde is taking care of the business without me."

"What are you doing to fill your time?"

"Twice a week I go to the Sufi dancing meditation class, the one that was on your list of suggested activities."

"Do you like the experience?" I asked.

"Yes. It's made me aware that the information I received about religion from Aunt Isobel was distorted by her political viewpoints and her relentless atheism. I've decided to do some reading about various religions and make up my own mind on the subject."

"Have you made any friends in the Sufi group?"

"All of the people in the group are friendly toward me."

I remembered Fitz telling me right after Angela's death that he didn't make enemies. My suspicions were that he wasn't making friends, either. I asked, "Do you have any close friends that you see regularly?"

"No."

"Have you begun or resumed a relationship with a woman since Estelle?"

"Who?" He appeared puzzled.

"Estelle Zimmer, the professional mummer."

"NO," he shouted, then turned red and looked apologetic.

"Fitz would you be willing for me to join you at your next Sufi class? I've done it before so I won't have trouble finding the group rhythm and the teacher knows me."

Fitz paused briefly, then said, "Fine."

"When is the next meeting?"

"Monday evening, but I'm not sure I'm going. Clyde invited me to a lecture on reef and aquadome structures that I may go to: I'll screen you if I decide to go to the Sufi class."

The remainder of the session moved along as if our therapeutic relationship were in a holding pattern. I had to get closer to Fitz. Joining the Sufi class would help, but I had to see him more often than once a week. I hoped my lapse in judgment hadn't created an impediment to his therapy; if so, it might be time for me to reevaluate my own career.

Maybe I should refer him to some other practitioner? No. He needed someone who understood his grief. How would he feel if I recommended another therapist? He might decide no one could help him, or wanted to. Fitz had experienced enough rejection in his life, and I wasn't about to contribute more. I would stand by him to the end—as Angela had wanted.

When Fitz didn't call on the following Monday I assumed he went to the underwater architecture lecture with Clyde. During the week I had compiled a list of activities that I could suggest to Fitz as joint adventures: The Hidden Wonders of India Tour with the beautiful Shirali twins; The Little Big Horn Powwow; an exploration of the newly discovered underwater temples in the Tuamotu Archipelago; Bastille Day celebrations in Martinique and Haiti; the Lawrence Durrell readers tour of Alexandria, complete with actors to portray the characters in his Alexandria Quartet; or the Western European gourmet's junket of major cities. If he showed a lack of interest in any of these earthbound entertainments, I'd get a printout from Off-World Travels or Labyrinth Tours. The Labyrinth was an enormous alien structure discovered in the asteroid belt almost twenty years ago.

I was determined not to let Fitz remain an uninvolved bystander in life.

I was still lost in thought, considering various vacation plans, when the screen chimed. I answered it and was greeted by Serge.

"Phillip, how are you?"

"Fine. And you?"

He smiled and shrugged his shoulders.

From his telltale actions I knew he needed a favor. "What's the problem?"

"I have a patient here at the clinic that I'd like you to talk to."

"Is it serious?"

"No, she's going to be okay. Just a case of too much nutmeg in some apple pie eaten on an empty stomach."

"Is this another of your romantic Latin schemes to get me involved with another woman?"

"Phillip, I'm as innocent as a virtuous altar boy. Besides the woman is happily married and old enough to be your great-grandmother. The nutmeg overdose, in addition to making her sick, gave her some kind of religious, mystical experience. She wanted to discuss it with someone and, knowing your interest in such things, I thought of you."

"Thanks, Serge. Is tomorrow morning a good time?"

"How about 1100 and then you and I can have lunch together afterward?"

"Fine, Serge. I'll see you tomorrow."

"Ciao, Phillip."

At 1150 the next morning, Serge and I were sitting at a small sidewalk restaurant near his clinic, eating huge submarine sandwiches and drinking coffee. Between bites Serge asked, "So you reassured my patient, convinced her that her experience was completely normal?"

"Completely normal but uncommon. I told her about Bucke's *Cosmic Consciousness* and some of the more recent books that detail mystical experiences. It was a very positive event in her long life; she's lost her fear of death now that she's had what she considers a preview of the after-death existence."

"Thanks, Phillip. I knew I could count on you." Then, in his jocular manner, he asked, "Are you going to apologize for suspecting me of ulterior motives."

"Of course not. You always have ulterior motives. It's part of your alleged charm."

"Alleged charm!" he cried out, like a Scientific Hedonist accused of chastity. Then he laughed, putting a sparkle in his eyes and showing his large, white teeth. "You look and sound good, Phillip. How goes the practice?"

"Well, or at least reasonably well. I'm not making as much progress with Fitz as I had hoped, but I think it will work out. Setbacks have to be accepted for what they are. Karl Kashubian, the holowriter, is doing better."

"Setbacks. What setbacks?"

"I took Fitz to New York to go through Dr. Spellman's womb expulsion therapy. It was an unpleasant experience for him but it may have provided some valuable data."

"My friend, when you talk of an unpleasant experience and possibly valuable data, I suspect a catastrophe that stopped just short of disaster. Tell me about it, Phillip."

"Neither Dr. Spellman nor I noticed that Fitz didn't remove that golden PT boat he wears on a chain around his neck. When the birth simulation was taking place, he almost strangled on the twisted chain. We had to stop the therapy."

"How did Spellman miss his chain and PT boat? That's not an insignificant item on a naked man—I assume he was in his birthday suit for this so-called therapy."

"I fear the good doctor acted in a less than professional manner."

"Phillip, cut out the circumlocution. What exactly is 'acted in a less than professional manner' in lay terms?"

"Dr. Spellman was too busy ogling his erect penis to pay attention to her job."

Serge threw up his hands. "His erect penis! Phillip, where do you find these so-called therapists? You spend way too much time on the Coconet! What brought all this about—if there is an explanation?"

"Spellman's a Kennedyophile, in love with the late John F. Kennedy. She has some fantasy about going back in time and helping JFK with the Civil Rights Movement. She saw Fitz, noted the uncanny resemblance, and lost her focus on what she was doing."

"Lost her mind is more like it! Are you going to file charges with the APA?"

"It's hard to prove and the most they'd do is write her up; the Association is just about worthless these days now that anyone with a shingle can set up practice."

"What data did you get that justifies this kind of danger?"

"We didn't know there was any danger. We weren't doing any trade-off analysis between danger and data. The data suggests Fitz had a difficult birth. That explains, or at least helps explain, the distance between him and his mother."

"Phillip, are you telling me you believe that Fitz's inability to adjust to Angela's death is directly tied into his relationship with his mother? No, don't tell me you've taken to reading Templeman."

I tried to ignore Serge's cheap shot and swallowed the bite of sandwich I'd just taken—it went down like an oversized wood chip. I took a deep sip of black coffee and then said, "Fitz's mother is a very complex woman. She's been an erotic terrorist all her adult life, intent on making herself a living legend at the expense of the truth, other people's belief systems and behavioral norms. She's an extraordinary woman, vibrant, erotic, attractive, and quite devious.

When I stopped talking, Serge didn't say anything. I was unable to decipher the look on his face. I took another sip of coffee; he remained silent. "Say it."

"Say what?"

"Whatever you're thinking, Serge. Whatever's behind that pensive look."

"The situation got out of control with Fitz's mother, didn't it?"

"What makes you think that?"

"Phillip. You call me a romantic Latin, but there's a strong romantic streak in you. I know you, Phillip. From the way you spoke of her, I knew that you'd seen her. But it's gone further than that, hasn't it? She seduced you. It shows in the way you speak of her and the way your face is turning red."

I looked away as he answered, feeling a growing sense of shame. Where was my life heading? Angela's death had put me into this slide. Or had things always been this way? Angela had never had any trouble working her wiles on me. Yes, I had enjoyed letting her have her way—as long as I had gotten what I wanted. But when she had tried to maneuver me into joining her clinic, I had shut her out. My professional life had always been my last bastion—now it was slipping out of my control, as well. Maybe it was time I started taking more direct control over my life, or at least admitting my own culpability. "Am I that obvious?"

"To me, you are," said Serge. "But, perhaps, not so obvious to others. How are you going to handle it when Fitz learns you've had intercourse with his mother?"

The way Serge said it made it sound ugly, sad—maybe even pathetic. "He already knows. I told him. He wasn't even surprised."

"How did you handle his anger?" he asked.

"He showed no evidence of anger. Fitz knows his mother and her predilections. Not every man resents every lover that his mother takes."

Serge slowly shook his large head. "Not showing and not having are two different things, my friend. Even if he knows from a logical point of view that he shouldn't reject you or be angry with you, he may still resent your sexual knowledge of his mother. That's especially true if he has memories of being rejected by her."

I kept my voice calm so I wouldn't sound as defensive as I felt inside. "Serge, I don't deny what you say. Fitz does feel that his mother rejected him, but he seems to accept her active sex life. I can't believe that he will allow my encounter with his mother to stop his progress. I may be having problems finding the right approach to helping Fitz, but I am getting closer. He's had problems with every woman in his life. Right now, I'm beginning to learn about those difficulties. I've met his mother, the aunt who raised him and the mummer surrogate he hired to emulate Angela. I believe he has to understand the relationships he's had with all the important women in his life so that he can cope with the loss of Angela."

"Phillip, you may be right. I hope you are. I'm tempted to believe you have everything under control, but I don't quite buy it. There's a tenseness about you I don't like, and you're having a hard time meeting my eyes. I'm not personally convinced you've come to terms yourself with Angela's death. Friend...she did you no favor by wishing Fitz on you as a client. She couldn't help him enough for him to function without her, or maybe that's the way she wanted it.

"Sometimes I get the feeling she's controlling the both of you from the grave." He laughed in a way that sent chills up and down my spine. Then he asked, "Can you tell me how much of your investigation into the women in Fitz's life is motivated by your desire to compare them with Angela?"

"A minuscule amount. I've come to terms with her death. I've even accepted that the relationship I had with her was more limited than I fantasized it to be."

Serge reached over the table and put his hand on top of mine. "I remember the talk we had about her just before she died."

In a sudden burst of memory I recalled the feelings I'd had that evening, the certainty that Angela would soon be mine. I had to bite down to keep the tears out of my eyes.

"Since Angela," I blurted out, "I haven't pursued many women. The relationship with Charmaine has made me suspect my grief is ending... other times I feel it never will." I felt as if there was a void inside, an aching hollowness that could never be filled... Tears started tracing their way down my cheeks. *I don't want to do this.* I took my hand away from Serge's and used my sleeve to wipe away the tears "I'm sorry, I don't know what got into me."

"You don't have to apologize to me, Phillip. I understand and I care about you. I feel you need some kind of closure for your love. I don't see you getting that closure through Fitz. I think you should seriously consider getting Fitz into some cathartic therapy that—"

"Serge, I know you think the type of therapy that Oscar Kemple's anger termination team does would give Fitz release for all the anger he's holding inside. But I don't think you can help a patient by brutalizing him. Fitz and I will work it out ourselves."

"As you wish, my friend. He's your patient. But please remember, I'm your friend, and I'll help you anyway I can. Don't hesitate to call."

We grasped hands and squeezed tightly. "Thanks. I'll remember."

He smiled and we stood up to leave. I promised to keep Serge informed on my progress, or lack of progress, with Fitz. I left with the warmth of the sun on my back, and in my heart too.

CHAPTER 16

CLIENTS IN TROUBLE

Trouble is my business.
William Chandler

"About forty minutes before my next appointment with Fitz, I received a call from another client, Karl Kashubian, the holly show creator who felt he was being persecuted by a conspiracy of holly programmers. On the screen he appeared calmer than he had ever been in my office.

"It's not your fault, Phillip," he said. "I know that. It's them. See those rejection forms?" He gestured behind him where the wall was covered by printouts from holly distribution webs.

"I see them."

"There are thirty-seven of them. All for my first independent show, *Giants and Dwarfs*. I did fifteen of those inane *Huburban Home* shows for the mass audience. I paid my dues. Then I did *Giants and Dwarfs*."

I nodded. This was all too familiar.

"Thirty-seven of the thirty-eight major networks rejected it. Did I tell you how I got the thirty-eighth web to buy it?"

"Yes," I said, stalling for time. Despite his surface calm, his voice was slurred and his gestures stilted. "You forged a note from the netweb's chief webspider that said, 'This is a sure lure.' and left it on the programmer's desk with your demo while he was out to lunch."

"That worked and I got almost eighteen percent of the available audience. *Huburban Home* gets ten to twelve percent and it's still on. I've proved myself to those failed artists who call themselves programmers and to the spiders of all the webs. I finished my new show, *Bisexuality Through Surgical Androgny*, and did simultaneous submission to all netweb's and commercial networks."

"Karl, I thought we had agreed to talk over submission strategy after you finished the project. Didn't we agree that I would be the first to see it?"

"Yeah, but I decided I didn't need to. Everything was going so well..."

"Karl, have you been drinking again?" He had almost crossed the line into alcoholism while working for *Huburban Home*.

On the screen, I could see he was unsteady. I hoped that he hadn't regressed.

"No. The doctor mus...n't worry. Karl Kashubian will never be a drunk." His eyes looked unfocused.

"I want to come over right away. I want to see your new show." I didn't know what kind of help he needed, but I was going to provide it.

"Fine, Doc. That's jus' fine. You'll have to run the holly by yourself. I won't be here."

"Stay there. I'm leaving right now."

"Doan matter, Doc. I'm almos' gone..."

"What have you taken?"

He shook his head, as though to clear it, and sat up straight. "I've taken as much rejection as I can stand. Ever one of the netwebs rejected my show."

"What stupid drug have you taken? I'll bring an antidote."

"Infectious lepromin. Got up the nerve. Massive multiple doses.

Catalyst booster. All nerves gone soon. I jus' called to cancel..." He started to slide off his seat.

The screen went blank.

I called the mobile medic unit in my complex and told them I'd go with them to Kashubian's address. I dashed outside and ran down to the ambulance area; the resident doctor told me there wasn't much of a chance for Kashubian if he'd injected infectious lepromin in quantity, but she had a retardant that might help if the dosage was small. I tried to push Kashubian's last words about multiple doses out of my mind. I wasn't going to let him die.

We sped from the Century City Constellation to the Fringes with flashing blue and yellow lights and the low frequency siren wailing. Fringe emergency services were inefficient where existent. It seemed to take a *long* time to arrive at the small frame house on Franklin where Kashubian lived and worked, but my watch showed less than ten minutes time had elapsed. I leaped out of the ambulance and started toward the front door. The mobile medic doctor was right behind me, followed by two attendants carrying an isolation litter. We were all wearing quarantine suits.

The door wasn't locked. I rushed in, taking the steps two and three at a time. His studio was on the second floor, where he was collapsed in front of the screen, his head lolling to one side.

The doctor and I checked him for vital signs: No pulse. No respiration. No heartbeat. No encephalic pattern.

"He's dead," she said. She saw the look on my face, the look of despair, the death of hope. She turned to the litter bearers and said, "Zip it up. Quarantine Morgue delivery." To me she said, "He took a painless way out of his pain."

There was no consolation for me in those words. They were true; leprosy is painless because the nerves die first. Karl was out of his pain—at least for a while. I suspected, and more or less believed, that certain kinds of pain can't be avoided, that suicide only delays the pain until sometime in the next reincarnation.

I was supposed to have helped him through that pain. I had failed. Had I wanted Serge to recommend that I refer Kashubian to Angela? Had I failed professionally because of problems in my personal life? What made me think I could get other people to handle their own garbage when my mental closets were full of my own? What would my mentor, Dr. John Benway, say about the way I'd mishandled this case? Maybe I needed to go back to him for therapy.

It felt as though my life were spiraling beyond my control.

I stumbled down the stairs after the two litter bearers and the medic. We stepped outside to see a small crowd of disaster addicts clustered around the ambulance's open doors. Their statements seemed like personal indictments.

"All zipped up. Watch out for the zippers."

"Shit, a deader!" cried a zebraman.

"It's that crazy Kashubian."

"Whose bode and booze can we commandeer for a wake? 'Ol Karl there was the Huburban burg cod."

"Then why'd he live here with the losers?" one sad-faced man asked, talking more to himself than any of his neighbors.

A trio of street musicians—players of flute, harmonica and tambourine—began to play, while some union beggars began to hustle the crowd. I heard the tambourine man start singing with, "'Til we meet again on the astral plane…" Two dwarfs and a Krishna Temple prostitute began to dance around the other fringers.

The rest was lost as we drove off. I felt lost, impotent, angered that an artistic genius had come to me for help and I had failed him—failed myself.

When I entered my office, my first thought was that Fitz might be waiting for me. I felt relieved that he wasn't, although I hoped he wasn't upset when he found I was absent. Communicating my mood to him would have done neither of us any good.

Fitz had been my only appointment for the rest of the day. There was no message from him on my answermat so I called his home and left a message: "Fitz, call me tomorrow and let's reschedule our next appointment. Sorry, if I missed you, but I had an emergency." Then I left my office and walked back to the solitude and comfort of my bode.

In my meditation alcove, I lit the orange candle in the custom holder and watched as it flickered. The sensor in the rim of the holder used the heat of the flame to raise the candle higher periodically to keep the tongue of fire visible above the rim. I pressed the button to start the candle meditation tape and concentrated on the flame as my own voice at random intervals asked me, "Where are you?"

When the tape ended, I went to the exercise room and systematically used up most of the readily available energy in my body. When my arms were leaden with fatigue, I had a fresh salad and a cup of tea before falling into bed.

Before going to sleep I recited a Buddhist prayer that seemed appropriate:

"Birth and death are faces of life's golden coin. They represent spaces where all forces join. If we can understand what one soul can feel, then we can let one hand choose to turn life's wheel."

Fitz never returned my call. The next morning I screened Clyde Burbank and he told me Fitz hadn't been in the office for almost two months. I asked him if Fitz had gone to the lecture with him and he told me that Fitz had declined the invitation. Next I contacted Juanita Delgado at her law office and she told me she hadn't heard from Fitz since he had unsuccessfully tried to purchase Angela's house and personal possessions from her relatives. On the off chance that he might have communicated with the trustees of the Rebirth Center, I called Charmaine; she said she hadn't seen or heard anything about Fitz. I confirmed that I'd see her therapeutic dance debut next week.

Where could Fitz be? Before Kashubian's death, I wouldn't have been so worried, but now I felt unsure about all my clients. I had to find Fitz, make certain that he was all right. Icy fingers of fear clutched my stomach. I vaulted out to Key West.

Fitz was not on his boat; it looked neglected, the teak was beginning to peel.

I screened Estelle Zimmer. She was eager to help and eager to see Fitz again but she hadn't seen him since they saw *The Crying Clown Rites* together. Her bruises were almost gone.

I spent the next few days in agony over what had happened to Karl and in fear over what might happen to Fitz. Late at night I would wake from a fitful sleep clammy with fear, unable to remember if only one or both had died. I contacted everyone who knew Fitz; no one knew where he might be.

It was a long wait until the next Monday when Fitz's Sufi class was meeting; I arrived about fifteen minutes early at the old mansion in the Los Angeles Fringes where Husein Medina taught the form of meditation known as Sufi dancing. I was admitted by a short, rotund man who looked as if he might be a eunuch. He was dressed as a harem attendant but that was just part of the stage dressing Medina used to attract students.

Husein greeted me warmly. He was tall and thin, very Semitic looking with a prominent curved nose and intense dark eyes. His scarred face looked as if it had been strip-mined. There were many rumors about Husein's origin and background; I suspected that he'd started most of the rumors himself.

"Phillip, have you come to explore the mystic aspects of Sufism with me, or merely to investigate the rumor that this establishment is a front for a seraglio where nubile slaves of passion await the pleasure of your company?" His voice was deep and resonant; as cultivated as the sonorous sounds of the holly late-night guest pests.

"I hadn't heard that rumor. The latest one I caught was that you are really Jewish and this establishment is a front for a shill that teaches the Torah."

For just an instant a strange expression flickered across his face and I wondered if he were from a Jewish background. I knew he'd never tell.

Then he said, “I suspect that you are here to check on the progress of the student you sent me. Let us see if he is here.”

We walked out of his study onto the balcony that overlooked the main floor dancing area. About ten people of different colors, sexes, sizes—all nude—were in a circle with joined hands. They leaned backward and turned their faces toward the roof and shouted “Ya Hai!” Then they moved forward until they were bent to face the floor and shouted “Ya Huk!” The continued movement was like the opening and closing of a flower, as heads and ten pairs of joined hands went up and down in unison.

Fitz was not among them. I said to Husein,” Fitzgerald Baker isn’t here. Have you seen him recently?”

“No, not since last week. Has something bad happened?” His face was twisted as if he expected bad news.

“I don’t know. Have you heard anything?”

“No, but he is a nice man. Sometimes the eternal force selects such a person for terrible things…”

I shook my head. “I don’t know. I do know I can’t find him anywhere. May I ask the students if they know where he is? After class, of course.”

Husein said, “Follow me.”

We walked down the stairs and over to the dancers, where Husein began to clap his hands. The sound bisected the time between the dancer’s shouts. They heard it and came to an almost uniform stop.

“Do any of you have factual information on where Fitzgerald Baker is tonight?”

There was no response. Husein said, “Continue to hold hands. Close your eyes. Try to visualize Fitzgerald Baker in the place where he is at the moment as I count back from ten. Ten…Nine…Eight…Seven… Six…Five…Four…Three…Two…One. Keep your eyes closed. All your mental focus should be on Baker.”

Husein removed a datacom from the underarm pocket of his purple robe. He opened it and slipped the needle pointed stylus over his right index finger. He made a number of quick motions with the stylus and then said, "All who saw him in a public place, incline your heads forward."

Two heads bent forward. Husein said, "Heads back. How many saw him in a private place?"

Five heads inclined. Husein said, "Heads back. Did anyone see him in transit?"

One head inclined. Husein said, "Heads back."

In the same manner, asking yes or no questions, Husein narrowed the parameters of his psychic search for Fitz. When he was finished, three of the five who had seen Fitz in a private place had indicated that they saw him nude in a private, single residence with which he was very familiar.

"Resume dancing," Husein told his students. Then he inserted the datacom in a printer and gave me a printout of the results, saying, "The first place to look is his home."

"Let me know what happens."

I thanked him without commenting on his methods and left as soon as a Fringe cabby picked me up. He took me the ten klicks to Fitz's home in Baldwin Hills. I didn't ask him to wait. That's when I realized how much I had been caught up in Husein's mixture of charisma and charlatanism; I hadn't even checked to see if Fitz was answering his portal screen.

The walls around Fitz's lot were too high for me to catch a glimpse of his house. Although I hadn't asked him to put me on his home access list, I checked to see if the outer door would open on presentation of my keycard. There was no response to that or to my repeated ringing of the bell.

Scaling the four-meter-high walls seemed improbable but just to determine if it was worthy of consideration, I made a paper airplane from a page of my pocket notebook and sailed it over the top of the gray stone barrier. My plane burst into flame like flash paper when it triggered the laser guard. The nearest tree that looked climbable and tall enough was easy to locate by the glowplate at its base.

I walked over to it and, being a compulsive reader, scanned the illuminated plaque. It read:

MORETON BAY FIG TREE PLANTED CIRCA 1988

DECLARED HISTORICAL CULTURAL MONUMENT NO. 52332

BY THE CULTURAL HERITAGE BOARD

MUNICIPAL ART DEPARTMENT

CITY OF LOS ANGELES

Climbing the one-hundred-year-old tree added some dark gray smudges to my beige, brushed cotton shirt and pants combo and caused me to skin several knuckles. Yet, despite the slight pain and exertion, I felt a sense of exhilaration I hadn't felt in a long time—at least since Angela's death. I was tempted to keep climbing till I reached the top, but stopped when I reached a point high enough to see over the walls; I looked and saw nothing but some shrubbery and a portion of the outer walls. My sense of duty reasserted itself and I climbed as high as I could, but without the earlier thrill until I saw the atrium of Fitz's underground home. The lights and shifting shadows in the open courtyard indicated that someone was moving inside or that the holly was on.

I scrambled down the tree, fast enough to snare one pants leg and create crotch seam pain in my groin. I let out a low groan and then limped over to the bell. There was still no answer. I let it ring for a long time, and while my bell finger was tiring, the solution came to me.

I rapidly walked the five blocks to the house Fitz had rented for Estelle. She was at home and came to the door promptly. This time I was ready for her uncanny resemblance to Angela and wasn't startled when she opened the door.

"Phillip, what's the matter? Has something happened to Fitz?"

I quickly ran my fingers through my hair to give it some semblance of normality and then replied, "I don't know. He hasn't answered the screen and hasn't responded to any of the messages I've left for him. No one's seen him for over a week. I climbed a tree to look over his yard and saw shadows of movement in the courtyard. No one answers the bell. Would you come with me and see if his door will open for you?"

"Certainly. Let me put on a shawl."

We rapidly walked back to Fitz's house. The door opened to Estelle's keycard. We walked over to the railed steps that led down to Fitz's underground house. On the tiled floor of the atrium, we could see a moving pattern of lights and shadows that came from the large living room. I looked through the glass door and saw Angela! It took me a few seconds to realize it was not Angela I was seeing but her letting-go hologram. It took a few more moments before my hands stopped shaking.

Estelle stepped forward, pressed her keycard to the doorplate and entered. I followed. Fitz lay on the floor. Estelle rushed over to his side and got down beside him. Fitz looked up at her, unshaven, hair mussed and painfully thin; he had lost at least fifteen kilos since I'd seen him last.

He looked at Estelle and tried to speak, but all that came forth was a harsh, thin croak.

"What's wrong, Fitz?" Estelle asked, as she brushed at his forehead with her fingers.

He coughed and then looked into her eyes. "Angela, you've come back from the dead! I knew that if anyone could do it, you could."

Estelle pulled his head tightly up against her breast; I could see the tears begin to trickle down her cheeks. I felt queasy inside and my legs were shaky. I staggered over to the viewscreen and called Serge. He answered on the fourth ring.

"Phillip! Are you all right?"

I nodded. "It's Fitz. I need an ambulance at the northwest corner of La Cienega and Stocker. I'm checking him into your clinic."

Serge picked up his direct line to the clinic and made the arrangements. Then he said to me, "Are you sure you're okay?" I nodded.

"You'll be coming in with Fitz." It sounded like an order.

"Yes. I'll transfer my files on him to your computer as soon as I disconnect."

"Good. I'll meet you at the clinic."

I made the data transfer and then looked at Fitz again. His head was in Estelle's lap. She was making soothing sounds to him in Angela's voice. I felt my head spin. The operating diode on his Noanx medpack was glowing beneath the black market safety override he had attached to it. Despite Estelle's attentions, the red light was still glowing when the ambulance copter came to take the three of us to Serge's clinic.

CHAPTER 17

BREAK TIME

One with the dance! Let joy be unconfined.
Lord Byron

Estelle and I stayed at the Recovery Clinic until Serge had Fitz sedated and in bed with intravenous feeding connections and complete electronic medical monitoring. When Serge came out of Fitz's room, he said, "Fitz is asleep now. He's suffering from exhaustion and malnutrition."

"Is he going to be all right?" Estelle asked.

Serge answered, "He'll be recovered physically within a week if he's a cooperative patient. He will still have to cope with whatever trauma led him to this state of physical and mental deterioration." He turned to me obviously waiting for me to introduce them.

I made belated introductions. Serge said Fitz would be asleep for hours. I was thankful that we'd arrived in time, and that he was going to be well again, at least in the physical sense. I thanked Estelle for her help and told her I would keep her informed of Fitz's condition. After making certain that she felt right about returning home, I put her into a pedicab and returned to Serge's office to talk about Fitz.

It seemed like one of the longest walks I'd ever taken. Serge was reading the data on Fitz that I had transferred to his computer when I walked into his office. "Sit down," he said without turning, "and have a cup of coffee. I'll be finished reading the data on Fitz in a moment."

While I was pouring the coffee, I tried to read the emotional content of Serge's voice; it had been studied, neutral, professional, yet with warmth there had been no hint of the censure I had expected, and certainly deserved. I sat down and tried to keep from slumping, but I felt drained and weary; it took a conscious effort to keep it from showing on the outside. To keep my thoughts at bay, I looked at the photographs of Naples on the wall. Serge had taken them last year when he visited his great-grandparents. I sipped my coffee and shifted my attention to the frown lines on Serge's handsome face as he turned around.

Looking at me with his knowing Neapolitan eyes, he said, "You really take the rough ones, Phillip. One more client like this and you'll have no time for yourself."

"I failed Kashubian too. He committed suicide. I overextended myself. I didn't realize that either he or Fitz was in such a depressed state. I should have listened to you, should have paid more attention to what I was doing."

Serge leaned back in his chair and closed his eyes so tight that I could see lines radiating across his temples. "Phillip, you have got to get ahold of yourself. It's not going to help anyone if you're consumed with guilt and..."

His voice drifted off and I waited for the words 'self-pity' to follow. Both my ears were ringing.

Serge slowly poured more coffee into his cup. "I'm very sorry to hear of Kashubian's death. Suicide is the ultimate act of a depressed person locked into a passive-aggressive behavior pattern. We're going to have to watch Fitz closely." The way he looked at me with his pensive eyes made me wonder if Serge thought he might have to watch out for me, too.

"You're right," I said. "It never occurred to me that Fitz might be putting on an act of improvement to get my approval. It appeared I had lost some of my objectivity since Angela died. I should have expected it, *damn it.*"

Serge jumped. Without realizing it, I had slammed my fist down on the table, rocking the coffeepot.

I mumbled an apology and then continued. "Fitz hasn't been making enough human contact. I'm practically the only person he's seen since her death, other than Estelle—and that was a disaster! He must have been trying to make every contact a success. To please Angela, if nothing else."

"You've had your own difficulties adjusting to Angela's death. Phillip, you can't expect yourself to be right all the time. No one's omnipotent."

I sighed. "You're right. I know, I know. But I've made too many mistakes. What do you think we should do with Fitz? Should I transfer him to another therapist? If I transferred him to you, it might be for the best—"

"Whoa… Slow down, Phillip. Let's look at this calmly and rationally for a moment. We're in no rush to make any decisions today. The most important item we have to consider is what would be best for Fitz. And I'm not convinced that changing therapists is in his best interest at the moment.

"The first thing we have to do is get him back on his feet. He ought to stay here at the Clinic for at least a week. Why don't you take that week off? You've had two traumatic experiences recently—three counting Fitz's collapse. Don't expect to perform like a machine. You need to get away from Fitz and his problems so you can renew your own spirit and purpose."

"But what about my responsibility to Fitz?" I asked.

"You can't carry out your responsibilities by yourself anymore. In the morning, you can tell him he will be here for rest and observation for the next ten days, and that you would like for him to cooperate with the staff in some research that is being done here. Let him think he's doing you a favor. By the time he's ready to leave, I'll have more data on him than the Universal Data Bank does. Then we can sit down and decide whether you should continue as his therapist. If you do, we can discuss what therapy to use when he's ready to leave.

"Serge, do you really think it's best for him?"

"Definitely. We can tell him that we're making every possible test to determine the cause of his symptoms. We'll let him suspect that we believe he has a viral infection that causes sleeplessness, loss of appetite, fatigue and ennui. It may help change his mindset. Is there anyone who is apt to want to visit?"

"Estelle Zimmer. But he shouldn't see her."

"Call her tomorrow and tell her that I'll give personal reports on his progress. I'll explain that she can't see him."

"Thanks. I'll screen her tomorrow and have her contact you. I could use a vacation myself."

I left Serge's clinic feeling as if a large albatross had flown off my shoulder. I decided to walk part of the way home in order to sort through the conflicting emotions and thoughts coursing inside my head.

I hadn't thought my love for Angela or my fantasies about her would interfere with Fitz's treatment. Had I failed him? I certainly hadn't saved Karl Kashubian, that intelligent, tortured artist. There were parallels in their cases. And I had not become aware of their desperation in time....

Was the ghost of Angela still haunting me? Was I unknowingly using some of my resources to shield myself from the vacuum her death had left in my fantasy life? The possibility of marrying her had never been as real as I had wanted it to be. Now that possibility no longer existed. I wondered if I had unknowingly avoided in-depth discussions of Angela with Fitz to protect myself from the realization that with her death I had experienced a fantasy loss greater than any possible reality we might have shared together.

It was time I found more professional help for Fitz and began to lessen the demands on myself. I arrived home and fell onto my airbed exhausted. Soon I dropped into a deep sleep of unremembered dreams.

When I woke up the next morning, I called Estelle and told her that Serge would call and keep her informed of Fitz's condition. After a quick breakfast, I went back to the clinic. There Serge and I talked to Fitz: I explained that I had to be away for over a week and that Serge would supervise his treatment during my absence. Fitz agreed to that and said he would be willing to cooperate in the research that Serge's staff was doing. "This experience may be what I need to make a change in my life. I can't go on this way anymore."

Back at my office, I rearranged my appointment schedule to give myself ten free days, left messages in all the appropriate places stating that I would be unavailable for a week and a half. After dinner, I vaulted to Mendocino to see Charmaine's dance therapy performance.

The Wykowski Center featured a small theater for performances; the seating was limited to less than one hundred so all would have a complete view of the stage. After presenting my keycard at the door, an usher led me to a reserved front row seat.

I was a few minutes early and looked around fruitlessly for familiar faces before reading the program. I saw Charmaine was first on a bill of five dancers. On the back there was a bold print notice that read:

BECAUSE SOME MEMBERS OF THE AUDIENCE ARE NOT FAMILIAR WITH THE MEANING OF THE POSITIONS AND MOVEMENTS OF SYMBOLOGY THERAPY, SUPRATITLES WILL BE PROJECTED ON THE BACKDROP.

This sentence relieved me, because the time I had allotted for studying Wykowski's symbolism had evaporated during emergencies. Now I could relax, confident I would understand whatever Charmaine chose to express. The houselights dimmed. Wykowski stepped out from behind the curtain and said, "Good evening, ladies and gentlemen. I am Anton Wykowski, the originator and teacher of symbology therapy. Each performer tonight has arranged a unique presentation designed to convey the essence of how one individual is relating to the circumstances of life through dance and the Wykowski Movements. During the dance each performer will reveal his archetypical essence, resolve conflicts with past roles and personas and—if in tune—merge with the collective unconscious…"

After several more minutes of neo-Jungian cant, he introduced Charmaine. The curtains pulled back to reveal a stage floor vibrating to the sound of music; Charmaine was standing motionless in the fifth position—feet turned sideways but flat on the floor, left knee in front of the right knee, left hand curled in front of her thigh, right arm extended as if holding an imaginary bar.

The music became louder; a piano played with a rehearsal hall sound, plunking out a tune that seemed vaguely familiar, perhaps an old Broadway show hit. The backdrop showed a cornfield under a hot sun. Charmaine began to dance and the supratitles read: **WHEN I WAS A GIRL IN KANSAS, MY PARENTS HAD ME TAKE BALLET LESSONS.** Jungian symbols of the anima and the animus superimposed themselves over the cornfield representing both the parents and the female and male aspects of Charmaine.

I was engrossed by the way Charmaine projected herself as a child dancing—for the first time in weeks my mind was off the doomed trio of Fitz, Karl and Angela. The tights she wore showed she had the body of a woman, but her movements were childlike as the supratitles read: **I DREAMED OF BECOMING A BALLERINA OR A FAMOUS DANCER**. Images of famous dancers obscured the field of corn—Marie Tagionli, Olga Preobrajenska, Isadora Duncan, Anna Pavlova, Margot Fonteyn, Maria Tallchief, Doris Humphrey, Martha Graham, Sally Rand, Carmen Delavalade, Peggy Prentiss, Olga Chemez, Shiela Satin, Kim Luanna, Yvonne Calvet. Charmaine did a brief imitation of each when the name and image appeared on the backdrop.

The sudden changes of dance styles and music were blended together in an overwhelming presentation. Then the music slowed to a dirge-like beat and the supratitles read:

THEN I LEARNED THERE WERE MORE STUDENTS OF BALLET IN THE AMERICAN MIDWEST THAN THERE HAD EVER BEEN SUCCESSFUL BALLET PERFORMERS. MY DREAMS WERE SHATTERED.

Jungian dream symbols of marvelous complexity appeared—a burning blue giraffe, a giant wheel-shaped spacecraft covered with blinking red, blue and gold lights in the shape of ancient runes, holograms of giant DNA spirals shooting overhead and turning into flat-headed sperm as they smashed into the backdrop.

The symbols turned into colored smoke and Charmaine began to dance again. The backdrop words were: **COULD I CONTINUE LESSONS UNTIL I BECAME PROFICIENT ENOUGH TO BECOME A TEACHER?** She danced a whirlwind of complicated forms and then stopped to the caption:

LEARNING TO DO SOMETHING MERELY TO TEACH OTHERS TO DO IT SO THEY CAN IN TURN TEACH OTHERS WAS NOT ENOUGH.

She was standing on the stage immobile except for her hands which first crossed over her stomach and then moved away in opposite directions, which in American Sign Language was the sign for not. Then she made a fist with her left hand with the knuckles pointing forward and the right hand flat on top. The right hand moved off to the right twice, a double motion for enough; she repeated the signs several times not enough. Not enough.

She began dancing again as I read**: I AM NOT A PROFESSIONAL DANCER BUT I HAVE BECOME MY OWN PERSON.** The music became more cheerful and was captioned:

I DANCE FOR PLEASURE. SO INSTEAD OF THERAPY I WOULD RATHER DANCE THE POLKA WITH MY LOVER.

There was a gasp of surprise from several members of the audience, but no one was more surprised than I was when Charmaine came over and took me by the hand. The music was now a cheerful polka and we danced joyfully. I could feel the floor vibrate to the beat as we whirled across the stage, Charmaine and I moving as one. I caught a glimpse of Wykowski frowning in the wings, but before I could react we were dancing wildly to the Beatle's classic *Glass Onion*. Never had I been so enchanted with Charmaine as I was now. We were both glowing with a manic vitality.

She whispered into my ear, "Go toward your right. Let's dance right out the door."

With an outstretched hand, she opened the door; the music stopped and the applause began. She closed the door. I grabbed her, kissed her and held her in my arms, for at that moment she was the most desirable woman in the world. I told her so.

"More, sweet Phillip, more. Consider the lengths to which I've gone to capture your attention. First I lured you here with the promise of therapy in flower." She pressed her wrist to her forehead in a pseudo-tragic gesture. "Then I plucked you out of your dignified observer stance into the mad whirl of a life-celebrating dance. Such an alive body! You do the polka so well."

She kissed me and took my hand, pulling me along. "To complete our escape, my chariot awaits—a rented Dakota to whisk us to the vault station before we are missed by the mad dancers."

More likely the mad doctor, I thought as I entered the hydrogen-powered car. "Wykowski may be the maddest of the dancers. He may dance a fit."

Charmaine laughed, and then said, "Wykowski once told the class that the teacher who can't take a joke is a disgrace to the profession. He also said that expressing our desires and feelings in real time is the best therapy. I listened to my teacher. If he doesn't like my joke, he has a good system at hand for dispersing his emotions."

"Charmaine, you have incredible style. Let's go somewhere and celebrate for days, maybe a week; I've got some time off."

There was a strained note to my last words; she tactfully ignored it. "Pick a place, Phillip. I'll go anywhere with you."

We left the Dakota at the vault station and teleported to Alexandria where we joined a Durrellian tour.

CHAPTER 18

STAGES OF GRIEF

All the world's a stage and all men and women are merely players.
William Shakespeare

Charmaine left Alexandria to go to a cousin's wedding in Warsaw; she invited me to go along, saying I would have a great time at a Polish wedding even if I didn't speak Polish. I assured her that I was certain I would enjoy myself anywhere on or off Earth with her, but that I had to go back to Los Angeles and see Fitz. We arranged to see each other when she returned from Warsaw. I vaulted back to Los Angeles and made a luncheon date with Serge.

Over eggplant parmigiana at La Dolce Vita, Serge said, with a smile that made vertical lines in his cheeks, "As I mentioned on the screen, Fitz is recovering as well as could be expected. Before we go into his case, tell me what you've been doing. Because whatever it is, it's been good for you."

"Charmaine Dwoskin and I did a Durrellian tour of old Alexandria. You've read the *Alexandria Quartet* by Lawrence Durrell?"

Serge nodded yes and I continued, saying, "We visited Scobie and drank his arak."

Recognizing the cue, Serge asked, "How did it taste?"

"A bit turgid. As if someone had peed in it. But we were among the fortunate who were not poisoned."

Serge laughed. "Nothing like authenticity. And Scobie's parrot?"

"In better health than the old sailor."

"How is the lovely Charmaine?" he asked.

"As intriguing as Justine and without the neurotic flaws."

"She must be good for you, Phillip. You look more alive than you have in months. You also look slightly different. Haircut?"

"Yes, a haircut and beard trim from the actor who portrays Mnemjian."

"Was this mock Mnemjian true to the character as Lawrence Durrell described him?"

"Completely," I said. "A dwarf with a hunchback, violet eyes, spit-curls of black hair and an incorrigible gossip who knows everything that is going on in Durrell's Alexandria. He told me that Justine was having an affair with Darley, that I should not let Capodistria get a glimpse of my beautiful companion, that Pombal was wildly infatuated with a young female friend of his acquaintance who had just been released from the lunatic asylum in Helwan. And he introduced me to Ludwig Pursewarden."

"What was Pursewarden like?"

"He's a pale, short, overweight Englishman with blond hair. He was suffering from a hangover so I invited him to our rooms for some brandy and hash. He accepted, saying that he couldn't stay for long because of other things he must do. We talked for a while. He was eloquent and full of gestures when excited. Just before he left, I told him I had read and enjoyed his writings. He replied, 'I set out to create fictional art and created a mirror of life. Much of what I have learned, I didn't know I knew until I had one of my characters say it. Then I discovered my knowledge. A bit too late sometimes. I once had one of my characters realize, after years of putting up with people who didn't care, that it was God who didn't care, that God didn't care one way or the other. That is entirely too true!'

"As if determined not to leave on that somber note," Pursewarden then told us an amusing anecdote about encountering a prostitute friend of Pombal's while he was staying at Pombal's flat. He left us with smiles on our faces."

"It sounds like you had a fun vacation. Just what you needed," Serge said. "Now I'll tell you about Fitz, if you're ready."

"I'm ready."

"In the guise of checking Fitz for symptoms and doing research, I've had my staff gather information on Fitz's emotional states during his stay. "Serge pulled a datapad from his pocket and said, "Let me read you the ones on the top of the list: sadness, emptiness, indifference, bitterness, inadequacy, denial and insecurity. What does that signify to you?"

"Grief."

"Right. Now we both know five stages of grief that people usually experience: the order of occurrence varies, but for most people all five stages transpire—denial, depression, anger, bargaining and acceptance. From your point of view, which of these had Fitz passed through?"

I paused for a moment to get my thoughts focused on Fitz and then said, "He's still experiencing the depression, or at least he was when I saw him last. His hiring of a mummer surrogate was a type of bargaining in my opinion, as if Fitz could use his power in this world to create the best imitation of Angela that credit could procure. According to what he's told me, he had an initial period of disbelief when Angela died, but he experienced that disbelief again when he saw Estelle just before we brought him here. He thought she was Angela. He expressed anger at Estelle when he terminated her Contract and I assume that he released some anger when we were at The Whole Body Center together. I've been trying to guide him toward acceptance, but he has a natural acting ability which enables him to present the facade that the other person wishes to see. I've only recently realized that."

"Fitz is still depressed," Serge said. "I believe the major source of that depression is anger, anger turned inward against himself. He's angry at

Angela for deserting him by dying. He's angry at Angela for controlling his life and angry at himself for having let her control his existence."

Serge paused, took a sip of red wine and brushed his brown, thick mustache with a napkin.

I finished the last bite on my plate before saying, "Convince me."

"I have all the evidence. Whenever he showed any of the signs of anger—increased heartbeat, rapid pulse, changes in respiration, increased muscle tension, flushed face—I have the words that he was reacting to. All the tests—thematic apperception, holographic archetypical projection, word association, sensual distortion, personal interaction—show that he is terribly angry. His anger toward Angela is something he cannot admit. Emotional amplification therapy shows that he is hostile to women in general. It is as if he has let his anger toward Angela prejudice him against any meaningful exchange with any woman. A most regrettable situation for a young man of heterosexual inclinations."

I poured us both more wine while saying, "I'd like to examine your evidence before you give me your recommendations for his further treatment. Not that I doubt you, but I need to absorb the data you've collected. I need to experience as much of the reality of Fitz's anger as I can."

"Of course, Phillip. Let's finish the wine and then we'll go to the Clinic."

During our walk—the clinic was only a few blocks away, I pondered over the question of what to do with Fitz: Should I terminate our relationship and turn him over to someone better schooled in suicides and depressive grief reactions, or should I keep searching for the therapy that would reverse the self-destructive course of his life? During my Alexandrian vacation I had purposely put Fitz, Karl and Angela out of my mind. Now I found, that if my conscience would have permitted it, I would have left him in Serge's capable hands. However, I was only too aware that Fitz's greatest problem was that the most significant people in his life had the habit of dying or skipping out just when he needed them most.

No, I would not desert Fitz. Not because Angela wouldn't have wanted me to, but because I didn't want to. He needed my help and, even if I couldn't be the one to cure his problems, I was going to help orchestrate that cure. A sudden all over sense of well-being told me I had made the best decision.

Back at the Clinic, I reviewed Serge's data on Fitz; repressed anger was evident in many of his reactions. He was hostile to the Asian doctor who was Angela's sex, age, size and shape. In the thematic apperception tests, he saw manipulation in most of the pictures of female-male situations. His perception of his anima—the female element of his psyche—was personified as a witch or priestess, someone who was in league with the forces of darkness. He showed signs of anger when he heard the word angel. His responses to questions asked by females were shorter and less informative than if a male asked the same question—regardless of which person asked the question first.

I told Serge, "You've done a thorough job, and I agree with your conclusion. Fitz has a serious problem of repressed anger. It is handicapping him in dealing with the world in general and with women in particular. I know you have some suggestions for his treatment, and I'm ready to hear them."

"Phillip, I know you're a man who has experienced a great deal of anger and that you've found your own ways to deal with it. Am I right?"

"Yes. My exercise program is designed to work off the anger I am unable to vent in any constructive way, as well as to maintain my muscle tone, body shape and vanity."

Serge smiled, and then grew serious again. "Phillip, do you experience anger as an unpleasant emotion?"

I nodded. "Anger sometimes gives me the energy to deal with the circumstances that brought it about, but I don't enjoy being angry at all."

"Do you think Fitz feels the same way?"

"Yes, from what he's told me, I believe he does. That's the most common cultural response to anger among middle-class Americans of northern European extraction. With your Latin heritage I imagine your experience might be quite different. Is it?"

"Yes. I feel anger as a pressure, something like gas; when it builds up, I let it belch out and then the pressure is gone. But I want to get the conversation back to your response to anger: you find anger painful. You are certain Fitz finds anger painful. You've tried to spare him that pain, Phillip. Your kindness has been misdirected.

"Fitz needs some experience that will make it impossible for him to mask his anger. He needs to vent it, get it all out. Then he can, with your guidance, learn to deal with anger in some more constructive manner. If he keeps on repressing it, it will kill him through suicide or some stress related disorder."

"Then you think I should continue as his therapist?"

"Of course, Phillip. I never meant to imply that I felt you were incapable of treating Fitz, only that your perspective was skewed—your emotions and personal involvement were obscuring your objectivity. Or at least your therapeutic distance. Fitz's withdrawal was the jolt you needed to shatter your old assumptions, and the vacation has given you the rest you needed to approach his case from an objective viewpoint."

"Thank you, Serge, I appreciate your support. I want to continue as Fitz's therapist, not because Angela wanted me to, but because he needs me. Fitz has a history of being abandoned by the primary figures in his life. Fitz still believes that I want to help him, and I want to live up to that trust."

"Good, because Fitz needs you. Other than Clyde Burbank, whom Fitz feels estranged from because of his lifestyle crisis, he believes there is no one else he can turn to. And, as an objective party, I think he's right. He's either alienated or severed every important relationship in his life. In light of this, his attempted suicide was to be expected."

"I know. His fear of rejection has made him a very lonely man. Clyde understands his problems since he went through his own mid-life crisis a few years back."

"This fear," Serge said, "is there because of all the anger Fitz is suppressing. If he doesn't care about anyone, then he can't be rejected, and therefore cannot be put in a position to be angry. From what I know of his case history, he has some beautiful reasons for blowing his boiler."

"Yes, but how do we convince him of that? I asked. "How do we get Fitz's anger out in the open where it can be dealt with?"

"I believe Oscar Kemple's anger termination team is the answer."

"Incredible! Do you expect me to lie to my client about what he's going to experience and then toss him into a weekend group encounter where he is the only patient and the rest are Machiavellian attack therapists? I've never lied to a client."

"Never?" Serge asked, his eyebrows raised. "Not even in the client's best interest?"

"Honesty toward the client is my basic approach."

"Phillip, are you going to let your principles prevent you from doing what is best for your client?"

"You're using my own brand of Zen on me as if it were judo."

"Didn't you tell me that you accepted Fitz as a client because it was the last request that Angela made of you?"

"Yes, but there was more to it than that. Fitz's case had all the drama that too few cases offer. Plus, focusing on his problems helped take my mind off Angela and how much I missed her."

"But the real question, Phillip, is have you forgiven Angela?"

"For what?"

"For being less than the goddess you wanted her to be. For asking you to help the disturbed man who held the place in her life that you wanted. For being petty in a very human way and making you angry."

"Serge, I think I'm really coming to terms with who Angela was and what she did. I'm not pretending she's still alive."

"But Fitz has been, and you've got to help him or refer him to someone who can."

I pressed the fingers of both hands to my temples. "I know you're trying to help Serge and I appreciate it. But Kemple?"

"He's the one who can do it. Not just for Fitz. You are going to benefit also."

"Me?"

"When the marathon is over, Fitz is going to want to tell someone about it. That's you. He's going to tell you how much anger he had stored away, anger against Angela. You are going to have to listen to it twice..."

"Twice?"

"Twice. The first time will be in the communications center with Kemple. That time will be when it is happening for Fitz. The second time is when he tells you about it, not knowing that you watched the entire scene via closed circuit holly. That second time will benefit you; it will be your closure for the relationship with Angela. You and Fitz will both be through with Angela and be able to get on with your lives."

"You really believe this whole scheme is necessary?"

"As your good friend, Phillip, I tell you from my heart that it is what I see as the best course of action for you and for Fitz. Angela was important to both of you, but the two of you can't spend your lives looking backward to what is over or looking sideways to avoid seeing her ghost. Am I not telling you what you already know?"

"Yes, Serge. I'll call Kemple and then I'll see Fitz."

"I'll punch Kemple's number for you."

Kemple's face appeared within seconds on the screen. He was either a small man or had a huge desk. His hair was blond, his cheeks smooth and pink. The lines in his forehead made him look like an aged cherub.

Serge made introductions since Kemple and I had never met. Kemple said, "Counselor Wendell, Dr. Dicori discussed your client with me earlier. If you wish, we can schedule your client for a marathon weekend on Retreat Island next weekend."

I cursed Serge sotto voce and then turned back to Kemple. "Doctor, I've read about your results. I'd like to know exactly how this marathon will be set up."

"The marathon will be held on a small island next to Asateague Island off the Virginia coast. I have the entire island under surveillance by microdot cameras. You and I and my assistant, Dr. Evans, will monitor the events from the adjacent island. There will be communication with all members of the anger termination team as required. Your client will never suspect that all the other members of the group are professionals. I have complete control over the direction and actions of everyone except your client."

Kemple obviously knew what he was doing. After being assured that this dramatic and expensive procedure would trigger a cathartic experience for Fitz, I told Kemple that I would confer with my client and call him back.

"You really had that one all worked out, didn't you?" I asked Serge.

He shrugged his shoulders, and gave me the-cat-who-has-just-eaten-the-canary smile.

"One of these days you're going to find yourself shipwrecked on the shoals of your own connivance. But thanks."

I gave him a quick embrace, and then he took me to Fitz's room, a bright room with off-white walls, bright blue trim and natural blond wood furniture. Fitz looked healthier than when I had seen him last. His color was better, he had gained some weight and was paying attention to his personal appearance.

"You're looking much better, Fitz."

"I'm feeling better," he said, but his tone of voice wasn't convincing.

After we discussed his symptoms and how they had been treated, I asked, "How would you like a change of scenery?"

"I guess so. Where would I go?"

"A weekend group therapy marathon on Retreat Island. I think the experience would be good for you. You haven't seen many people outside of Serge's staff lately. And it won't be for another week."

"Good. Will you be running the group?"

"No, but I'll be dropping you off and picking you up. I think you'll benefit from the experience most if I'm outside the group."

"All right. I don't have anything else to do. You're completely sure that I should do this? I don't have any group therapy experience."

"Yes, I'm sure that it's in your best interest." At least that part was true, but the other lies left a foul taste in my mouth. I hoped Serge was right about the effectiveness of Kemple's anger termination therapy, because I didn't know where to go next. And no idea how I would justify my lies to Fitz.

CHAPTER 19

NUMBER THIRTEEN

They've given you a number and taken away your name.
P.F. Sloan & Steve Barri

Evans, Kemple's assistant, met Fitz and me at the vault station in Chincoteague, Virginia. He was black, just barely taller than Fitz and had bulging muscles that filled out his sailor's denims and chambray shirt. With the assured motions of someone who is accustomed to taking charge, he led us to the boat that would be taking us to Retreat Island.

"Nice boat," Fitz said. "Well maintained."

Evans replied with a thank you. "I selected it and supervise the maintenance. You know boats?"

They talked technical nautical details while Evans cast off and headed toward Retreat Island; I was pleased to see Fitz responding again to his surroundings. I began to have a better feeling about the therapy that we were about to undertake. The ocean was greenish blue and calm with a sea breeze that added a hint of salt to the air. Soon there was a holiday mood aboard as Fitz helped Evans maneuver the boat.

It seemed the trip had just begun when Retreat Island appeared as a brown squiggle on the horizon.

Just before we reached the dock, we could see a sand soccer game in progress along a sandy strip that girdled the island. The background was dominated by an old castle made of cement blocks.

Evans brought the boat gently against the dock fenders and Fitz threw a line around a wooden stanchion. One of the soccer players came running over to help; he was wearing a bright orange sport suit with a large number six emblazoned on it. The sport suit was one of those deflector padded garments complete with see-through helmet and face protectors. He was carrying what appeared to be an identical suit looped over his shoulder. He helped secure the line and then said to Fitz, "I've got your sport suit here. Number thirteen. You're just in time to join the game."

Fitz examined the speaker, a well-built, handsome man with fair skin, chestnut brown wavy hair and bright blue eyes beneath a wide forehead with supraorbital ridges. Then Fitz looked over at me.

"Go ahead. Join into the spirit of the group."

Fitz stepped below to change and the man on the dock said, "You can leave the jumpsuit on the dock. We've got everything he'll need at the castle."

When Fitz stepped back on deck, I said, "We'll be back to pick you up on Sunday."

Fitz bid us goodbye and joined the soccer player on the dock.

We cast off and headed for the next island, approximately a kilometer beyond Retreat Island where Dr. Kemple would be waiting for us in his communication center. I said to Evans, "I'm glad that came off well."

"You don't have to worry about Number Six. He's got an excess of Irish bonhomie and reassures everyone; he could convince a libertine that he was the great god Pan or persuade an Irishman that he was St. Patrick in person."

When Evans referred to the man as Number Six, I remembered that Kemple used numbers instead of names for the depersonalizing effect in the group. Dr. Kemple wasn't a personable man. It would be a weekend of last names—Evans, Kemple and Wendell—until I returned for Fitz who would spend his weekend as Number Thirteen.

I felt a twinge of guilt at leaving him alone in the hands of Kemple's disciples. Fortunately, the brisk ocean breeze soon restored my earlier high spirits.

Kemple's second island was much like Retreat Island except for its uninhabited look. Kemple had his communications center, a building with all the charm and style of a concrete bunker, hidden in a grove of stunted trees. Evans led me to the door and Kemple ushered us in.

Gesturing toward the far wall of the square interior where row after row of repeater screens winked, Kemple said, "Three-hundred and eighty-five monitors. Each one of them connected to a microdot camera, which is triggered by movement, body heat or by the contacts built into all the sport suits. You can get a holly close-up from any of these six monitor consoles; the rest are all video."

I sat down at one of the consoles, looked up at the monitors and punched up a three-dimensional image of Fitz running along the sand in pursuit of the soccer ball.

Kemple stood beside me, just barely taller than me when I was seated; I tried to keep the distaste his proximity generated from showing on my face. I had to remember it was Fitz I was here for, not myself.

Kemple pointed out the multiple features of the console and said, "You and I and Evans will monitor the entire weekend from here. Either Evans or I will be awake at all times to make certain that every word and action from Baker is recorded. You will get two copies of all recorded material; you can decide later whether or not your client should receive one of them—that is your decision, but the price of two is included in the weekend. Sleep or rest whenever you want to. Food and beverages are available in the autokitch over on your right. Any questions so far?"

"Not at the moment," I replied.

"Then we'll begin."

Kemple sat down at the console, selecting a close-up of a blonde woman wearing a sport suit marked number one. Kemple plugged in his throat microphone and said, “Kemple here, Number One. Blink twice if you hear me”

Number One blinked two times.

“As soon as you can end the game and frustrate Number Thirteen at the same time, do so. Then call for a social meeting in the castle recreation room. Blink twice to acknowledge.”

After her reply, Kemple said to me, “The new communication implants are an improvement. Watch Baker. The therapy has almost begun.”

Kemple, Evans and I all watched as Number One continued to umpire the game of sand soccer between the odd-numbered team and the even-numbered team. Number Three scored a goal and Number One announced the score as twelve to eleven in favor of the evens. Play was resumed.

During the next few minutes, I familiarized myself with the console and learned to get the images I wanted as fast as I required them. The miniature figures appeared lifelike on the center holly stage. I could tell Fitz was playing well by the energy with which he pursued the soccer ball. With a quick feint he took control of the ball. If he scored now the game would be tied.

“Kick it in, Number Thirteen,” Number Three yelled, “and we’ll have them tied.”

Fitz drew back and was already into his kicking motion, when Number One blew a painfully piercing whistle.

“Game’s over! Evens win twelve to eleven. Everyone report to the castle rec room for the social.”

Fitz nearly lost his balance as he completed his kick and sent the ball veering off. All the other players were moving toward the cement castle.

Number One looked at Fitz and said, “The game is over, Number Thirteen. Report to the castle recreation room.” She turned on her heels without waiting for a reply.

Fitz’s face was a portrait of frustration.

With an eye on the movements of the players and nimble fingers to select camera output, I followed their progress from the sand along the concrete path to the castle, past the sign reading RECREATION ROOM to the double doors that opened into a room large enough to be called a ballroom. It was furnished with a variety of chairs, cushions and couches that would seat maybe twenty people. All the furniture was in a circle; Number One was seated in a throne like chair. Showing impatience, she said, "Sit down everyone and I'll read you your rules."

They all sat down.

"The rules are very simple," Number One said. "We do it my way. You all have gone to a great deal of expense to be here so let's not have any crap about not having problems. We all have problems. My problem is I have to deal with yours. So I've made it easy for myself. I don't want to have to remember your names so for this weekend your names are your numbers—that's a rule. I don't like violence, so I've minimized the possible effects by requiring you to wear your sports suits except in the cleanser or the lav. Wear your suits—that's a rule.

"We are going to focus on one person at a time. Get that person's story and help that person deal with her or his set of individual problems. We'll do it my way. I'll ask for feedback when I see that I need it. If I ask you, give me your reactions to the best of your ability—that's a rule.

"Food and coffee are over there." Number One pointed to a dispenser that was against the wall in back of her and to her left. "You get all the coffee you want because you won't get much sleep this weekend. All the food dispenser modules are keyed to your number. If yours is empty, that means you don't eat. Eat your own food only—that's a rule."

I have never liked overtly authoritarian social organizations or their leaders; I found myself beginning to loathe Number One. I wondered if she might be overplaying her role, but Kemple appeared content with whatever group dynamics he was watching.

There was a bit of restless stirring after Number One's last pronouncement. She looked around to see who was doing what and everyone settled down. Number One continued: "Now, I don't want any challenges to my authority. You are going to get all the authority that you paid for. I can't force you to listen, to help yourself or to get you to help others. I can and have made it the path of least resistance.

"You can't get transportation off this island until Sunday afternoon. If you work at it, you might be able to spend part of this weekend all by yourself avoiding help. I'd like to see a show of hands of those who are that stupid."

No hands were raised.

"Good, I've got an intelligent group. I'll do my best to help you keep thinking that way about yourselves. You get to help."

She paused for a moment to let her words sink in.

"Now, I want to talk about questions," Number One began. "The important thing to remember is that I ask them. You'll get answers, as you need them. You don't need to know my theories, my fantasies or my expectations. Have I convinced you or is there someone who still thinks she or he has an important question?"

Number One paused and looked around at the dozen people in the circle with her. Number Eight, a young, thin black woman raised her hand in an incomplete gesture and said, "I'm Harriet Ar—"

"You are Number Eight," shouted Number One. "Start over and get it right."

Number Eight was visibly cowed. "I'm Number Eight and I want to know what it is I'm supposed to do while the focus is on someone else."

"You don't need that answer now because the focus is on you. I want you to tell me and the rest of the group about you—not your name, address, citizen's number, screen number or nonessential statistics. Just tell us what your life is like, what your thoughts are and what is bothering you."

Number Eight looked sorry that she had spoken. She hesitated before answering. "I don't know where to begin."

"We can't tell you about your life, yet. Tell us about it first. Who do you live with? What do you do with your time? What in your life makes you feel it's worthwhile? Or is it?"

"I live with my husband and daughter. I love them both very much.

My husband is a camera operator for *The Allen Heart Show*. He's, ah, good at his work, but he doesn't like Mr. Heart very much."

She paused as though waiting for a laugh that never came. Everyone around her looked uncomfortable, as if they might next be on the hot seat or have to remember her responses for a test. "M…my daughter attends the huburb union school but lives in our bode. She's a pretty child. She's eight. I don't know what else to say."

"What do you do with your time?" Number One asked.

"I keep the bode straight, play with my daughter and talk to my husband about his work."

"What do you do with your time? The rest of your time?" Number One was insistent.

I kept Fitz in my field of vision while Number One kept hammering Number Eight's statements into a recognizable shape, the shape of a very conventional life with large empty spaces. The material was quite ordinary, but Fitz seemed fascinated, probably because he had never seen a superior attack therapist at work before. Attack therapy is not one of the techniques I use, but I have enough therapy experience to recognize Number One as a determined and talented practitioner.

She was so good I had to keep reminding myself that Number Eight was not a patient but a trained therapist playing a role.

Over the next hour or so, Number One peeled away the onion skin layers of the persona that Number Eight presented, inviting other members of the group to make suggestions to, or ask questions of, Number Eight. Playing her part with conviction, Number Eight soon had several supporters in the group who were giving her sympathy for her problems.

"All right," Number One said. "That's enough of that. Some of you got sucked into Number Eight's game. She's got you going in a circle. She says that no one ever talks to her. You talk to her and all she says boils down to her claim that she doesn't know what is going on. You tell her what is going on and she claims she doesn't understand. No matter how much you explain, she claims to still be confused. If you ask her why she's confused, she says it's because nobody ever talks to her."

Number Eight was blubbering and saying through sobs, "That's not fair. I am confused and hardly anybody ever talks to me."

"FAIR," Number One shouted. "Who in the universe ever told you that life was fair? Life is not fair. It's a challenge and you are sitting in your nest and trying to avoid taking that challenge. That's what *you* are trying to do. And it is not working. That is why you are unhappy. You wouldn't be unhappy if you were living. You might get a little joy out of life once in a while."

Sobbing, Number Eight asked, "What am I going to do?"

"You can start by being honest with us. Is your husband old enough to be your father?"

Number Eight's head seemed to shrink into her shoulders. Her voice resembled a squeak when she answered. "Almost."

"And your daughter is what, eight or nine?

"Eight and a half."

"When you play with your daughter, do you play the role of a child most of the time?"

"Yes."

"If your husband comes home, does the game stop when he arrives? Stop not to be resumed?"

"Yes."

"Before the birth of your daughter, did you and your husband play little girl-big daddy games?"

"H...How did you know?"

Fitz was hunched forward, intent on every word. There was no movement among the group members as Number One proceeded to get to the center of Number Eight's problems.

"Are most of the arguments with your husband generated when you take your little-girl role?"

Number Eight burst out crying and nodded assent.

"Is the gap between you and your daughter most noticeable after you win one of the childish games you play with her?"

"I think so."

"Don't slip back into crap, Number Eight. You know that's true, don't you?"

Number Eight's tears continued to flow.

"Now tell us what is really going on in your life?"

After drying her eyes with a tissue, Number Eight said, "I act like a child when my husband wants a wife and when my daughter wants a mother. That's what's making all the confusion and unhappiness. I compete with my daughter to see who can be the biggest child, and I always win because I've got more practice."

Number One, with a caring in her voice that had not been obvious previously, said, "If you're winning the games that you're playing and it isn't making you happy, what should you do?"

"Give up the games. Get involved with my husband as a wife and with my daughter as a mother."

Number One opened up the floor for people to give their suggestions to Number Eight. They brought up family therapy, sharing activities, behavioral changes. Number Two, an Asian man with a pockmarked face, suggested The Temporary Friends Association to Number Eight as a means of practicing friendship as a giver instead of a taker. Fitz was paying attention but didn't say anything.

Kemple turned to me and said, "There won't be much going on that you'll need to pay attention to now. Evans will monitor."

Evans nodded affirmatively towards me.

Kemple continued with, "Number One will call for a coffee break after she sums up everything for Number Eight. Any conversation that Baker gets into before the next group focus will be manipulated to reinforce the image of Number One as a powerful and competent leader."

"I'm favorably impressed so far," I replied.

"Yes, Number One is good. She will use fatigue, lack of sleep, distorted time sense, sudden awakenings, exercise periods and a number of psychological techniques to create the proper atmosphere for Baker to experience an anger breakthrough."

"When will the group focus be on Fitz?"

"Probably not until Sunday morning or afternoon. It could be earlier if something unexpected occurs. Number One will keep him from getting too comfortable until he is ripe, and then she will make sure he gets very uncomfortable, uncomfortable enough to be ready to change."

When Number One called the group back after coffee break, she asked, "How do you feel, Number Eight?"

Number Eight's voice was calm and more pleasing to the ear than it had been previously. She said, "I feel like I'm in low gravity, like the weight of the world is off my shoulders, like I am out of a self-made trap."

"Good, Number Eight. Now you know what to do when the group focus is on someone else, don't you?"

"Pay attention and help when I can."

"We're ready to focus again. Who's next?"

There was a flash of panic on Fitz's face. Then Number Six's hand went up and Fitz relaxed.

Kemple said to me as we watched the monitors, "Baker may have established the illusion of rapport with Number Six. This is designed to dispel that feeling."

Evans left his monitor and lay down on a cot. This was obviously familiar to him. I watched with interest.

Number Six told an engrossing tale of the factors that had led him to become a freelance mercy killer and how his avocation had complicated his personal life, especially in the area of establishing a new, durable sexual relationship. Fitz seemed both fascinated and repulsed as Number Six told of his activities.

"When did you have your last long term satisfactory sexual union, Number Six?" Number One asked.

"It began over twenty years ago and endured on an on-and-off basis for almost eighteen years. We met through a common interest in the circumstances that cause death. I knew that we were falling in love so I confessed to her that I performed mercy killings on a religious basis—

I'm a follower of Jesus Ortega, of course. She told me that she, too, dealt in death, but that her motivations were philosophical. We accepted each other completely.

"After a few months we began living together but maintaining a certain separateness that allowed us to perform our deviant acts in secrecy. I'm not saying our existence was idyllic; I saw that it was better for me than I could have imagined any commitment being. We filled our joint life with activity so we would not miss the absence of philosophical and religious discussions.

"Almost three years ago in a drug roulette group, someone substituted Truthtalk for some genuine Brazilian yaje and my lover ended up taking it. To my amazement—and it is hard to be amazed when Sodium Pentothal is being time-released into your bloodstream—my lover began telling these friends and strangers about receiving instructions through a triple-blind mail drop to assassinate someone on the Berkeley campus of the University of California.

"She said that the unique aspect of this assignment was that she wasn't give a name or description of the target, just told where to stand, where to aim the laser and what exact time to squeeze the beamer—"

I had a close-up of Fitz's face on my monitor; he looked enraged as he yelled, "Did she kill Dennis Nash?"

"Shut up, Number Thirteen," shouted Number One. In her regular tone of voice, she said, "Go on, Number Six."

Fitz persisted. "Did she kill Dennis Nash?"

"Number Thirteen, I can easily gather enough support to shut you up. We are going to do this my way. You are going to shut up. Your only choice is whether it is voluntary or involuntary."

Fitz's stance and countenance were the essence of impotent fury. He struggled to speak, repressed the effort and gradually resumed his former seat.

Number One nodded to Number Six and said, "Continue."

"One of the strangers who recognized that she was not hallucinating began asking her questions which she answered candidly. It seemed insane. She was building a fund to finance a secret change of identity and a life of great wealth by assassinating persons with a potential to become politically dangerous. I can understand killing someone whose life is a burden—I do that myself. Because I have a reverence for life. But to kill someone over politics! You might as well kill them over a lapse in good taste."

Number Six paused. Fitz was listening intently, anxious to get every word. I turned to Kemple and said, "That was unexpected."

A smile played at the edges of Kemple's smug mouth. "Good research pays dividends."

"I must have nodded off soon after that," continued Number Six. "When I became aware of externals again, my lover was gone. I asked my host and hostess if they knew where she was and they told me she had left with the stranger who had asked her all the questions. Then the hostess pulled me aside and asked me if it was true that I was a freelance mercy killer as my lover had revealed before leaving, because if I was, she—my hostess—found that very exciting and would love to watch some time, perhaps with a small group of friends. I left immediately."

Shaking his head as if to dislodge disturbing images imprinted in his mind, Number Six continued, "I went back to our bode. It was absolutely bare: no personal possessions of hers or mine: no furniture, no food, no dishes, no computer, no viewscreen. The fabrics had been stripped from the walls and the rugs from the floors. I knew I couldn't stay so I activated my own new identity—surgery, conditioning, habit pattern switchover, new papers, new reality. As soon as my identity was power proof, I began a discrete search for her.

"I know she could have changed height, weight, color of skin, sex, personality, character. None of that makes any difference to me. I still love her and I still want her. My search has led me to this group. Someone here is her! Please identify yourself to me. We can work it out. I bear no grudges. I make no more judgments."

Most of the group was open-mouthed in surprise. Fitz looked bewildered. I said to Kemple, "Nicely done. What happens next?"

"Number One works on Number Six to get him to face the possibility that his search brought him to the group so he could learn to accept the improbability of ever locating his former lover who might be long dead. She gets him to admit that reestablishing the relationship is unrealistic and he gradually appears to convert to her point of view, somewhat. Meanwhile, he continues to look at some members of the group as if they might be out of his past."

"What will he say to Fitz on break when Fitz asks him about the Berkeley assassination?"

Kemple smiled and said, "He'll suspect Baker of being his lover disguised with a sex change. He'll say that he doesn't have any more information than he revealed. That will add to Baker's frustration."

"As long as you are going to record it, I'll just sleep through that. Unless you think the next focus is going to contain information or reactions pertinent to Fitz?"

"No. We're going to keep Baker interested enough to stay awake, but the small frustrations and confusions we have slated for him you can review tomorrow at your leisure. Either Evans or I will call you if something significant occurs."

I stretched out on the cot easily, letting my fatigue fall into the rhythm of sleep. Whatever I thought of Kemple as a person or his therapeutic methodology, there was no doubt that he was highly competent and somewhat devious. However, Fitzgerald Baker was one of the most resistant patients to therapy I'd ever encountered. Kemple had his work cut out for him. I only hoped that he was as successful at triggering Fitz's anger as his confidence suggested. Sleep soon dropped its soothing veil over my magpie mind.

CHAPTER 20

ANGER TERMINATION THERATY

Things do not change; we change.
Henry David Thoreau

During the night I awakened once, prompted by a full bladder. Kemple was asleep. Evans was monitoring. The group focus was on Number Four, a blonde, buxom actress who had spent the last three years in the residential Shakespearean company in the New Deal Enclave, which was, according to her, "a place where culture is respected without being enjoyed and where social stagnation is supported by the endless opportunities for boredom." Just hearing about the New Deal Enclave again was enough to put me back to sleep.

When I awoke in the morning, the group had been up all night and Number One had them out on the sand doing wakeup exercises. During the exercise period and their breakfast break I had some coffee and toast while looking over the taped material on Fitz. The exchange between him and Number Six went just as Kemple had planned it.

Just before noon, after two hours of harassing a tall, lank man with limp hair and mustache who was a conspiracy buff, Number One called a food break. I wondered if her persecution of Number Five, who believed he was being snooped on by a master organization of conspiracy control called ACE, was her attempt to bring Fitz face-to-face with his own paranoid tendencies. All the members of the group got up except Number Eleven who was asleep in his chair. Number One said to let him sleep.

When the break was over, she woke up Number Eleven and said, "It's your turn and you don't get to sleep through your own life unless it's so boring that it puts all of us to sleep." Fitz appeared suitably impressed and increased his coffee consumption. Kemple was sleeping and I told Evans I would be back in a few minutes. I walked around the island twice to keep my muscles feeling alive.

The low point of the afternoon was the problems of Number Twelve, a woman of approximately thirty-five who had tired of her life as a dentist. She had managed to get a government grant to follow an original line of research to find a way to counteract the loss of tooth color brought about by the repeated use of Tranzokeen, a drug which induces mystical trances. So far Number Twelve had developed a recovering agent less effective than the ones on the market; however, she had also become a habitual user of Tranzokeen.

Kemple coached Number One and she tried to use the session to get Fitz to confess to his Noanx overuse—it didn't happen.

Kemple looked at me afterward and said, "The structure is strong enough that not every trick has to work." I was relieved to find that the great man was fallible, like the rest of us, and hoped for Fitz's sake that his anger termination therapy was as effective as he and Serge seemed to believe.

Watching so many fatigued people had a tiring effect on me. I took a break for a sandwich, glass of apple juice and a short nap after checking the schedule with Kemple. The most probable schedule said it would be another ten or twelve hours before the focus turned to Fitz unless he demanded it.

Number One called for an exercise period in the late afternoon to be followed by a meal and a short sleep period. During the exercise period,

Number Twelve tried to interest Fitz in the wonders of Tranzokeen and he became quite agitated. He avoided her during the plain meal of stewed vegetables. Number One watched via monitor to determine when Fitz went to sleep; she ended the sleep break one hour later.

Tempers grew shorter as the evening wore on or at least they appeared to under the authority of Number One and the occasional direction of Kemple. Differences between members of the group caused minor emotional flare-ups; Number Nine and Number Eleven got into a major dispute over which of them would be the next focal point of the group. Number One ordered the others out of the way and let the two men indulge in a useless bit of fighting. Soon both had worn themselves out by punching sport suit deflector plates. Then she gave them both a symbolic kick in the pants by announcing that Number Seven was next.

I watched Fitz. He had a look on his face I had not seen before as if despite the fatigue he was alert and attuned to the gestalt of the group. There was no way I could be sure, but I suspected Fitz was prepared to reveal his problems to the group.

Number Seven, a rotund middle-aged man with mismatched blue eyes, presented a formidable intellectual defense system. As Number One with the assistance of other group members began to dismantle the structure, Number Seven began raising new walls to be stormed, each of the new barriers having less foundation in reality. Number One finally drove Number Seven into a position where he said, "I failed because I wanted the experience of failure to help me mature as an artist."

Number One asked the group. "Will those who believe Number Seven's last statement raise their hands?"

No hands went up.

Number One asked, "Can any of you imagine any adult of average experience and intelligence believing Number Seven?"

Again no one replied.

Turning her pale eyes on Number Seven, she said, "Insecurity can be cured. The first step in the cure is admitting that you have the symptoms."

The mental housecleaning Number Seven needed took until 0400. At that time Number One took a coffee break.

I asked Kemple when he thought Fitz would be ripe for the focus; he estimated about six more hours. I said that I was going to get some sleep.

Evans woke me up, saying, "This is something you ought to see." I felt as if I'd hardly slept. I sat down at the monitor and saw that the time was 0430.

Coffee break had just ended and Fitz was saying to Number One, "Are you especially hostile to me because of something I've done or is that just the way you deal with everyone to avoid meaningful communication?"

"Me hostile toward you?" asked Number One. "You are a fine one to ask that. You are hostile to all women, particularly to any woman who has authority."

Fitz came to his feet shaking his head. "You're wrong. My lover had authority. I loved her but she died. She was murdered. I can't think about anything else."

I heard Kemple say to Number One. "Go with the script. It's earlier than we planned but he's ready." Then he turned to me saying, "We're off and running."

"I'm not wrong," Number One told Fitz. "When someone tells me I'm wrong that means I've hit your resistance. Sit there." She pointed to the chair that directly faced her. "Tell me what you disliked about your lover."

"I didn't dislike anything about her. Angela was the ideal lover, perfect."

"Number Thirteen, no names. You know the rules: Follow them." She looked around the circle and said, "Is anyone here dumb enough to believe that Number Thirteen had a woman who was perfect?"

"Hmm. No takers. Not surprising. She wasn't perfect. She died. She left you alone. How do you feel about that?"

I looked at Kemple and Evans; both were intent on their monitors.

I was glad they weren't looking at me. My face was reflecting how hard Number One's statements were hitting me. I had a momentary flash of paranoia, thinking that Serge had set me up for a dose of reality therapy. I banished the thought and brought my attention back to Fitz's tortured face.

Fitz was telling the group about Angela being buried alive as though he were there. He was certain there had been an attempt on his life.

Number One interrupted with, "Be responsive. The question is how do you feel about your lover betraying you by dying?"

"I'm grieved by her death—there's a spinning black whirlpool at my feet and I've been slipping into it ever since she died." Fitz banged his hands down on the table and then froze. A few seconds later he shook his head, like a swimmer coming out of a pool, and then began to speak. "I've been in pain and mourning since she died, but I don't blame her. She was the perfect lover that I'd always searched for. I found her and lost her. It's the greatest loss in my life, but I don't blame her."

"I ask you what you feel and you tell me what you think," said Number One. "That's non-responsive. Emotions aren't subject to a logic framework. Of course you blame her even if you can't accept it. You say she was the perfect lover that you had always searched for."

She turned to Number Six. "Number Six, you're the local expert on searching for an alleged perfect lover. What has it done for you?"

"It gave me a false front to hide behind, a way to avoid living while waiting for death." His blue eyes were on Fitz's face as if looking for clues.

Number One made a continuing circular motion with her hand while saying to Number Six, "What else. Come on. Get it out."

Number Six dropped his eyes from Fitz to his own hands. "It was my escape clause. I used it to escape from the real image in the mirror, to avoid looking at who I am regardless of what has happened to me."

In her group instruction manner, Number One said, "That's called displacement behavior. Very common. Very negative to her." She paused and then in a sympathetic voice asked, "How many other women have betrayed you, Number Thirteen?"

"My mother left me with my aunt when I was school age; my mother wasn't into parenthood. She only had me to pull my father closer to her. When he died, she didn't need me anymore."

"How complete. Your authority figure lover leaves you through death. Your father died and your mother abandoned you. Did you know that parents are the only authority a child recognizes in the early years? Parents are the godlike figures who rule every aspect of the only existence a child knows. Your mother was the authority figure because your father didn't care. The two most important female authority figures in your life desert you and you say you have no reason to be hostile to women in authority.

"I'm a woman. I have the authority here. Can you tell me what you think or feel about me?"

Fitz looked her in the eye and replied, "You're a cold-hearted bitch. I take that back; bitch means female and bitches go into heat. There's nothing female or warm about you. You get a sick thrill tearing people apart. You don't care much about how they are put back together, what you haven't destroyed. You're a predator looking for victims."

"A very average reaction for the unaware," Number One stated, shaking her head in mock solemnity. "You want someone to hold your hand and say 'Poor baby?' What a shock I must be. You would take any gesture of comfort and use it as support for your immature behavior. You don't like me because I confront you with the truth. I'm the star of this show, the queen of the attack therapists. You are the star of your fantasies and I'm destroying those fantasies with the truth you need to begin living again. I'm the best in the business. I've got the talent, the education, the training and the experience. You've paid for the experience you're getting because you need it.

"You can waste your time, energy and credits fighting me, but it won't help you. Only I can help you. You don't have to like me and I don't have to be bothered about irrelevant matters such as whether I like you or not. It's time for you to take an active part in your own life. Tell me about your aunt."

Number One was pushing too hard; I could see the resistance on

Fitz's face. I wondered if I wanted on some level for her to fail. After all, if she succeeded that meant I was the failure. Or was it that simple…?

Fitz slumped back in his chair and said, "She didn't die and she didn't abandon me. She encouraged me in my political inclinations. She fed me. Clothed me. Provided the only real home I had until I designed my own."

"What else did she do?"

"She often spoke at political rallies, and took me along. She's a militant atheist, opposed to organized religions. Sees them all as scams and power trips. She always said, 'The god dodge is a confidence game.' She wanted all religious tax advantages revoked and the 'Jesus Merchants' put out of business. She's an inspired speaker and considered an expert on government subsidies to religious organizations."

Fitz shot a meaningful look at Number One and added, "That's the only area in which she's a genuine authority."

"Ah. There were other areas where she wasn't expert?"

"I never doubted my aunt's love for me, but she didn't know how to express it. She couldn't cope with my puberty; I learned more about sex by chance from my mother and her friends than my aunt ever knew. Since some of my classmates knew that my father was Zach Baker—pardon me—that my father had been a sex star in the auggies, they expected me to know all about sex. I didn't really. But I managed to see all of my father's auggies and got some ideas, and some help from one of my teachers. When I put some of those ideas into practice with my union mates, there was a lot of flak from their parents."

Kemple said to Number One, "Hit him with being able to act without a woman's direction then and not being able to now."

"So you used to be able to act on your own. Without a woman to tell you what to do."

Anger blazed in Fitz's eyes. "No woman has told me what to do in a long time."

"I truly doubt that. How did your aunt react to the flak from the parents?"

"She refused to discuss it. She punished me by putting me on restriction. All of my time was structured with supervision or close accounting."

"How did you feel about that?"

"I was frustrated. I felt like a prisoner. How would you feel?" I could see the vein over Fitz's temple throbbing.

"I'm not here for therapy. You are. What did you do about it?"

"A sympathetic teacher helped me get transferred to a boarding school so I could escape from my aunt. So we could have weekends together. I escaped from my aunt. She didn't abandon me."

"Oh. How hard did she fight to keep you?"

Fitz, obviously proud of his actions, said, "She wasn't my legal guardian. I signed the papers myself."

"You're blocking again. Answer the question."

"She didn't fight at all. She barely muttered a goodbye."

"But you have no feelings of betrayal over your aunt's actions—or, in this case, lack of actions. Let's have some feedback. Who wants to tell Number Thirteen how they'd feel about that aunt in that situation?"

"I'd have wanted to kick that old jade in the ass or smash something," Number Nine said. He slapped the seat next to him with a resounding whack.

Number Seven said, "Number Thirteen's too intelligent for that kind of behavior and so am I. I'd submerge my anger in fantasy. Invent some mysterious reason for her behavior. Like a family curse with all adult members sworn to secrecy, pledged not to reveal the romantic, tragic details. I've done that kind of thing in my own fantasy life."

"Okay," Number One said. "Enough. We have one vote for violent reaction and one vote for self-delusion. Respond, Number Thirteen."

"I'm not inclined to violent aggression. Number Seven is closer to the truth. There are secrets in my ancestry, secrets that even my mother won't talk about. Events shrouded in mystery."

"We will deal with your fantasies later," Number One said, "the important thing for you to face now is that given a choice of reactions, you chose to turn to another woman to solve the problem. The woman was a teacher, an authority figure. Do you see the pattern beginning to emerge? You seem to have both an attraction and repulsion for female authority figures."

Fitz, frowning in anger, replied, "Do you have to talk about me as if I were a case history?"

"Who is currently repulsed by a woman of authority. What happened to your teacher lover?"

"She just didn't show up one weekend. She didn't screen or anything; I called her home and got no answer. I was hesitant to screen the school. She didn't come the next weekend and when I called her screen was disconnected. I wrote a letter to her and it came back marked: 'Addressee Deceased.' I used the school computer to find out what happened. She had died in an accident."

Number One started to speak, but Fitz made a negative shushing motion with his right hand and continued, "Yes, that's another betrayal in your terms, but I didn't think of it that way. After that I avoided any serious involvement with women. I worked hard in school and went to the university. After I graduated and became an architect, I got much satisfaction in meeting the challenges of my profession. When the challenge was gone, my life became terribly dull until my lover came along. Then I felt alive again."

"Back up. Say it right: To solve my problems, I turned to a dominant woman again."

In a louder than usual voice, Fitz said, "I didn't turn to her. She came to me for a business project."

"But you know very well how to ignore women. You chose to become involved with this particular woman when your lifestyle was a problem to you. To solve your problems, you turned to a dominant woman again.

"Okay. Okay."

"Say it. Out loud. In those words." Number One stood up.

Fitz stood up and said, "When I have a problem, I turn to a dominant woman."

Number One sat down. "Whew. That's over. Now let's look at the process. The woman must possess certain attributes."

Fitz stood silent with clenched fists and his eyes scrunched up.

Number One used her fingers to call out her points. "First, she is outstanding in some way. Second, she is highly sexual. Like your mother. Third, she is verbal, able to express herself about the things she is comfortable with—that may leave out the important emotional things, of course. Fourth, she is a bit of a fanatic. Your aunt was like that wasn't she? Fifth, she is successful in her chosen field. Your lover was well known wasn't she?"

Fitz nodded.

"Your teacher accomplished what she intended under adverse circumstances—How many teachers get to spend sexual weekends with young students? Your aunt is prominent among the many, in your own words, who wish to end the privileged position of religion in government. Your mother is selfish and manipulative. You certainly don't look for the helpless types, do you?"

I could hear the grinding of Fitz's teeth.

Number One took a deep breath and continued. "Most important of all, however, is that the women are flawed. Their path is pitted with trouble. There is little hope for a well-adjusted, joyous personality to emerge. Disaster always waits around the corner."

I had never looked at Angela as actually flawed before—not that I had considered her perfect, just that I saw her as a human being with some unresolved problems and great potential. A flawed person has character and personality traits that create daily problems that continue in the same form regardless of experience, a condition of zero growth. But that wasn't important now. I shifted my attention back to what Number One was saying.

"Meanwhile, Number Thirteen, you play the hapless child caught up in their dilemma. You are swept along. Trapped. Perhaps as a child you were. Then you rejected them. You tried to escape. But you have no pattern of your own. You are lost without an amazon, a woman with an image larger than life. So you found a lover to fit that image. She was not perfect; she just fit the inappropriate image you had in your head Can you see that?"

"Yes," Fitz mumbled. "I can see that."

Kemple said to Number One, "You've got him. Go for the Monroe obsession."

Number One said to Fitz, emphasizing each point by holding up a finger, "Sexy. Powerful. Successful. Flawed. Where does that pattern come from? Where did you get that overlay? Who is the model for the sexy, powerful, successful, flawed female? Tell us, Number Thirteen?"

"You mean my great-grandmother?" Fitz stammered out the sentence and then crimped his eyelids together as if that would hold back the tears.

"Tell us about her."

"She was the legendary sex goddess of the flatties. She married a famous athlete, and an outstanding playwright. She had an affair with and a secret child by the most famous politician of her time. Neither marriage was successful and the politician was assassinated in Dallas. She committed suicide while she was still young."

"Marilyn Monroe and John Kennedy? How exciting!" Number Four cried out.

"Out of order, Number Four. I ask the questions here. We all know about your martyr complex. If you had wanted excitement you would have been in the Camelot Kingdom. You chose to suffer in the F.D.R."

Number One turned back to Fitz and said, "You know about suffering, don't you, Number Thirteen. You've played the tragic hero in pursuit of the unobtainable goal. You aren't mourning your lover except on the surface. Inside you are mourning your great-grandmother. Do you see that?"

"I always wanted to know her," Fitz cried out. "To tell her that I loved her, wanted to understand her, wanted her to live. She died so young. She needed someone to comfort her, to touch her with caring. Someone who could have convinced her to live, not to take the pills. I could have been that someone."

Kemple said to Number One, "Let him talk with Marilyn Monroe in a psychodrama."

"You're going to have that chance right now," said Number One. "Pick someone from the group to be her."

Fitz looked confused. What do you mean?"

"You are going to pick the person in this room who most reminds you of your great-grandmother. That person will act the part. You will have the opportunity to have a face-to-face encounter with your great-grandmother. You will not pick me."

Fitz, with an offended tone, said, "You'd be my last choice." He looked around the group and picked Number Four the blonde actress with the prominent breasts. Now, I understood why she was in the group; I had underestimated Kemple. He had, during his research, come up with an aspect of Fitz's disturbance I had never considered. I had suspected that Number Four's purpose would be something to do with Estelle Zimmer, which I could now see was just a distorted reflection of his relationship with Angela. The real problem lay much deeper.

"What? Ahh… What do you want with me?" the blonde asked in a little-girl voice.

"Number Four you get to play the most famous actress of film and screen."

Number One turned to Fitz and began setting the psychodrama scene. "Where does the meeting take place?"

"A cottage in old Hollywood," Fitz replied.

"Describe it."

"There's a path to it with other cottages on both sides and a number of tall palm trees."

Number One said to the group at large, "Bring up the extra chairs to line the path like they were palms. Move all these chairs back. This area in front of me will be her cottage." Then she turned to Fitz and asked, "Is your great-grandmother's cottage at the end of the path?"

He nodded yes.

"Number Four, get someone to help you move that couch over here." Number Nine and Number Six both helped her move the couch.

"Number Four, sit on the couch and look sexy. Number Seven you'll be Number Thirteen's double; he can talk to you like he was talking to himself about what he is doing. You can echo, amplify and expose his thoughts and emotions."

"The rest of you stand near the cottage, just off the path like you were palm trees. Follow the action and the dialogue. Be ready to speak and act whenever I call on you."

Number One turned to Fitz and pointed at Number Four. There's your great-grandmother waiting for you to come. How do you feel?"

"I'm shaking," Fitz answered, in a subdued voice. "My knees feel weak. My stomach hurts."

"Talk to your double. Tell him what you want to do. No, don't turn around. He's right behind you and can hear you. Look down the path to the woman of your dreams. Tell your double what you're thinking."

"I'm afraid! What if she's…What if she's less than great?"

Number Seven responded, "She's the most beautiful woman in the world, the yin and yang of desire and satisfaction."

"Yes. Yes. I will really see her and touch her."

"Tell your double what you will say to her," Number One ordered.

"I will tell her how much I love her, how much she means to me. Perhaps I'll ask her about the child she had, the child she wasn't allowed to rear. I'll ask her about my great-grandfather and the love she had for him."

In a confidential voice, Number Seven asked, "Will you stop her from taking the pills?"

"I will comfort her. Tell her that I love her. I will not let her die feeling alone and unwanted." Fitz looked toward Number Four; he seemed dazed and his body swayed back and forth as he began to walk down the path.

"You people along the path tell him about her," ordered Number One. "Tell him what he's doing. Don't stop."

The words overlapped and intertwined: "Only a dream."

"She's beautiful but phony."

"So completely fantastic."

"Unreal!"

"Everyman's wet dream."

Fitz slowed and his steps became steady.

"Mad fool."

"Your unappreciated great-grandmother. "Did she really have a child?"

"I'm in love."

Like a bass rhythm, Number Nine chanted over and over while tapping his foot to his own internal beat, "Fuck her. Fuck her. Fuck her…Fuck her…Fuck her…"

Fitz reached the end of the path and moved toward Number Four.

Number One blew her referee's whistle shrilly. "Stop! Now!"

Fitz froze.

"Double, stay with Number Thirteen. Numbers Four and Thirteen stay where you are. Everyone else go sit." She stepped between Fitz and Number Four. She turned to Fitz, she asked, "How do you feel?"

"Why did you do that? Why are you trying to hurt me? Why did you stop me?" Fitz's face was growing red.

"Do I have to remind you that I ask the questions? You answer them. How do you feel?"

"Cheated. Angry! You promised me more."

"We're not through yet. We are looking at the last place that she lived in. The room where she died. I want to know how you feel about her, about actually being here where she died."

"I'm all...I...I don't know. It's hard to talk about it. I feel compassion for her…a desire to make everything right for her."

"Go ahead, Number Thirteen."

Fitz spoke with a soft sadness in his voice as he looked at Number Four and asked, "Why did you take the pills?"

Number Four took a deep breath causing her large breasts to

become even more prominent. "Because nobody loves me. Many men love my body but nobody wants to know what's inside. I said yes to a great number of men. They fulfilled their fantasies with me, but none of them cared about what I wanted. My old friends won't talk to me on the phone. They even took my baby away—told me it was for my own good. I'm all alone."

Fitz took a step forward and said, "You're not alone. I'm here."

"I can sing, dance and act," Number Four said in a melancholy tone. "I feel most alive when I'm entertaining. Everyone pushes me into dumb-blonde roles in films and in life. If I could only get the right part I could prove that I'm more than just a dumb blonde. I'm an actress and a human being. If I could just get the right part I could show that I'm a real actress and a real person."

"I know you are a great actress," Fitz said. "I believe you're a real person. I love you."

"You love me. Men always tell me that. But it's never true. They lust for some fantasy. I want someone to want the real me."

"Tell me about the real you."

"I have trouble with that," Number Four said. She must have been a great actress because the illusion of Marilyn was there, even for me who hadn't seen one of her flat, faded image movies for years. Like Fitz, I wanted her too. I could feel the stirrings in my loins. Number Four continued in her little-girl voice, "The real me is hard to find. The image is so strong. It's so easy to give the image and get temporary acceptance. And so hard to show anyone that I'm vulnerable. Scared. Afraid that I'll say or do the wrong thing." A tear ran down her cheek toward her mouth.

Fitz moved to the couch and sat beside her. "Don't be sad. Lean against me." He stroked her hair, smiled and said, "I care about you."

"Who are you? I can't tell. Future and past are all mixed-up in this place. Who are you?"

"You mentioned having a baby."

"Yes, my son. They wouldn't let me keep him. Are you him? Have you cared enough to come back to me?"

"I'm your great-grandson, your son's grandchild."

Number Four burst into tears. Fitz said, "It's okay. You don't have to worry." He stroked her hair.

"Number Thirteen," Number One said, "you only have a few more minutes with her. Then you have to say goodbye to her forever."

I watched Fitz, waiting for him to tell her not to take the pills, but he didn't say anything. He pulled her closer; he was crying. "I have to go soon."

I was still waiting for him to tell her not to take the pills.

"Someone prompt Number Thirteen."

I looked at Fitz's double. Number Nine began chanting, "Fuck her. Fuck her…Fuck her…Fuck her…"

Fitz's reddened face turned from sad to lustful.

"Yes." He reached for the presfast at Number Four's neck.

Number One's whistle screamed. Then she shouted, "Restraint. Separate them." Number Six and Number Seven grabbed a struggling Fitz.

Fitz turned to Number One. "You dirty bitch. You set me up for this. I'll tear you apart."

"Number Nine, get the foam rubber bats," Number One said. "You two," she said, looking at Numbers Six and Seven who were still holding Fitz, "hang on until the bats are issued. Form a circle around Fitz, everybody. Grab a bat. The battle goes on until Fitz has enough."

The melee that ensued was formidable. Fitz grabbed a bat when his captors released him and started for Number One. Number Nine and Number Eight hit him simultaneously, their foam bats bouncing off his skull and shoulders.

Fitz swung wildly, no longer caring who he hit. Number One and Number Four stayed outside the circle. Soon Fitz disappeared in a mad whirl of bodies and thrashing bats.

He finally slipped to the floor exhausted and sobbing. When his cries had subsided, Number One said, "Now we know Number Thirteen wants to fuck his great-grandmother."

Fitz looked up. "You manipulated me."

"Just to show you what you are doing. You want to fuck your famous great-grandmother. You want what you can't have and you pick substitutes like the mummer surrogate you hired. You can't have the real thing and so you seek substitutes. None of the substitutes can be her so you're doomed to failure. You cling to the failure because it bolsters your image of the tragic figure with the tragic background. Tragic backgrounds are as common as potatoes. They don't matter compared to who you are and what you do.

"Instead of finding out who you are, everything you say and do is a reaction to other people. You live your life by default. You operate in the passive-aggressive mode. You see the things that you 'think' are done to you because you aren't doing anything with your life but playing the tragic hero. And you are not too good at doing that. Open the curtain. Watch the hero tear out his hair, swallow booze, down pills, weep in anguish and chew the scenery.

"That is what makes you feel special. You have been destined by the stars to suffer. What a pathetic role. No one buys a ticket for that. You can see it for free in almost any bar any day, in every beginning therapy group, in every addict's theater of the mind. You're the tragic hero in your own mind and a bystander in life. You let others take your personal power and run with it because you are afraid to act. You have set up a game where you cannot possibly win and when anyone suggests a change, you say, 'I can't give up this game. Look how good I am at playing it.' You've gotten very good at losing just like you have gotten good at victimizing women."

"What do you mean?" Fitz looked shocked. "I don't victimize women."

"Any woman who takes you as a lover is in trouble," Number One stated. "You pick a woman ripe for disaster and then serve up your personal disasters to her as a love offering. Have you thought that maybe you wanted your lover to die? That you wanted it to be your fault because it would reinforce your dumb tragic hero role?"

"You're wrong!" Fitz shouted.

"I'm not wrong. You've set up a pattern of repeating your great-grandmother's problems. You can see the pattern with your last lover as proof. She was ripe for betrayal, obsessed with death. Her son had died. She was building a monument to death and you were helping her. She had alienated a son, divorced a husband, and, with your help, she discarded a lover…."

The abandoned lover phrase gave me only a small twinge.

"Marilyn Monroe was ripe for tragedy and she died. But you don't mourn for her. You mourn for yourself, for the *you* inside that you will not bring to light and life. Let your great-grandmother have her pattern. You have adopted it. Your homework is to take that pattern home and break it if you cannot leave it here."

Fitz stood up to his full height, took a deep breath, and said, "You think you did your homework before you came. You know more about me than I told you. Everyone here does. I know I was set up for this, but I'm not a prisoner and I don't have to take any more of it. But I do have something for you to take and chew on. Something you can take home with you. You talk a lot about lovers and loving, but you wallow in hate. You don't know anything about love. You attack to hide your defenses against love. You sit here on your throne and pronounce judgments, but you don't question who you are or why there is no love in your life. Here's a mirror for you. Who in this group would take Number One as their next lover?"

There were hoots of laughter and scattered applause.

Kemple cried, "*Blow that damn whistle*!"

I hoped this didn't destroy everything Number One had accomplished.

Number One blew her whistle and said, "Coffee break."

Fitz bypassed the coffee machine and determinedly marched out of the rec room. Kemple looked at me and shrugged apologetically; I almost felt sorry for him.

"I am sorry, Dr. Wendell, there appears to have been a lapse of professionalism among the team here. It's most unusual for a patient to elicit so much sympathy from the staff. I wonder if a few of them are beginning to forget they are playing parts here."

Number One was talking angrily with a group of staff members. Number Four was in tears. Number Seven and Number Six were leaving to look for Fitz.

I punched the new camera images up rapidly as Fitz left the castle in the predawn darkness. He began a loping run down the path toward the sand. Then he began a clockwise circuit of the island, always making frequent glances toward the sea.

Kemple was saying to Number One, "*Just stay where you are and call back Number Seven and Number Six. He's just running around the perimeter of the island. I'll keep you informed.*"

Fitz made a complete circuit of the island and then stopped, looking toward the island on the right which had a bridge leading to the mainland. He stripped off his sport suit, entered the water and began swimming toward the lights that were fading in dawn.

"Do you think he can make it to the mainland?" I asked Kemple.

"It's possible, but he'd have to be a very strong swimmer," said Kemple, his face lined with worry. "I think we had better pick him up. We've only had one incident like this before, and that one we had anticipated...."

When Evans and I left for the boat, Kemple was still standing in the same spot with a distracted look on his face. One of the difficulties of a rigid mindset is its inability to respond to sudden change; it looked like Kemple was caught in the middle of a mental earthquake.

After ten minutes of searching with the boat, we pulled up beside a tired Fitz who was swimming furiously. I helped pull him aboard, wrapped a blanket around his cold body and gave him a cup of hot coffee.

Through chattering teeth, Fitz said, "It was a setup, wasn't it?"

"Yes. Are you angry about that?"

"Very," he said, "but I can handle it."

CHAPTER 21

CONFRONTATION

To thine own self be true.
William Shakespeare

My next therapy session with Fitz took place three days after his island marathon experience. I wanted enough time to pass for Fitz to reflect upon his catharsis but not so much time that he would be able to reconstruct his emotional defenses. Also, I needed time to integrate my new insights with my previous assumptions and misconceptions. I had been certain that Fitz's breakdown had been brought about by Angela's death, but Kemple's team had shown me that the genesis of his disturbance went much deeper and was linked to the unique tragedies of his past.

Then Fitz strode into my office, his face was grim and there was a hollowness around the eyes that showed he had not recouped the sleep he had lost during that long weekend. His first words were: "You set me up, Phillip. There was no way I could have escaped that island without being carved up by that school of trained sharks."

"Do you feel I've betrayed you?" I asked.

"You're damn straight, I do."

"And you're angry about it, aren't you?"

Fitz raised his fist and shook it.

"How does it feel, Fitz?"

"Like shit! I want to destroy something."

"Good. Use that energy to destroy those defenses that have been draining you of life. You've been so energetically maintaining your defenses against appropriate emotional reactions that you've had little energy for anything else. Tell me, is feeling angry worse than feeling defeated and helpless?"

Fitz sat down in the captain's seat and began massaging his forehead. "No," he finally said, "It's not worse. But I don't feel as angry now as I did when I came in."

"No, of course not. You've recognized it and dealt with it in a direct manner. Our emotions only control us when we refuse to recognize them, or disavow them. If you can express your anger without creating problems for yourself, you've started on the path of smart emotional management."

"I still resent the hell out of having been the only mark in the group. And I don't like the nonchalant way you eased me into that school of head-shredding sharks."

"You have every right to be angry, Fitz. But if I seemed nonchalant, it's a tribute to the acting training I've received. I've got to promote a confident bedside manner; assurance is part of the treatment." After my unexpected baring of the soul, I felt a sudden euphoria. What I was saying was as important to me as it was to Fitz. By trying to be omnipotent, I'd become impotent. I needed to sever the reins of the past as much as Fitz did.

"You?" Fitz looked at me as if seeing me for the first time.

"Therapists have problems, too," I continued. "I had just learned that I'd failed a client and that I'd never have a chance to help him again. Then I thought I'd lost you. Perhaps I have."

Fitz shrugged his shoulders.

I settled myself in the office chair, turning it slightly so I faced Fitz squarely. "I let Angela influence me too much. I'm sure you understand how that could happen, because it happened to you, too. Honoring Angela's last request, accepting you as client, was so necessary for me as an act of closure that I did it despite my own personal and professional conflicts."

Fitz sat up abruptly and asked, "What conflicts?"

"I was obsessed with a fantasy, although it seemed quite real then, of marrying Angela after she had her suicide center functioning. I resented the place you held in her life and fully intended to replace you in her affections."

Fitz's eyes grew wide and he rose halfway out of his seat. "You wanted to marry Angela?"

"It was a fantasy that goes back a long time. I didn't realize how unreal my plans for us were until she died."

Fitz sat back down. "I can't blame you for loving her because I did, too. But I thought there hadn't been anything between you and Angela for years. She told me several times that that phase of her life was a closed book."

I winced. "There wasn't anything going on, but I had hopes. Damn, it doesn't matter anymore." I swallowed hard and looked Fitz in the eyes. "I believe that I've come to terms with her death, and the end of my romantic fantasy about our relationship."

"I wish I could say that," Fitz replied, as tears began to well in his eyes. "But I'm not lying to myself anymore. I realize she's dead—that her time in this world is finished. I think I can learn to live without her. But I'll need help. And I think you're the one who can best help me. You understand what I'm going through better than anyone else. I want you to help me through the changes, the changes that you understand."

"I'm not convinced any longer that I'm the best person to help you through them. I've already made some decisions in your case that don't seem professional as I review them. I know that I was partially blinded by my own grief, but I was unaware of how little progress we had made in your case until it was almost too late."

I slumped in my chair, recalling the feeling of defeat I experienced when I had found Fitz collapsed in his underground home.

"Phillip, are you really free of Angela? For good?"

"Freer than I've been since I first fell in love with Angela, or my fantasy of Angela."

Fitz looked forlorn. In a soft voice, he said, "Angela had that unique ability to be what every man wants a woman to be, and yet be herself too."

"Like a prism," I returned, "but only reflecting those bands of light the viewer wants to see. There was always more just out of sight...I wonder if either of us really knew her, truly."

Fitz brought me out of my musings with his next words. "You said before that you accepted me as a client as an act of closure for your relationship with Angela. Can you deny yourself that closure? Don't you need that as much as I need your help?"

"Fitz, I don't know that I can help you. I haven't done a satisfactory job so far—"

"You can do a lot better now that I have some hope, now that I'm willing to cooperate with you. Before I was just going through the minimum motions, following the path Angela had charted for me. Now, I see that I can change. Maybe I can even find happiness. But I need help, Phillip, just as you need to feel you granted Angela her last request."

I started to speak but Fitz went on before I get could get out the first word. "I'll do it your way, and I won't hide anything from you. I'll tell you what I do, what I think and what I feel. I've survived the death of Angela because you cared. I need you now that you've given me hope. Don't desert me now. I couldn't survive the death of hope."

"Are you going to be as honest with me as you're capable of being?"

"Yes. Just try it until the end of the month. If either one of us is dissatisfied with the progress I've made, you can refer me to someone else knowing that you have fulfilled your final obligation to Angela."

This was the first time I'd been exposed to the Baker charm and persuasion, the charisma I'd heard others speak of. I didn't want to let it rob me of my professional judgment. "Do you resent the position I held in Angela's life?"

"No. I always saw you as her friend. Never as my competition."

I sighed, thinking about the future that might have been. Then I shut off my interior babble, asking, "Are you still angry with me for leaving you on Retreat Island?"

Fitz brought his hands together with a loud smack. "Of course, I'm still angry!" Then he closed his eyes and shook his head. "But more with myself than you. I'm the one who mucked things up so badly that you had to deceive me to get me to come to terms with my own feelings."

"Then the anger you feel toward me, the anger that could get in the way of treatment, must be your resentment of me for having sex with your mother. Is that it?"

I'd caught Fitz off guard; the muscles of his face went slack, unsure of what expression to make. He stammered. "My mother behaves in accordance with her standards and I accept that. I shouldn't get angry about that."

"But you are. No matter what logic tells you to think about it you feel angry about your mother copping with me instead of you."

"But Mary offered to cop with me anytime. Why should I be angry? You aren't getting anything I couldn't have had. Could have now, if I wanted it. Mary would think it a *grand adventure* in defying conventional morality—what little there is left of morality these days..."

"Even so, you experience the anger of lost expectations. As a child, can you remember wanting to be special to your mother?"

"Of course."

"When she offered herself to you, you knew her sexual attitudes. You were aware that she was open to a wide spectrum of sexual activity. Isn't it possible that you didn't take her offer because you feared that the act itself would not be special enough to make you the most important person in her life?"

Fitz's hands were trembling. "I...I never thought of it like that, but that could be true."

"You wanted to be her lover, but you were afraid that you might lose her for good if your performance wasn't spectacular. Another faceless body among the legions of her lovers. Yet, you wanted her. Didn't you?"

"SHUT UP!" Fitz rose out of the captain's chair menacingly.

"You wanted her all for yourself. But it didn't work, did it? You lost her anyway." I was operating with more intuition than usual and it felt good to be making real progress on my own.

Fitz had fallen back into the captain's chair and was sobbing. "She... She never wanted me. All I was to her was an anchor to my father...but he didn't want either of us... He was the smart one. Maybe I should have fucked the bitch—"

"It's all right, Fitz. That time is over. You did the right thing. Not only did it gratify your immature desire to return rejection for rejection, but it kept you from a situation that might have caused you more problems than you're dealing with now."

Fitz was crying openly, releasing the confined rage and frustration of a lifetime. When his sobs had turned to shudders, I went over to him and held him in my arms.

After the flow of tears had dried up, Fitz blew his nose and then asked, "Phillip, what did you mean by more problems? It's hard to believe that anything Mary and I would have done could have made things worse than they are now."

"If you had slept with Mary and the experience had been just an ordinary sexual encounter, you would have considered it another failure in your efforts to get and keep her attention. That would have been bad enough. Suppose the sexual experience was exceptional for either or both of you? The result would have been much more complex and problematical—both of you would have been involved in some form of scheming and manipulative relationship. And with Mary's history of promiscuity, any relationship based on sex would have been doomed from the beginning. To say nothing of the guilt and anxiety that would have resulted, at least on your part; after all, you were raised—not by Mary—but by a sexual prude, Isobel Grant. Can you see that, Fitz?"

Fitz shook his head like a deep-sea diver coming up out of the water. "Give me a few moments to assimilate what you've just said. I've never looked at it in this light before." He was looking toward the window but the gaze of his attention was turned inward. His eyes were dry, but puffy and bloodshot.

I had a good feeling, maybe the first since Fitz had disappeared, about the future of our relationship. At last I had an awareness of the many factors in Fitz's maladaptation. Kemple's therapy had broken down Fitz's defenses long enough for me, and possibly him, to look around and examine some of the inner clockwork.

"Phillip, I'm not through thinking over what you said about Mary and me. I may want to talk with you again about it."

"Certainly."

"Does that mean I'm still your client?"

"Yes. But I want you to commit yourself to taking an active role in living. No retreats. No turning back."

"I don't want to go back, Phillip. What do we do next?"

"We'll devote the next session to a review of your experience on Retreat Island. As you know, I watched the entire scene on a monitor. I know it was a painful experience, but it was a necessary one and we must make the most of the information we got from it."

Fitz nodded. "Because of that weekend I've decided to sell my boat. That was part of my life with Angela."

"I applaud your decision, Fitz." It was a good decision for it showed not only an acceptance of Angela's death but—I hoped, since the boat was a replica of John F. Kennedy's PT 109—a lessening of the Kennedy fixation. He still had the Monroe obsession, which was obvious from his encounter with her in the psychodrama. He had been so overwhelmed by the encounter that he forgot to stop her from taking the pills—was it because he hadn't come to terms with his own suicidal impulses?

"I also plan to redecorate my house to help me get Angela out of my everyday thoughts. I'm going to do that right away. Then I want to see Estelle Zimmer and apologize to her."

"Are you thinking of resuming a relationship with her?"

"No. I want to wait until I'm more certain about my feelings before I begin another relationship."

"I think that's wise for the time being. Estelle will probably invite you to see her in a musical comedy based on the exploits of the Green Jinni; Serge and I are going."

"If she does, shall we all attend together? Make up a theater party?"

"That's a great idea." I was pleased to see Fitz take an interest in something outside of his obsessions. This might be the right time to risk asking him about the Monroe encounter. "Fitz, can you tell me why—during the psychodrama on the island—you didn't try to stop your great-grandmother from taking the pills?"

Fitz looked down at his lap and began rubbing his hands. "I...I'm not sure. Maybe I didn't think I had the right...I don't know."

I debated running him through the scenario with his surrogate great-grandmother, but decided against it. One major trauma per session was enough; I didn't want to scare him away now that we were making progress. I said, "We'll look into that later."

He gave me a thankful look.

CHAPTER 22

THEAPEUTIC DECISIONS

Life is just one damned thing after another.
Elbert Hubbard

During the next two sessions, Fitz and I went over the tape of his session on Retreat Island. He was coming to terms with most of his experiences there, although he still felt uncomfortable viewing the scene with the surrogate Marilyn Monroe. He had given me a number of possibilities as to why he hadn't tried to convince the woman who played Marilyn Monroe in the marathon not to commit suicide—being overwhelmed by the experience, being uncertain what to say or do that would seem genuine to her, being overcome by his own fantasies, being unsure that his own attitude toward life was strong enough to deter suicide. It was obvious to me that he still had ambivalent feelings about living and I felt if we could resolve this issue he would be well on his way to a healthy and stable lifestyle.

Two days before our next session, Fitz called to tell me he had redecorated his house and invited me to stop by on Thursday morning around 1000 and see the new decor prior to a joint breakfast. I had only seen his geotecture home once and that was under dark and adverse circumstances. I was pleased by his invitation and accepted, thinking that this would be the right time to talk with Fitz about his architectural career.

On Thursday morning I got off the La Cienega tramline and walked past the huge fig tree to Fitz's gate, which opened to my keycard. As soon as I started down the stairs to the atrium I could see many differences. The Spanish look was gone, replaced by a gestalt that I would term Japanese-Mondrian: lots of white space, horizontal and vertical lines enclosing patches of red or yellow or blue with minimal furniture also in primary colors.

"How do you like it?" Fitz asked.

"I'm impressed. You did all this yourself?"

"Some I designed. Some I selected. I did all the painting but hired a carpenter to create the built-in furniture.

"What do you call this look? Japanese-Mondrian?"

"That would be a good name for it. They're two of my sources, as are the Scandinavians. I wanted to create a comfortable atmosphere with the feeling of spaciousness and solid geometry. My former decor was intended to make the house comfortable for Angela. One of the traps I built to prolong the relationship."

"I find it an encouraging sign that you can mention Angela's name in a realistic context. Do you think you have finally let her go?"

"There are two things left in this house that symbolize Angela. A copy of her letting-go ceremony and about three fingers of Spanish brandy. I thought you and I would finish the brandy while I burn my copy of the ceremony in the barbecue as an act of closure for my relationship with Angela."

We toasted Angela and then tossed the glasses into the disposer to follow the bottle. Perhaps that is the modern version of breaking the glasses after the toast; to me, and to Fitz, it was an act of completion. Outside Fitz tossed the data wafer onto the gas grill; the fire flared-up with blue and red flames followed by a quick explosion of multi-colored sparks.

We walked eight blocks to the Egg Keg for breakfast. Inside we showed our keycards to the scanner, punched out our orders on the menu terminals and, in a few minutes, were eating our omelets—mine with truffles and Fitz's with onions and mushrooms—and drinking black coffee from brown ceramic mugs.

Over a second cup of coffee, I asked Fitz, "Have you decided whether or not to go back to work with your partner?"

"I haven't made up my mind yet."

"Have you thought much about it?" I inquired.

"Yes, but I haven't made up my mind."

"Fitz, I'd like for you to tell me what factors are involved in that decision. Maybe I can help you to clarify your thinking."

"I'm not sure what the factors are. I'm still not certain what's important and what's not."

"Have you talked it over with your partner?"

"No. Clyde took over what work was left on Angela's Center when I couldn't continue. He's handling everything."

"How do you feel about that? About letting go of your work on Angela's Center?"

"It seems okay. I've done all the creative work. That was the important part. I was very interested in all the details when Angela was alive—she had that way about her, you know. With her gone, it's become just another project with a few loose ends. Clyde's good at handling loose ends. He's a different kind of architect than I am."

"How's he different?"

"Clyde comes from a family that made their money in demolition work. He had more of a creative streak than anyone else in the family so he decided to build structures rather than destroy them. He enjoys the whole process from the initial examination of the site through the final touches that make the building ready for use."

"What parts of the process do you enjoy, Fitz?"

"Primarily, creating the design. Looking at the site and examining all the engineering data are just necessary preliminaries. When I'm at my drafting screen with all the information in mind or at hand, that's when I get lost in my work, that's when I really enjoy it."

"Isn't seeing the final structure important too?"

"In a secondary way. It's a validation of my design, but it's not as satisfying as actually creating the design. Once construction has been completed all that's left is fine tuning the details, which any competent contractor can take care of."

"I've seen your home and I was impressed by it. But I'd really like to see some larger structure that you've designed, something you're pleased with."

"You mean now?"

"Sure." I said.

"How about the pyramound in Calm Springs, which is one of my favorites because I was given a large area to choose from and was allowed artistic freedom."

"What is it used for?"

"Western headquarters for the Nutritional Research Institute."

"Let's vault there now."

We left the Egg Keg and began walking to the nearest vault station. There was a spring in Fitz's step I had never observed before. I was glad to see he was feeling very alive and pleased that he was ready to talk about the status of his career. The marathon weekend had renewed the wellspring of his vitality. If I could get him to examine his career now, he would be able to view it in perspective. After that step—a comparatively easy one—I would have to get him to deal with his flirtation with death. That was going to be difficult, and I wasn't sure that either one of us was ready. Angela, who had been the best suicide crisis therapist in Los Angeles, hadn't been able to counteract Fitz's suicidal tendency; she had merely kept him from acting it out.

Finally, I had faced that fact; Angela hadn't cured Fitz of his self-destructive behavior. But why hadn't she cured him? Was it because she couldn't, or because she wanted to keep him tied to her apron strings? Had she wanted to recreate Jason in Fitz?

I dropped the thoughts of Angela as we entered the vault station. An assorted party of six, all wearing faddish after-midnight makeup of

Chinese red, emerged, talking about a festival they had just attended in Hong Kong. They headed for the cleansers as Fitz and I went to the terminals, pressed our keycards to the scanners, punched in our destination and went to our respective vault booths.

The vault stations, which ran along the Earth's magnetic lines of force, or ley lines, were inoperable anywhere else or under a distance of less than eighty-five kilometers. Inside the darkened cubicle, I experienced a lightless flash as I was transported via the energy force lines to the foothills of the San Bernadino Mountains. I emerged from a similar cubicle into the Calm Springs station, which differed from every other vault station only in its signs. Automatically, although if I had thought about it I would have realized I hadn't changed time zones, I checked my watch against the clock showing local time.

Fitz—having, of course, arrived at the same time and emerging from his booth—saw me look at my watch and said "Local time is 1148." As far as I could tell he hadn't glanced at the clock and he wasn't wearing a visible watch. I asked, "What told you the correct time?"

"It's one of my tricks. I always know what time it is wherever I am."

"How did you learn that?"

"I've always had that ability."

"Can you teach it to me?" I asked.

"I don't know how it's done, but I suspect everyone has the ability. If I ever work it out, I'll tell you."

As we left the vault station I saw the pyramound about two klicks away. I had seen it before but saw it through new eyes now that I was standing next to the man who designed it. The hemispherical top was the mound that collected the maximum solar energy for utilization in the modules below, which were assembled in the form of an inverted pyramid. Each outside corner was supported by a large tube that housed both a lift and a baffled gravity drop which could be used for people and equipment. The pyramound was visually appealing and blended harmoniously with the nearby foothills and mountains. With unspoken agreement Fitz and I boarded the tram that ran from the vault station to the building.

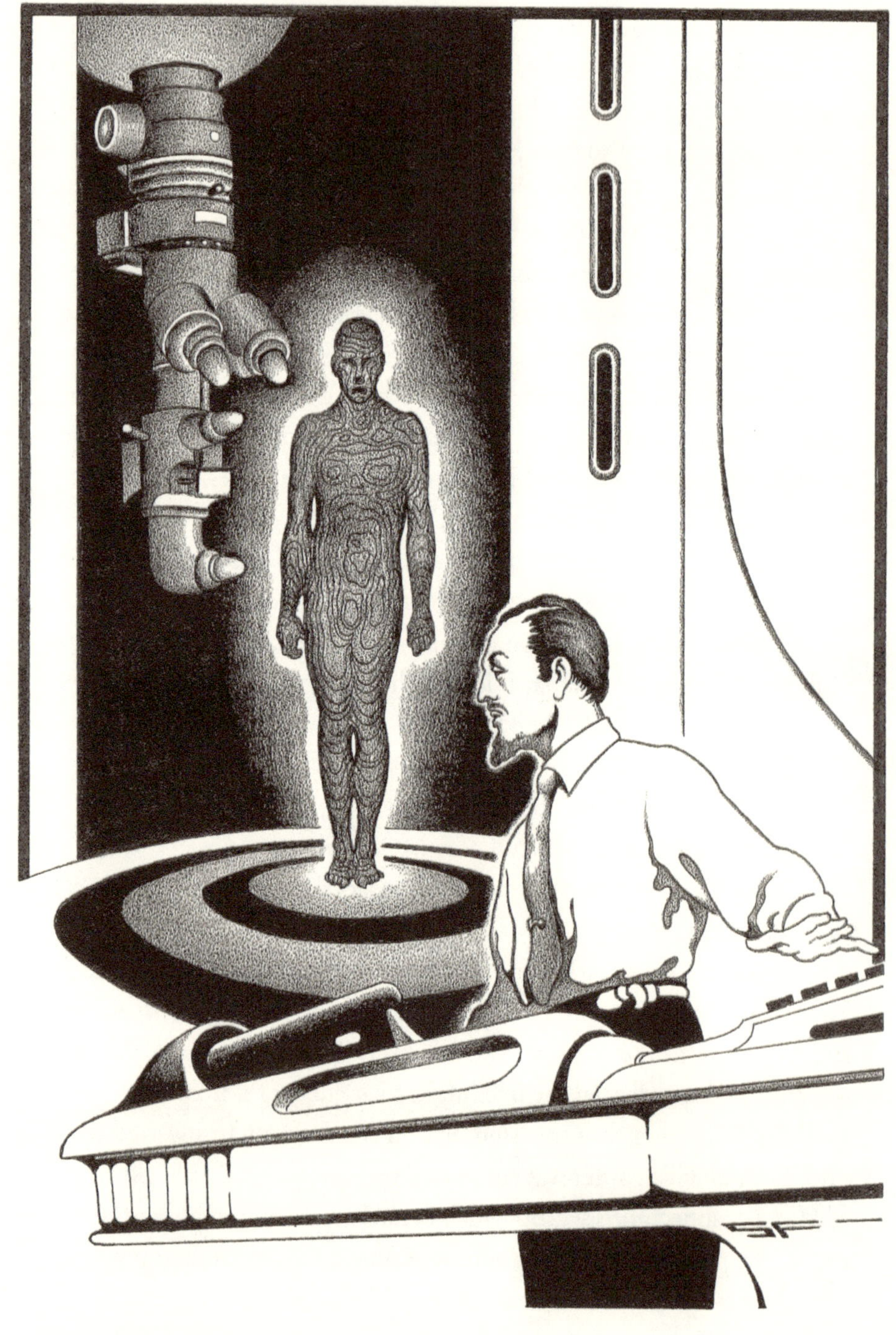

Fitz was looking off into the distance, perhaps at the top of the mountains. I got his attention by saying, "I compliment you on your achievement."

"Thank you. It's one of my better efforts."

"It looks as though it was designed for this location, was it?"

"Yes. This was the best location of the ones where the dowser found water."

As we neared the first tube, I asked Fitz if he had invented the concept.

"Oh, no. The idea of powered lifts and gravity drops have both been around for some time; I just modified them for the pyramound. When the techies were responsible for most architectural design, or what John Brunner called 'shitabrick phase architecture,' there were no gravity drops. That meant that a power failure would trap the people on the upper floors inside the building—it was the same kind of shortsightedness that produced the neutron bomb."

I was pleased to note a touch of anger in Fitz's voice; he was dealing more openly and honestly with his emotions with each passing session. When we reached the terrace, I put my keycard in the voucher plate and dialed two cups of coffee from the automatic dispenser. As we reached for our cups, Fitz asked, "Phillip, can you name one architect from the last century who has an admired work standing today?"

"Frank Lloyd Wright."

"Good choice," Fitz said. "Can you name one of his works that you've seen?"

"The Mayan Temple on Glendower Avenue in the Fringes."

"Ahh, the Ennis House. You are hereby awarded two points, would you like to try for four?"

"No, I'd rather concede that most of twentieth century architecture was uninspired and not well adapted to human needs, values or aesthetics."

We took our coffee cups to a nearby table with a view of the dry, brown mountains. I mentally reviewed what Fitz had said previously about architecture before speaking again. "At an earlier meeting you commented that you were bored with architecture. Would you be willing to expand on that thought?"

Fitz nodded. "Sure. We were just talking about twentieth century architecture, but not all of it was low-tech wood frame housing or stucco shoeboxes. There were some very innovative and provocative architects: Buckminster Fuller, who created the geodesic dome and the city sphere; William Moruan, the father of the underhome movement; Francisco Carbajal de la Cruz, whose inexpensive modular houses sprouted like termite mounds throughout Africa; Steve Baer, the originator of the Zomeworks un-homes; Paolo Soleri, the designer of the first arcology, Arcosanti, which is now being completed by the Pueblo Indians or even Claes Oldenburg, who built the Dream Cathedral—a fantasy temple thirty stories high—during the twenties. For all their efforts, what do we have today: the tall-wall, the huburb, the city stalk, the home dome, the archplex…need I go on?"

I shook my head.

Fitz continued, "I was fortunate; early on, I worked on several projects like this one which established me as a young and innovative architect. Not a major talent, but someone to watch. I occupy a comfortable niche and get one or two interesting projects a year to work on, but nothing too important. Like the pyramound, my best work seems behind me now. This building, with its replaceable modules, will, most likely, last longer than I will.

"When I was young, I wanted to build cities and arcologies that would live and procreate… Earthworks that would incorporate art and life. But what have I been doing: designing tinker toy towns for the rich. Do you know what Clyde wants to work on now?"

"Huburbs and other large multipurpose structures, I suppose."

"Yes. He feels stifled and wants to expand. My God, the first huburb was built seven years after I was born! Working on huburbs is like reinventing the wheel. The only major design question is what style:

Egyptian, Mesopotamian, Persian, Greek, Roman, medieval, renaissance, academic, baroque, functionalist, technic—or some combination of any number. The idea of doing that kind of work makes me feel dusty inside."

"You don't have to do what Clyde wants. Start your own firm, Fitz."

"Five years ago, maybe. Or even if Angela was still alive...she could have made any kind of life worthwhile. Now it seems so fruitless."

"But how about the new project you were working on, The Pantheon of Prophets?"

"Yes, it's exciting all right, but I only got that commission because they thought they might be able to use me politically. Because of my ancestry, there's always someone or some group that thinks they can make me into a politician. I went into architecture to get away from all of that."

Fitz walked over to the terrace railing and looked down. I rose up slowly, trying not to show the alarm I felt. The railing came up to just above his waist; his hands were gripping the rail so tightly the knuckles were white. My heart flip-flopped inside my rib cage as I moved closer. Reaching his side, I put my hand on his shoulder and said, "Fitz, you are free to pursue architecture or not as you choose. There is no law that says you have to engage in any occupation; you're a registered citizen entitled to receive the allotted annual energy credit. You have much more than you need. If you feel that working is a compulsion rather than an interest, we can work on that. You can do what you want with your life. Nobody is looking over your shoulder directing you. Your life is yours to do with as you see fit."

Fitz turned, taking one hand off the rail, and said, "Remember in *The Crying Clown Rites*, during the initiation scene, when one initiate said, 'I don't have to go through this; I can die,' and then tries to commit suicide by holding his breath?"

I exhaled slowly and then said, "Yes, I remember. And he failed."

Fitz went on as if he hadn't heard me at all. "I tried that before you took me to your friend's clinic. I held my breath. I passed out from lack of oxygen. When I lost consciousness, my body betrayed me by automatically breathing again. I woke up with a malignant headache."

"Of course, it's impossible to commit suicide by holding one's breath." I steered Fitz back to the table. He didn't resist. I asked, "Are you troubled by suicidal thoughts often?"

"When I left Retreat Island, I knew there was a possibility I might die trying to swim to the mainland. I didn't care."

"I think you do care about living, that not caring is a mask you've worn for protection from the past. The past is over and I can show you that you want to live."

"You can? How?"

"Through pharmodrama. Are you familiar with it?"

"No. What is it?"

"Pharmodrama uses pharmaceuticals and technology to create a drama that takes place in the minds of the client and the therapist. With drug doses tailored to their body chemistries and with sensor skullcaps on their heads, the two enter a reality shaped by the information fed them via a neuro-modulator. The client is the protagonist, the star of the show; the therapist's own reactions are suppressed to allow the client's reactions, transmitted as they occur, to dominate the therapist's experience spectrum."

"That sounds interesting, if I'm really in charge."

"It's the client's drama, not the therapist's. However, the procedure does have certain risks built into it."

"What risks?"

"For the drama to be effective, you would have to identify strongly with the protagonist's role. I would have to be receptive to everything that you experience and yet still be able to initiate a sequence to bring you back to this life. The risks are that you might suffer terminal identification, an inability to return completely to this reality. If I fail to break my identification with your experience, I could suffer reverse transference, which requires long and arduous treatment."

"You said 'you' and 'I.' That means that you're willing to take those risks for me?

"Yes."

"Have you done this before?"

"Twice. I consider both times successful."

"You believe that you can overcome the risks?"

"Yes, Fitz, I do." I didn't want to tell him that he would be identifying with the role of John F. Kennedy because that would increase the possibility of terminal identification. I didn't want Fitz to think about being Kennedy while I made the preparations for the pharmodrama.

"This will tell me, convince me that I want to live? Wipe out the suicidal urge?"

"I'm sure of it," I said, realizing that I was asking Fitz—who felt betrayed by everyone he had ever trusted—to trust me. I felt a core of strength inside me. I desperately wanted that strength to be enough to do for Fitz what Angela hadn't done, rescue Fitz from his self-imposed limitations.

"Phillip, I want that."

"I'll make the arrangements." I said it calmly, but I was aware of how much responsibility I was taking for Fitz's future. I had to create the drama, prepare the script, hire the actors, make the recordings necessary to make Fitz realize that he wanted to live. If I succeeded, Fitz would be ready to live fully. If I failed, Fitz would be lumbered with a hard-to-dispel pseudo John F. Kennedy persona while I would be suffering from an incapacitating reverse transference.

CHAPTER 23

CONSULTATION

Oh, I get by with a little help from my friends.
John Lennon & Paul McCartney

Dr. John Benway, a tall, slender man dressed in a gray worsted formsuit, welcomed me into his office saying, "Come in, Phillip. It's been a long time since you've visited me here in the secluded corridors of academia. What's on your mind?"

"I'd like to discuss a client with you. Actually, I want to discuss the therapy I have planned for him."

"Sit down," said Dr. Benway. "Help yourself to some Thai tea."

I sat down in the imitation leather visitor's chair and poured myself a cup of tea. He asked, "How have you been faring? You were obviously suffering distress the last time I saw you."

I sipped the tea, enjoying the vanilla flavor. "I've finally managed to accept Angela's death. For a while I wasn't sure I ever would. She was closer to me than any other person in the world."

"Are you sure that it isn't her that you've come to talk about? There aren't many people with whom you have had that kind of emotional bond. Losing one is always difficult."

"Thank you, John, but I really need to talk about my client, Fitzgerald Baker." Calling him John came easily to me now. Years ago I had called him Dr. Benway because he was the teacher and I had been the student.

"Then there is a connection to Angela. I thought there must be one because I kept thinking of her. Baker's the architect who designed her center, isn't he?"

"Yes. She told him that if he felt the need for therapy to see me. He's done so and I've helped him some, but I'd like your opinion on the procedure I have planned."

I took another sip of tea and looked at my white-haired mentor whose face was lined and serious as he said, "Give me a brief summary of everything that's happened so far."

He listened in nonjudgmental silence as I told him of my sessions with Fitz, the interviews with the women in Fitz's life, the grief release experience, *The Crying Clown Rites*, the Noanx use, the womb expulsion therapy, taking Fitz to Serge's clinic and the marathon weekend. My tea became cold during the telling.

"What do you plan to do next?" he asked.

"I'm going to do a pharmodrama to convince him that he wants to live. I've found what I consider is a great way to both lessen his Kennedy fixation and reveal his desire to live at the same time"

"Have you given him the 5-HIAA Test?"

"Yes, it was administered during his stay at Serge Dicori's Recovery Clinic. His serotonin level is within the normal range."

"Good," said Dr. Benway. "The prognosis for individuals with a low serotonin level in such a pharmodrama as you propose is very poor. Zimelidine is usually best for those genetically predisposed toward suicide. Tell me more about your proposed pharmodrama?"

I gave him the details as I had planned them. When I finished, he asked, "What signs do you have that the Kennedy fixation is lessening? You don't want to strengthen it. It could be very dangerous for both of you."

"He sold the boat that was a replica of Kennedy's combat boat."

"The PT boat, yes. But is the fixation completely gone?"

"No. He still wears the miniature golden boat on a chain around his neck, but he doesn't talk about Kennedy anymore."

"You're taking chances with this therapy, Phillip. I've always encouraged you to take risks because a no-risk position for you is also a no-win stance. Have you really come for my seal of approval on this procedure?"

"Yes."

"You still see me as an authority figure?"

"I do. And as a friend."

Dr. Benway sighed. "I suppose there's nothing inherently wrong with that; it's not as though you come to me for advice very often. Although you could come around more often, just to remind me how well I taught you."

"I promise to accept your next social invitation," I answered with a smile. Deep within me I felt real warmth for this old man who was probably the only family, real or otherwise, I had.

"And does Fitzgerald accept you as an authority figure now in much the same way that Angela was? I mean that in the psychiatric sense."

"At this stage in our relationship, yes."

"Then here is what you have to do, Phillip, to get my sanction. First, have Serge Dicori standing by in your office. Out of sight but keeping you and Baker under surveillance. Dicori must be ready to intervene if Baker decides not to live, to retain the Kennedy identification. You will be in no condition to handle terminal identification yourself. Second, you will have to make two recordings instead of the usual one and set them up to play in synchronization. Baker's recording will have a command at the end in your voice to return to present reality.

"Your tape will have the same command but it will be in my voice. Third, when you need my voice I will come to your office and we will do a complete run-through with me taking Baker's part. And when I say complete, I mean that I want Serge Dicori standing by. Fifth, I'll want to know when you start and I'll want a call from you when you finish.

Provided you do all of that as well as take all the professional care that is necessary, you have my blessing."

I thanked him and left to begin my preparations.

I spent the next week doing research, reviewing and studying every recording and book on and about John F. Kennedy. On the following Tuesday we did the run-through with Dr. Benway taking Fitz's part. It went without any glitches. While Dr. Benway was satisfied, Serge still had reservations about tomorrow's pharmodrama.

"Phillip, is there anything I can do to talk you out of this session tomorrow?"

"I don't believe so. I've come close to losing Fitz three times now; in his home, in the ocean, and on the pyramound last week. I don't believe that he really wants to die, but, if he keeps making these suicide attempts, he will eventually succeed. I don't want to take that chance."

"Yesterday," said Serge, "when I ran him through the physical you ordered, I had a chance to talk with him. Physically, he looks fine; he's gained some weight and his color is back. Even his reaction time has improved. Regardless, I'm not convinced that he's really gotten over Angela yet. She's still the primary focus of his conversation, and I think he may be subconsciously misusing this pharmodrama of yours as a way of joining her."

"That's a serious assertion," Dr. Benway acknowledged. "Do you have anything to substantiate your feelings?"

Serge shook his head. "While I was taking his holo-encephalogram, I used the alpha projector to put him into an REM sleep. Nothing unusual turned up; the usual REM ideographs on the dream recorder: large fish of some sort, possibly cetaceans, some clowns, Fitz riding some sort of hump-backed long-horned bull, a megalith, and a burning blue giraffe—that was about all we could decipher."

A burning blue giraffe! Where had I seen that before? Yes, during Charmaine's symbology dance. Fitz wasn't there; how did he pick up on that symbol?

“The blue giraffe. Has either of you seen that symbol before?”

Serge said no, but Dr. Benway looked thoughtful. “I’ve seen that figure before, in a museum I think… Yes, it was a painting by Pablo Picasso.”

I sighed in relief and Dr. Benway looked at me quizzically. “I’ll explain it some other time, John.” Then I turned to Serge and said, “I don’t see anything in those symbols that would indicate that Fitz was still preoccupied with Angela.”

“I know,” said Serge, “but I think I could find something if I gave him the full battery of tests again.”

“I disagree. Right now he has expectations of resolving his inner conflicts tomorrow during that pharmodrama. Delay would probably be the worst thing we could do.”

“What do you think, Dr. Benway? Serge asked.

“I agree with Phillip. He has taken every possible precaution and, while there is no guarantee of success, I believe that it would be in Baker’s best interest to brook no further delays.”

“Okay, okay,” Serge said, throwing his hands out. “But I’ll tell you this, I’ll be interrupting this pharmodrama in a flash at the first sign of trouble.”

CHAPTER 24

PHARMODRAMA

Life is real! Life is earnest! And the grave is not the goal.
Henry Wadsworth Longfellow

The next day everything was ready. Serge was standing by in the room next to the one in which the pharmodrama would take place. Fitz arrived at exactly 1100; he appeared anxious but in good spirits. I ushered him into my office, had him strip and step into the diagnostic analyzer. I needed an up-to-the-minute printout of his metabolic state to be certain that I administered exactly the right amount of drugs tailored to his body chemistry.

While waiting for the prescriptor to formulate the proper dosage for the two of us, I gave Fitz some additional information to keep his mind off the coming ordeal. "I'll administer the drugs here. We'll be sitting in these recliners with the sensor skullcaps on."

Fitz, who had just finished dressing, asked, "Can I sit there now?"

"Certainly. The recordings we will be listening to will be identical in most respects. Except that you will be the star of the drama. I'm going to see the same scenes but I will be tuned into your reactions to the experience. Serge Dicori is in the next room monitoring all that takes place. If we want to stop the pharmodrama at any time, either one of us can press this button and he will take over."

"Is this going to tell you whether I wish to live or die?"

"It's going to tell both of us."

"Good. What else do I need to know before we start?"

"When the drugs begin taking effect, you will experience a shrinking of identity. You will feel your conscious personality—what you consider you—slipping away and may be surprised to discover that you still exist when all that represents you to you is gone. As soon as your reactions to this loss self-stabilize, an identity thread will be fed into your brain via the skullcap to create the temporary persona that you will assume for the drama. I'll be outside of your own awareness but tuned into everything that you experience, ready to handle any problems—if there are any."

The prescriptor beeped.

"Are you ready?" I asked.

"I'm ready," he answered with a slight tremor to his voice.

With a hyposprayer I injected the drug mixture into his upper right arm, adjusted the controls so that only I could read the monitor output and waited for the temporary chemical dissolution of the facade that Fitz presented to the world.

When the readout confirmed that Fitz was ready, I fed the identity thread into his skullcap. As soon as positive pickup registered, I took the maximum dose of Empathol—or empathy plus as it was popularly called—for someone with my metabolism and empathy quotient and waited.

As the Empathol coursed through my bloodstream, I could feel my own personality receding, enabling me to identify with the star of the drama I was creating, a drama based on some of the known facts in an historical event. I put on my skullcap and verified that I could detect and empathize with the thoughts and emotions of my client, who now believed that his name was John Fitzgerald Kennedy and that he was the thirty-fifth president of the old United States.

The drama began with the voice of a reporter coming directly into our brains, a voice with most of the regional accent lost through announcer's training, but the rhythm of the speech was definitely American Southwest and the hint of a Texas drawl hovered over the words like a hummingbird seeking nectar from a flowering plant. At some deep level I knew it was the voice of an actor hired by me to record the message he was delivering, but now I was hearing it as Fitz heard it—as an announcer's voice coming out of the open-topped vehicle's radio, saying, "For those of you who just tuned in, November 22, 1963 is a pleasant day here in Dallas, just right for a presidential motorcade. I'm here at Dealey Plaza and according to the schedule I was given, President Kennedy should be coming into sight any moment now."

A scanner transferred my client's thoughts via computer into my skullcap as input, thoughts that became mine as my personality submerged and I became the pseudo John Fitzgerald Kennedy. I was waving to the crowds, hearing them cheering, hoping that the presence of Governor Connally and his wife in the car would help convince skeptics that I had patched up the differences between conservative and liberal factions of the Texas Democratic Party.

With excitement in his voice, the announcer said, "Here comes the lead motorcycle turning onto Elm Street. There is the presidential limousine now, a blue Lincoln coming this way. The President is waving to the crowds who seem very excited. The President's wife is sitting beside him. Just in front of them, in the seat behind the driver are Texas Governor Connally and his wife. I've never seen the people of Dallas give anyone a more enthusiastic reception."

Mrs. Connally turned toward me from the forward seat and smilingly said, "You can't say the people of Dallas don't love you, Mr. President." As I started to smile at her in reply, there was a loud noise. I seemed to be riding the crest of a shockwave—

What's happening? I can't think straight. Did I have too much to drink? Never liked heavy drinking parties anyway. Remember Charley at Harvard. Always lushing it up, especially after midterms. I remember his favorite toast:

Drink it up!
Drink it up!
Drink it up!
If you die young,
What's the diff?
The coeds will say,
As they lay you away,
That's a good-looking stiff.

The shockwave hit me again! What the hell? It's that Japanese destroyer. It's run into our starboard side! The wheel is being torn out of my grasp. Jesus!—MY BACK. I just hit the rear of the cockpit. Somebody is saying something, but I can't understand it.

It's Johnston saying to someone who's moaning, "Aw, shut up. You can't die. Only the good die young." That's right, Johnston, you tell them. I can't die now. I'm still in my twenties. Only the good die young. Like my brother Joe. Joe was good. His death made me resolve to do better. Wait a minute. Joe died in 1944 and I was on Olasana Island with Johnston in 1943.

What's going on? There's blood all over Jackie's pink suit!

I hear that voice again: "Those loud noises were shots. I can't tell whether the President has been hit or not. He's leaning forward and his wife is bending over him as the car continues down the hill. I think that Governor Connally has been hit. It looks like he was driven downward to the floor of the car. Did you hear that noise? That was another shot!"

Last effort to make sense of this. Got to clear my head. Someone is yelling something about Parkland Hospital. I can take it all in now, all of it. There's more blood on Jackie's suit. The crowd seems to be running in different directions, screaming yelling and pointing.

What are those people doing?

They're picking up bits of bloody bone!

One has a handkerchief.

It's like with Dillinger. They're souvenir hunters!

Where's that bone from?

Is it Connally's? He's slumped down and looks bad. But the hair is wrong. John's hair doesn't have that much color. Could it be colored by the blood? Could blood make it look that color of reddish brown?

The car is going faster. Can't see many details. Got to make sense of all this. Wind noise taking all the sounds away. Can't understand what they're shouting.

The air isn't hitting me in the face anymore. It's hot! Everything looks pink. Am I looking at Jackie's suit or is that blood in my eye? The pain is building into another wave.

Dear God! It's headed my way. Have to find a way to stop it. Feels like it's going to be as bad as that pain in my back. Oh God, I understand it now, but I'm not ready. I'm only forty-six and I'm dying young!

A new voice, familiar somehow, spoke to me, saying, "Wake up! Wake up, Phillip! Time to be alert. Wake up and come back."

The voice kept repeating the message. Was I Phillip? Had I been dreaming? Whose voice? Dr. Benway's? Had I fallen asleep in the lab?

I opened my eyes and looked into Serge's face. He was shaking me by the shoulders. I said, "It's all right, Serge. I'm back."

A final image of Jackie in a blood-spattered suit, her mouth open and twisted in horror, faded as Serge pulled off my skullcap. "Are you sure you're okay?"

"I'm coming around. How's Fitz?"

Serge turned to look at the monitor. "He's coming out of it now."

I paid attention to my breathing, calming the intense emotional experience with concentration upon the repetition of the inhalation crest and the exhalation trough. By the time Fitz's disconnection procedure was complete, I was breathing normally.

Fitz was still seated on the recliner, his eyes shut tight. I tried to stand but my limbs began to tremble so much I sat back down. It was almost as though a piece of myself had died with him. I knew I would never do a death pharmodrama again.

I was worried about Fitz, but afraid to speak, afraid I might catch this moment in amber for all time.

Serge injected the antidote into Fitz with the hyposprayer. Then he turned to me and said, "Should I make one up for you to?"

"No. I'm okay."

"Then what are you waiting for?" he asked, turning to look at Fitz.

Steeling myself, I asked, "Fitz? Can you hear me?"

Fitz groaned, and then turned and looked at me with wide eyes. "I want to live."' he shouted. Then in a lower voice added, "I really want to live, don't I?"

"There's no doubt in my mind, Fitz. Is there any in yours?"

"No," he said, "I wanna live. I was John Kennedy but the feelings about premature death were all mine. Do you think he felt as I did? Is it possible that our internal experience was the same?"

"It may have been, although we'll never know since there is no known reliable method of chronicling the unrecorded thoughts of the dead. Some of the religious groups are exploring that territory. Of course, very little of their data can be verified because of its subjective nature. Is knowing what John Kennedy thought as he was dying important to you, Fitz?"

"I don't know. I haven't quite recovered from my identification with him. I do know it's time to stop worrying about my past and start living in the present. I have most of my life yet to live."

"I think we both have." We exchanged smiles.

After a few more minutes of conversation, Fitz came to his feet and left. His movements were sure and unhurried, a reassuring sign. An intense pharmodrama experience can immobilize some of the crisis prone for up to forty-eight hours.

Serge turned to me and said, "Phillip, you did it! I'm proud to be your friend and I'm so proud of you. The sincerity and pride in his voice rang like bells as he spoke.

"Thank you, Serge. I feel like I overextended myself. I'll never put myself through that kind of experience again. I guess I needed it to feel right about my professional abilities, but I feel like I've just come back from the dead, resurrected by amateurs."

"Well, my friend, you can rest for a few hours after you call Dr. Benway."

"Thanks for reminding me, Serge. I promised I'd tell him the outcome of the pharmodrama. Hey, what do you mean a few hours rest? I might sleep for a dozen."

"Not until later tonight, my friend. Dr. Benway is hosting a congratulatory dinner for you this evening. He knew you'd be successful."

I was unable to speak for a minute so I didn't dial John Benway's number immediately. The lump in my throat was the emotional knowledge that I had the best of friends and mentors.

CHAPTER 25

REBIRTH

There is no cure for birth and death, save to enjoy the interval.
George Santayana

I didn't get the dozen hours of sleep that I'd told Serge I might need after the pharmodrama. The congratulatory dinner had induced a degree of excitement in me that I hadn't experienced for a long time, an excitement that kept me awake long after I returned home at midnight. My late morning sleep was interrupted by Fitz at my door. I let him in and started the coffee maker.

"Phillip, I dreamed about Angela. I woke up at dawn and I've been thinking ever since...."

I didn't hear the next sentence. I was still partially asleep, but awake enough to be aware of something new: I had truly let go of Angela Calderon. I didn't give a damn what Fitz had dreamed about her because to me, at last, she was only a memory, not an active concern.

"She was wearing the same clothes that she wore in the letting-go ceremony. She told me that she had come to say a final *adios*. That I didn't need her anymore because you had set me free. That you had done what she hadn't been able to do, free me to live a life of my own choosing."

"Fitz, could you slow down a little? Give me a chance to get some coffee into me. I'm not yet fully awake."

"Let me get it for you." Fitz moved over to the coffee maker as if he was bursting with unlimited energy. He got two cups from the cabinet and began pouring the coffee. How different he was, how alive. I had never imagined him free enough to make himself at home in someone else's kitchen.

"I'll fix some toast if you want some," he volunteered as I relaxed in the breakfast nook, rubbing my eyes and scratching my head.

"Just coffee, thanks," was my reply. I had eaten more than I should the previous evening with Serge and John. What I really needed now was more sleep but I was having coffee instead.

Fitz put a steaming cup of coffee in front of me and, as I reached for it said, "Let it cool a minute. It's hot enough to burn your mouth." I shook my head, trying to get the thoughts of sleep out, wishing I were more alert to appreciate the change in Fitz.

After setting his cup on the table, Fitz dropped into the chair opposite me and said, "Sorry to overwhelm you like this. It hadn't occurred to me that you might still be asleep. I woke up with the dawn, feeling as fresh and alert as if I'd been reborn. I owe it all to you, Phillip. You restored my life to me. I'll never forget you."

"Thank you, Fitz. It feels good to be appreciated." I felt the warmth of the coffee cup in my hand. I brought it to my lips and sipped a few drops. It was hot but I didn't burn myself.

"Are you ready to hear about my dream?" The eagerness in Fitz's voice was unmistakable.

"Sure. You dreamed of Angela, you said." There were no pangs of regret, no bittersweet pains of unrequited love as I said her name. If I were just awake and rested, I might feel as energetic as Fitz obviously did.

Fitz looked directly at me as he began speaking. His eyes had never seemed so clear nor his face so free from tension and worry lines. His voice had a depth and resonance that was new to me. For the first time I was seeing and experiencing the charisma that others had told me. It was as if the Fitz I had seen before was a pale imitation of the human being before me now, as if the Fitz who had sought help from me had been a prototype of the man who looked into my eyes as he spoke.

"At first, Angela seemed so real I didn't realize I was dreaming. She said, 'Fitz, you don't need me anymore.' She said it and the realization that it was true ran through me like an electric shock. Her next words were, 'Your need of me held me to the physical plane like a magnet. Now that you are free of that need, I am free to explore the afterlife. Death is nothing like what I expected. That was when I realized that she was wearing the same clothes that she had worn for the letting-go ceremony. That was when I knew that I had finally accepted her death."

Fitz paused for a moment, taking a sip of his coffee. I hadn't touched mine since the first sip. I'd been captivated by his story and the energy with which he told it. His eyes seemed more open when he talked to me, as if seeing me was a treasured pleasure.

"Phillip, I knew it was a dream then and I know it now but the impact of her words was real, regardless of the framework in which I heard them. Can you believe that?"

"Of course I can, Fitz." At that moment, I believed he could have sold voodoo charms to engineers. He spoke with a certainty very much like the glory shouters except the sincerity was not induced by a temporary group high. Fitz had blossomed overnight.

"In my dream, Angela said, 'Death isn't like what I expected. It isn't the enemy at all. I am embracing death just as you must embrace life. You must change your perspective, widen your horizons and stop cheating yourself of the variety of life's experiences. Come to terms with your past, explore your present and be ready to enjoy the future.' Phillip, her words seemed to solidify the results of the therapy with you. I feel free!"

I recognized many of the words and phrases Angela had said to him as the basic tenets of her motivational talks to suicidal patients. It didn't matter if Fitz had remembered them from Angela's papers and lectures or whether they had come to him in a dream. The important event was that those words now inspired him to feel free. I asked, "What are you going to do with your new freedom?"

Fitz raised his right arm in the air in a gesture of triumph and said, "I've already started. I called Clyde Burbank this morning to resign from the firm. We compromised on an indefinite leave of absence. I'm going to attend the dedication ceremony of the Pantheon of Prophets and then I'm through with architecture. The dedication will mark the end of this phase of my life and the beginning of another."

I wasn't surprised that Fitz felt that he was finished with architecture. It had been an occupation, never a passion. I could hear the passion in his voice now and I wondered to what ends he would direct it. "What do you plan to do next, Fitz?"

"Just what Angela recommended in the dream, which is the same thing all the therapy has told me: Accept the past, get involved in the present and embrace the future as it comes. Specifically, Phillip, I don't know exactly what I'm going to do next. I've realized that my past doesn't define my future. Angela dominated my recent past, but that is over. Currently there's no woman in my life—I've made my peace with Estelle.

"She's as interested in the Green Jinni play as she is in me. Not that I'm ready for a romance now. I've still got to come to terms with the other women who've influenced my life. I want to get centered and balanced and discover the things I've missed."

"Like what, Fitz?"

"I feel that my mother's sexual acting-out and Aunt Isobel's militant atheism limited my spiritual development. The closest thing I've ever had to a religious experience was at The Whole Body Center when that tall, thin man had his conversation with God. I'm going to explore the religious experience in whatever way seems right. I'm going to find ways to accept my past. Most of all, for the first time in the longest time, I'm looking forward to the experiences that await me. Do you agree that my lifestyle crisis is over?"

"Yes. Fitz. It's over."

He smiled at me, with gleaming teeth, and said, "The crisis is over and I'm living again. Since I may hit a few rough spots on my way to a new lifestyle, a new purpose, will you be willing to give a friendly fellow seeker a little professional help now and then as needed?"

"Of course, but you don't have to need help to keep in touch. I want to know what happens in your life."

"I'll keep you posted. Thank you for everything, Phillip, and thanks for listening to me today. I've got too much energy to sit still so I'm going to leave you here to drink your coffee in peace. I'll be in touch."

I saw Fitz to the door. We hugged each other in parting. I was pleased, almost smug, about how well things had turned out for Fitz. But I didn't go back to my coffee. I went to bed because I still wanted that dozen hours of sleep I'd longed for. I shut off the communications system and set the timer to come back on in about thirteen hours. By that time I'd have my sleep. More than twelve hours. Thirteen. A baker's dozen.

The End

www.ingramcontent.com/pod-product-compliance
Lightning Source LLC
Chambersburg PA
CBHW030424310726
48979CB00009B/1609/J

* 9 7 8 0 9 3 7 9 1 2 5 9 1 *